NOA

Mistakes We

Make

WITHDRAWN

Mistakes We Make

Jenny Harper

Published by Accent Press Ltd 2016

ISBN: 9781910939161

Acknowledgements

Some books are a joy to research, others prove more challenging. I have to confess that *Mistakes We Make* fell into the latter category – it proved extraordinarily difficult to persuade lawyers and accountants to describe a perfect fraud to me! One lawyer, after an hour of grilling, protested, 'You're making me think like a criminal.' To the various people who did dream up potential scenarios for me, therefore, I am incredibly grateful. They know who they are.

On the plus side, I discovered that lawyers and accountants make excellent interviewees in terms of research – their information tends to emerge immaculately organised, if not in numbered lists with sub-points!

I am most grateful to Bob Brown and Leonard Mair for general information on how law firms operate, and to Donnie McGruther, who directed me to The Law Society of Scotland for information about what happens when possible criminal activity is reported or detected in a law firm. I am indebted to the Society's Registrar, David Cullen, for outlining this process in detail.

As ever, my heartfelt thanks go to all those who support me and put up with me in my writing. They include my writing buddies Dianne and Jennifer and my long-suffering husband, Robin. I am eternally grateful also for the support of a wider community of writers, bloggers and reviewers – thanks to all of you. Writing would be a more difficult and a lonelier place without you.

And finally, thanks to the wonderful team at Accent Press, in particular Bethan James and my editor, Rebecca Lloyd. And – because I'm so thrilled with it – a special thanks to my cover designer!

Note on Hailesbank and The Heartlands

The small market town of Hailesbank is born of my imagination, as are the surrounding villages of Forgie and Stoneyford and the council housing estate known as Summerfield, which together form The Heartlands. I have placed the area, in my mind, to the east of Scotland's capital city, Edinburgh.

The first mention of The Heartlands was made by Agrippus Centorius in AD77, not long after the Romans began their surge north in the hope of conquering this savage land. 'This is a place of great beauty,' wrote Agrippus, 'and its wildness has clutched my heart.' He makes several mentions thereafter of The Heartlands. There are still signs of Roman occupation in Hailesbank, which has great transport links to the south (and England) and the north, especially to Edinburgh, and its proximity to the sea and the (real) coastal town of Musselburgh made it a great place to settle. The Georgians and Victorians began to develop the small village, its clean air and glorious views, rich farming hinterland and great transport proving highly attractive.

The River Hailes flows through the town. There is a Hailes Castle in East Lothian (it has not yet featured in my novels), but it sits on the Tyne.

Hailesbank has a Town Hall and a high street, from which a number of ancient small lanes, or vennels, run down to the river, which once was the lifeblood of the town.

In my novels, characters populate the shops, cafes and

pubs in Hailesbank and the pretty adjoining village of Forgie, with Summerfield inhabitants providing another layer of social interaction.

JH

PART ONE

PART ONE

Chapter One

Molly Keir always claimed that her success as an events manager was down to her passion for detail. Keeping control left little time for contemplation, and that suited Molly just fine – it was easier than thinking about the mistakes she'd made in her personal life.

Much easier.

In the middle of the Scottish Highlands, her mobile phone clamped to one ear, a large notebook open on her lap, a pen in one hand and her black-rimmed reading glasses perched on her nose, she was oblivious to the glories of the afternoon sunlight on the hills on either side of the car. Instead of connecting with the world around her, she was doing what she did best – organising a universe of her own construction.

'I'll do my best on the peonies, Miss di Constanza,' she said brightly, 'but the florist is telling me that peonies are out of season now and … No, I understand. I'm sure we can source them from somewhere, but they will have to be imported and I know you like to support local suppliers … Yes, yes, of course.'

She turned to Lexie Gordon, who was driving, wrinkled her nose expressively, then carried on without missing a beat.

'It's all under control, Miss di Constanza, I promise you. Yes, I will be away this weekend, but I have my phone with me, and you can always reach me. Everything is in place, you have my personal guarantee. … Thank you. … Yes, indeed. Goodbye. Yes, goodbye.'

'She seems quite demanding,' said Lexie, glancing across at her.

Molly shrugged. 'She's a prestigious client. Her lingerie collection is big business and this is the second launch she's done at Fleming House. It's a great name to have on our credentials so I can't afford to offend her. Lexie! Stop!'

'What the—?' Lexie stamped on the brake and they stopped a few inches from the rear of the campervan they'd been tailing.

The traffic heading west had been quite light. They'd just threaded their way through a small hamlet where the biggest building was a café that catered for passing tour buses. All around them were rolling hills, heather and bracken – but now they'd run slap bang into a long queue of traffic.

'Phew. That was close. You OK?' Molly asked.

Lexie laid a hand on her swollen belly. 'Fine.'

'What's causing the hold up?'

'I think there are roadworks somewhere.' Lexie craned her neck. 'I can see some lights ahead. We'll be through in a minute.'

Molly's phone rang again. She glanced at the screen and groaned. 'It's Jonquil Prosser.'

'Bridezilla?'

'Worse. Her mother.'

She switched into professional mode. 'Good afternoon, Mrs Prosser, what can I do for you today?'

'Patience of a saint,' Lexie hissed, slipping the car into gear and inching forward as the traffic began to move.

Ahead, a large sign announced ROAD CLOSED. LOCAL ACCESS ONLY. DIVERSION.

'Damn, it's sending us left,' Lexie said as Molly stopped talking abruptly.

'Is that bad? I've lost the signal,' she said, jabbing at her phone.

'It's a long diversion,' Lexie said, swinging on to a minor road with the rest of the traffic.

'You all right with driving? I know you hate it but I've got some more calls to make.'

'You're meant to be on a weekend off, Moll.'

'I know, I know! I just need to … Still no signal.' She opened her notebook again. 'Peonies,' she muttered, scribbling an addition. 'Thrones—'

'Thrones?' Lexie said, slowing to a crawl to take a bend. Behind her, someone tooted impatiently.

'That's what Jonquil Prosser was on about, before I lost her. Apparently, Ellen and Rob want thrones in the ballroom.'

Lexie snorted. 'Jonquil wants thrones, more like. Where are you going to get them?'

Molly added to her list. 'I'll have to hire them in. I bet one of the theatres in Edinburgh will have some in store somewhere. Bother, there's still no signal.'

'Your phone's trying to tell you something,' Lexie said, laughing. 'Come on, put it away. This is a holiday.'

'You're right. I can't do anything at the moment anyway; it looks as though we're in a dead area. I'll have to get hold of Logan at some point though. He's not answering his phone. I swear he sees my number and presses decline. Hey,' her face lit up, 'maybe I should get you to call him. You two have always got on well.'

She indicated left to signal the impatient car to overtake. It shot past in a blur of silver.

'Asshole. How far ahead does he think he can get? Anyway, what would I be calling Logan about?'

'I dunno. Some painting you want him to buy, maybe?'

Lexie snorted. 'Forget it, Moll, it isn't going to work. Just keep trying. He's probably busy.'

'He's always busy. I don't know how Adrienne stands it. Those boys must wonder who the strange man is when he actually does show up for supper.'

'Well, you can call him from the hotel.'

'Still not telling me where we're going?'

True to form, Molly had been reluctant when Lexie had announced she was taking her away for a weekend. 'I've got so much to do. Where were you thinking of, anyway?'

'Secret. And if you don't come, you'll never know. Come on, my treat. Patrick's in Madrid this weekend to sign the lease on his new art gallery, and it'll probably be our last chance for a girlie weekend before baby arrives.'

It was true. Once the Mulgrew-Gordon baby was here, their lives would be very different.

Lexie let another car pass, then glanced at Molly and grinned. 'You can call Logan from Loch Melfort.'

'Loch Melfort! You're joking.'

Lexie looked smug. 'I know you love it.'

Loch Melfort ... A glorious autumn day on the west coast of Scotland. The sun baking their arms and sneaking between the hairs on their heads to scorch their scalps. A pair of golden eagles soaring in the endless skies above, her man beside her and the bliss of new love requited. His hands cupping her face and his kiss, gentle at first, then unrestrained. She could remember how that kiss had ended up – naughty and naked and very, very nice on a bed of scratchy heather under the open skies.

She hadn't been back there in an age. It was beautiful –

but it was *his* special place. Could she stand being there without him?

Molly sank back on her seat and closed her eyes. So much had happened in the past three years. It had started with the gradual degeneration of her marriage, which had led to her brief, passionate affair with Lexie's brother Jamie, and had ended – tragically – with Jamie's death in a car accident. She'd given up her fast-moving career in marketing and beaten a retreat to Fleming House, where she'd hidden away and paid penance by working herself half to death for a fraction of her old salary.

Lexie had been through bad times too, but she had grabbed hold of all the difficult things in her life, shaken them to destruction and moved on. Whereas Molly – what had she done? Merely allowed herself to get stuck in a rut. It had to stop – and maybe this weekend away would be the perfect time to take stock.

'You may be a bit crazy, Lexie Gordon,' she said, yawning, 'but I think you have something of the genius in you.'

And as Lexie settled into a steady crawl through the spectacular scenery, Molly did something rare. She nodded off to sleep.

Adam Blair wasn't quite sure when or how he'd agreed to come away with Sunita Ghosh for what she called 'special together time', but here he was in the car, half way to the west Highlands. He had only been dating Sunita for four months, and even that had been something of a surprise.

It was six o'clock already, they'd just passed Dalmally, and now they were sitting at a red light in the middle of nowhere. Ahead, he could see a large notice saying LOCAL ACCESS ONLY, and a large DIVERSION sign pointing left.

'I'm tempted to risk it,' he said, glancing at his companion.

'Best not,' she said passively.

'If the locals can get through, why can't we?'

'Maybe it's closed further along.'

'Then how can anyone get to Oban, for heaven's sake?'

'They wouldn't put a sign there if it wasn't necessary,' Sunita pointed out reasonably.

They passed through the lights and reached the point of no return. Adam swung the wheel to the left with considerable reluctance.

'I know this road. This is going to add fifty miles. We'll be late for dinner.'

'Chill, Adam. It's our holiday.'

They were heading to the Loch Melfort Hotel, south of Oban, which was the only reason Adam had agreed to come. His parents used to bring him here when he was a child. They all used to come together, his family, Uncle Geordie, Auntie Jean and his cousin, Hugh. He'd brought his wife here on their first anniversary.

God, she'd loved it. He'd known she would; she was drawn to the outdoors, just as he was. She loved climbing the Scottish mountains – and not just to please him. She was like a mountain goat, lean and lithe, her long legs taking the steep slopes with easy agility.

He pursed his lips, thinking that he should not have accepted Sunita's invitation. It was too early in their relationship to spend a weekend together – but when she'd mentioned Loch Melfort, he'd wavered. It had been too tempting. Something deep in his psyche had yearned for the familiar beauty of the place.

A thought struck him and he glanced across at her again.

'Why did you pick this hotel, Sunita?'

Sunita's long black hair always seemed to shine, but in the low rays of the evening sun it had a particular gloss, almost purple, like a raven's wing. She turned her face towards him, her coal black eyes radiating innocence.

'They were offering a great deal.'

She looked away again, her lips curved into a quiet smile.

Adam's suspicions crystallised. He must have mentioned the hotel at some time, and Sunita had turned the information into a lure. She was a clever, clever woman.

It wasn't that he was reluctant, he told himself, not really. Sunita was beautiful, smart and pleasant company. He lifted one hand off the steering wheel and scratched the top of his head. His thick brown hair stood up in protest.

It was a relationship with definite promise. Her cooking was sublime, she was a goddess in bed, they had a great deal in common. Well, some things in common. They both liked cinema and – he searched his mind – curry.

'I'll call and tell them we might be late. I'm sure there'll be lots of people with the same problem.' Sunita leaned forward and retrieved her handbag from the footwell. Neat brown fingers tapped in a number, the burgundy-painted nails immaculate. How did she keep them like that? So sleek.

'You might not get a signal,' he warned. 'It's really poor in this area.'

Maddeningly, she was already talking. 'It's fine,' she said, slipping her phone back into her bag, 'other guests have been caught in the traffic too. There's not a problem.'

Adam focused his mind on the hotel. Forget the diversion, forget Sunita's astonishing competence. In less than an hour he'd be slouching comfortably on one of the luxurious sofas, holding a large glass of fine wine. A weekend in a beautiful retreat like the Loch Melfort Hotel was exactly what he needed – why had he been so resistant to the idea?

'This is where we turn right.'

'Sorry?'

'Slow down, Adam, this is where we turn right.'

He saw the junction up ahead and eased off the accelerator.

'You've been in a dream.'

'Have I?' He came to a halt behind the short queue of cars waiting to pull on to the main road north, reached across for her hand and squeezed her fingers. 'Sorry. We should be there in less than half an hour.'

'Good. I'm getting hungry. I can't wait to try this fantastic food you've told me about. You?'

'Definitely.'

Adam smiled at her. It was going to be all right. She was a pleasant companion. And he owed her some time.

Molly, sitting on the padded window seat in the lounge at the Loch Melfort Hotel, lifted her glass up to the light. Through the liquid, the view was ruby-tinted and glorious. The field that rolled down to the loch was home to half a dozen stocky Highland cattle with heavy fringes and jaunty horns, for all the world like Viking invaders. One lifted his head and seemed to stare right at her, placid but immoveable.

She laughed. 'That beast's got the right idea. Look the world in the eye and don't let anything shake you. Cheers, mate.' She raised the glass to the hairy animal, who stared back imperturbably.

The loch stretched to the horizon, blue as the sky, its stillness turning it into a mirror. Molly grinned. 'I feel like being a bit bonkers tonight. I've escaped! I'm free! For a whole weekend!' She took a deep draught from her glass and felt the wine course down, its effect as calming as the scenery. 'You were so right to drag me away, Lex. This is bliss.'

'Sorry to interrupt.' A waitress had arrived, unnoticed, beside them. 'I'm Kenna. Are you eating with us tonight?'

'You bet,' Lexie said, reaching for the heavy leather bound menus Kenna was holding. 'I haven't been able to think of anything else for the last hour and a half.'

'We were hoping we wouldn't be too late,' Molly said. 'There was a diversion. The road between Dalmally and Oban is blocked for some reason.'

'They're doing major roadworks. I'm really sorry.' Kenna smiled apologetically, as though the fault was all hers. 'It's been going on for weeks. Everyone's hopping mad – they always seem to start them at the height of the tourist season. Don't worry about it – we're still expecting guests; loads of people have been delayed. Kitchen's all organised. I'll leave you with these. Give me a shout when you're ready.'

'Thanks.'

Molly rummaged in her handbag and extracted her glasses. 'Yum, this looks amazing. Scallops, black pudding, gravadlax, sole paupiettes. Wow. I didn't realise how ravenous I was till I started reading!'

Lexie whispered, 'Molly.'

'Mmm? What do you think about beef?'

'*Molly.*'

Molly looked up at the note of urgency. 'What?'

Lexie's face had turned an odd shade, and her brown

eyes had a panicky look about them. She was staring over Molly's shoulder at the doorway.

Molly shoved her glasses onto the top of her head and swung round. A woman was walking into the room. She was Asian – Indian, perhaps? – and classically beautiful. Her hair fell in thick, shiny tresses halfway down her back, her eyes were dark as treacle and dramatically outlined in black. She was wearing scarlet. Afterwards, that was what Molly remembered most – the stunning silky dress, hugging a perfect figure.

For now, the dress and the woman faded improbably into the background because there was a man behind her. Not just any man – Adam Blair.

Molly's husband.

Chapter Two

Molly leapt up; the menu dropped from her fingers onto the table and sent her wine flying. Half of the contents landed in Lexie's lap, half on the carpet.

'Moll!' Lexie shrieked, staring as the blood-red liquid spread across her vintage cotton dress.

Kenna grabbed a cloth from the bar. 'I'll deal with this, don't worry, there's no real damage—'

Molly was oblivious to it all. She only had eyes for Adam, whose attention had been attracted by the commotion and who was now staring in her direction with his mouth wide open.

'Jeez, Moll!' Lexie hissed.

'It's Adam!'

'That's what I was trying to tell you.'

'He's seen us!'

'Well, that's hardly surprising, is it?'

Kenna said, 'If you'd like to change and give me your dress, I think I can get the stain out.' Lexie didn't move. 'If we deal with it quickly?'

Molly said, 'We've got to go.'

'Go? Go where?'

'We'll have to go home. We can't stay here.'

'Don't be silly, Moll. Let's be mature about this. Anyway, we were here first.'

'Who *is* she? I didn't know he was seeing anyone. He never said anything about seeing anyone.'

'Ask him. He's coming over.'

'Shit!'

Molly whirled round and made for the only other door, while behind her, Lexie hovered uncertainly, hampered by her pregnancy. She made it up to their bedroom a minute after Molly.

'We've got to get out of here.' Her friend had begun yanking at her dress frantically.

'Come on, Moll. It doesn't matter, does it? I mean, we don't have to see them or anything.'

'See them?' The dress finally yielded to Molly's tugging and flew up over her head. She seized a pair of jeans off the bed and hauled them on. 'In a place like this? Of course we'd see them, there's nowhere to go except the gardens, or out for a walk.'

'There's Oban – it's only a few miles up the road. And from there we can take the big ferry to Mull, or the little one to Kerrera. Or we could go the other way and explore Inveraray.'

'Then come back here for dinner? Sit a few tables from them? Or even *next* to them? I couldn't bear it. And what about breakfast?'

'What's really eating you, Moll? It's hardly the first time you've met Adam since you split.' She narrowed her eyes. 'It's *her*, isn't it? The woman?'

Molly zipped up her jeans and rammed her feet into a pair of trainers.

'Come *on*, Lexie. It's a long drive home, we've got to get going.'

Lexie flopped down on the other bed. 'I'm not moving.'

Molly's head appeared above the neck of a coral sweater. She pulled her long blonde hair free and flicked it back with her hands.

'I can't stay here.'

'Let's talk about it.'

'No. Sorry. I know you've gone to a lot of trouble, but I mean it. I'm not staying here. If you won't drive me, I'll call a taxi.'

Lexie sighed. 'Can't the two of you behave in a civilised manner? It's been two years, Molly, surely he's entitled to a new relationship – or a dirty weekend, if that's what it is?' She frowned. 'You're not jealous, are you? I mean, to be fair, you did leave him because you were having an affair.'

Molly was stuffing clothes into a case. She swung round, a pair of trainers in her hands. She stared at Lexie. 'I can't believe you said that, Alexa Gordon. I was *in love*. With your *brother*.'

There was a moment of heavy silence before Lexie crumpled. 'Sorry, Moll.'

'No.' Molly crossed the room and sat down beside Lexie. 'I'm the one who's sorry.'

Grief bursts its shackles without warning. Every time they thought they'd come to terms with what had happened, it reared up at them from another angle. Jamie Gordon's tragic death had nearly destroyed Lexie, her parents, Molly – and its shadow still lay across them.

Lexie, her voice small, said, 'I'll pack.'

Molly nodded. 'I appreciate it.'

They were unnaturally subdued as Molly, driving, turned the car north. 'We can find a hotel in Oban, it'll save us driving all the way home tonight. Anyway, I'm ravenous; we'll need to eat.'

'Fine.'

'OK?'

'Sure. Good thinking.'

'It doesn't have to ruin the whole weekend.'

'No.'

'We're going to have a great time.'

'Yes.'

Two miles up the road, a car flashed its lights at them.

'What's up with him?'

'Maybe there's a speed trap ahead.'

'A speed trap? It's impossible to do more than fifty on this road.'

Another car flashed as they rounded a bend and ran into yet another queue of traffic.

Molly braked sharply. 'At least we know why they were warning us. I wonder what's causing it.'

Minutes ticked by. The traffic didn't move. Ahead, two or three cars performed U-turns and headed south. Lexie opened her door. 'I'll ask the car in front if they know.'

While Lexie got out, Molly picked apart her emotions. Lexie was right, there was no reason for her to react so strongly to Adam's appearance. Their relationship wasn't exactly cordial, but they'd learned to be polite. It had taken her a long time to get over Jamie Gordon's death, but as the memories of the laughter and passion she'd shared with Lexie's brother gradually faded, it had begun to dawn on her that she was in no great hurry to legalise the separation from Adam.

Lexie opened the door and poked her head in. 'Apparently it's a convoy of wind turbines. They are massive and very, very slow. There were warnings, he says.'

'So we can get through to Oban?'

'Probably, if we wait long enough, but they're going at five miles an hour and they're too wide for anything to pass on this road – southbound traffic has been pulled off further up. So it could be a few hours before we get there.'

'Sheesh. What are we going to do?'

Lexie slid in and slammed the door. 'We can do a U-ey and head for Inveraray. We'll find somewhere there.'

'OK.'

An evening mist was rolling in from the sea, engulfing the road. Molly shivered. 'Wish I'd put my jacket on.'

'I'll ramp up the heating.'

Lexie fiddled with a control and a fan blew in some warmth. 'There's been nothing coming north for the last ten minutes,' she observed. 'People must know about that convoy.'

They neared the turn-off to the hotel.

'We could—'

'No.'

Molly drove on in silence. A few miles south of the hotel they rounded another bend.

'What the—?'

They jerked forward, wrenched against the seat belts, and slammed backwards into their seats as they narrowly avoided hitting the last car in another queue of traffic. Molly's head hit the headrest with some force.

'Ouch!'

'You all right?' Lexie sounded breathless.

'I think so. I'll probably have a bruise right across my body in the morning. Are you? Oh my God, Lexie, the *baby*!'

'Kicking like crazy. I guess she's OK.'

There was no sign of movement at all. Up ahead, several drivers had left their cars and were walking forward, presumably to find out what was going on.

Molly switched off the engine. 'Let's see what's happening.'

A broad-built man with red hair was wandering

towards them. 'Do you know what the problem is?' Lexie called.

He headed their way. 'It's bad news. There's been a nasty accident. Apparently a lorry has dropped a load of caustic acid. One of the drums trapped someone. And one has burst on the road.'

'Acid? Oh my God—' Lexie clamped a hand across her mouth and turned away.

Molly was pale. 'Someone's trapped?'

'Yup. And the worst thing is, they're not going to be able to get the fire engines or ambulances down from Oban because of the—'

'—wind turbines—'

'—and no-one's going to be able to move until they hose down the road. The caustic acid will eat rubber. You wouldn't be able to drive more than a mile or two before the tyres go.'

'What about the poor man—?'

'They've called for a helicopter. It'll have to come from Glasgow. But I think they'll have to send some trained firefighters with some equipment up as well. They might send a second helicopter so that they can free him, but to clear the road they'll need a fire engine with a water tank and hoses. I don't know if they have any in Inveraray, or Dumbarton. They might have to come from Glasgow. It could take a long time.'

Lexie looked grey. 'We're cut off.'

'Looks like it.'

'We have to go back to the hotel.'

Molly swallowed hard.

'We'd be several hours getting to Oban and heaven knows when we'll be able to move on south. If we get back to the hotel before others begin to think about it, we might just be able to get our room back. We can have supper sent up. We can have breakfast there too, if you want, then we can set off home tomorrow.'

'I'm not sure—'

'It's not a suggestion, Molly. It's what we're going to do. I'm shattered after the drive here, I'm starving, the baby's starving, and if we don't go *right now*, we could end up sleeping in the car.'

Molly pursed her lips but gave in as gracefully as she could. 'You're right. I'm being selfish. Let's go.'

Chapter Three

Molly seldom slept well. She'd never told Lexie this, although Adam knew, of course – it's hard to hide such things from someone you live with.

When she first met Adam, she'd never even thought about sleep – you don't when you're eighteen. And you certainly don't when all you want to do is have sex, sex and more sex till you can't help sleeping like a god because you're satisfied through and through. That was what it was like thirteen years ago, when she'd first started at uni.

She'd been with a crowd of girls at the bar – not that she knew any of them. They'd all met for the first time that day, so they were sizing each other up. Was the sporty-looking one really good at sports? Was the one with the pebble glasses a brainiac or was that stereotyping? How did that girl with the bob get her hair to look so sleek? And who would be friends with whom come the end of term, or even come next week?

Then the boys arrived and there'd been a change in atmosphere – still a lot of girly chat, but covert glances too, some not so furtive. One girl honed in on a well-muscled guy with a light dusting of facial hair who turned out to be gay, though she didn't discover that for two whole years. Another disappeared after an hour with a preppy-looking youth in a pristine Ralph Lauren polo shirt and pink chinos, setting a pattern that was to be repeated over and again for four years while she worked her way through students and staff.

Molly had arrived at uni the survivor of some short, intense experimental relationships, from her first kiss at the back of a cowshed in Switzerland on a school trip to her first tentative shag with a physics geek with spots and thick glasses, but a great sense of humour.

She turned restlessly. What she remembered most of all was the throbbing sexual hunger she'd felt the first time she'd clapped eyes on Adam Blair, that first night in the students' bar.

'Who's that?'

The girl next to her had shrugged. 'The skinny guy? How would I know?'

He wasn't skinny. He was lean. His limbs were long, his fingers astonishingly elegant. She examined the way they curled into the handle as he picked up his pint, marvelled at the square line of his jaw and the way the craggy broodiness of his face was transformed when he laughed. No, he was not skinny, though there wasn't an ounce of fat on him. She could almost see the muscles under the T-shirt, narrowing to the waist, all the power in the honed upper body, while the denim-clad thighs were compact and firm. Everything about him was exactly as it should be.

'Fancy him?' The girl was laughing. 'I'll fetch him over if you like.'

'No, stop! Don't!'

Her face reddened as the girl called out and waved a glass towards him in a wild gesture of invitation.

Across the room the youth's gaze locked with hers for one ecstatic moment – then some girl in skintight jeans and a slinky top appeared at his side, and awkwardness turned to an anguish so acute that she longed for the embarrassment again.

I don't care, she told herself, he's just one guy among hundreds. And she made herself carry on chatting to the girls as if nothing had changed.

When she looked again, he had gone, and her disappointment was so sharp she was forced to acknowledge it.

'Hi. Can I get you a drink?'

The touch on her shoulder was feather light. She whirled round, her insides detonating. Ka-boom! That had been it. Love at first sight.

Molly was getting stiff. She could feel the tension in her shoulder muscles and rolled onto her side to try to get more comfortable. In the other bed, Lexie was snuffling softly, like a spaniel contentedly chasing rabbits in its dreams.

She reached for her iPod and fumbled for the in-ear headphones. Under the covers, she located the right track of her audio book and set the timer to thirty minutes. If she was still awake, she'd set it again when it turned the player off. And again, if necessary, until sleep finally came.

Adam Blair. Sexy as hell and with a sense of humour so dry you could set light to it. She'd thought she'd be with him for ever. So how had it all gone so badly wrong?

A couple of hours later and three rooms away, the subject of Molly's reminiscences was alert and restless. Adam slipped soundlessly out of bed and padded across the carpet to the window. He eased one heavy curtain away from the glass so that he could steal a look at the morning world.

Inside his chest, his heart seemed to swell. This was what he had come for!

He inched the curtain back further, slipped between the

fabric and the glass and pressed himself against the cold pane, his hands spread above his head, his nose almost touching the window, as if he might absorb the beauty of the scene through every cell.

Already the early sun was glancing off the water. Across the vivid emerald expanse of grass, the loch was a wash of blue framed by the glinting grey of the rocks by the foreshore.

He could feel his breathing deepen. He'd become conditioned to city living. Day after day, he was hemmed in by Edinburgh's grand Georgian buildings. Day after day his eardrums were assaulted by the ceaseless noise of traffic. Day after day he was forced to thread his way through the crowds on the pavements or force a path for his bike between cars on his way to work or home.

He closed his eyes. He hadn't realised how much he'd come to loathe it.

Outside a curlew mewed as it flew across the loch and he opened his eyes again. The siren call of this vastness was too much for him. He had to get out into the fresh air, the wide spaces, the hills. He forgot about the curtain and whirled around in his eagerness so that a bright shaft of light fell across Sunita's slumbering form.

She stirred, threw a hand across her eyes and moaned softly. 'What are you doing?'

He dropped the curtain back into place. 'Shhh. It's all right.'

'What time is it? Come back to bed.'

He surveyed her curled body, so soft and desirable. There was no denying her beauty, and for a brief moment he was tempted to climb back into bed and wind himself around her. But he could have Sunita in his bed any time, while the opportunity for a climb was rare.

'Shhh,' he whispered. 'Go back to sleep, it's still early.

I'm going for a walk.'

She raised her arm, the silky brown of her skin stark against the white cotton cover. He slid briefly into her embrace, nuzzled the softness of her neck with his lips, then extricated himself gently. She was already almost asleep again.

'Back for breakfast?'

'I promise.'

She turned on her side and, almost at once, her breathing deepened.

Chapter Four

Adam missed his way, scrambled up a scree slope and strode across a large patch of heather before he found the path again. He didn't care. His walking boots felt like forgotten friends. For a moment guilt nipped his conscience. This was Sunita's weekend. Maybe he shouldn't have slipped away.

Despite this thought, he didn't stop climbing. At the top of the next ridge he halted, panting. A few years ago he would not have been out of breath.

Far below, he could see the Loch Melfort Hotel, the early morning sun just starting to pick out its white walls. Sunita would still be asleep.

Molly had never been like that.

He pulled a bottle of water out of his backpack and drank.

Correction. Years of stress had made Molly restless, and her wakefulness was contagious. She used to listen to the radio, or stories, to help her relax. Did she still do that?

Adam's jaw tightened. Seeing Molly like that last night ... he'd been shaken. He hadn't seen her for months, then to come across her so unexpectedly ...

She'd looked tired. There were dark circles in the skin below her eyes that had never been there before. And she'd been so shocked to see him that she'd run off.

That hurt.

Adam shoved the bottle into his backpack, straightened and turned up the hill again. No point in going back now, not when he was so near the summit. Sunita would understand.

He attacked the next few hundred feet with ferocious energy, trying not to think about Sunita, or Molly, or even Lexie Gordon, for heaven's sake – the link between those two was what had started all the damage in the first place. Besides, he had other worries. The unexpected phone call from his aunt a few days ago to be exact. He'd been working late – what was new? – when she'd called the office.

'Adam? Is that you?'

'Yes, hello?' he'd said uncertainly, trying to place the voice.

'It's Jean. Auntie Jean.'

'Oh, hi!' He'd pulled himself together. 'How good to hear from you. How are you?'

'Sorry to phone … You know how difficult—'

She'd stumbled to a halt.

Adam had stepped in smoothly. 'I know. You don't need to explain. So?'

He'd swung his chair round and stared out of the window. It was August and the Edinburgh Festival was at its height, but he couldn't see any of the fun from here. His cramped office in Blair King – the law firm started fifty years ago by his grandfather, Duncan Blair, and taken on by Adam's father, James – faced out into a narrow lane at the back of the building. It was an uninspiring view. All he could see was the grubby white-tiled wall of the tiny car park. He could have demanded one of the prime rooms upstairs, but Adam hated pulling rank.

'Are you all right?' he'd prompted, realising she'd gone quiet. 'Or—' he'd had a premonition, '—is it Uncle Geordie?'

'He's dying, Adam. That's what I'm calling about.'

Adam gulped and closed his eyes. He hadn't seen his uncle for three years, and then only at his cousin Hugh's funeral – and what a difficult, stilted encounter that had been, with his father and his uncle not speaking and only an unwelcome sense of family duty driving his father there at all.

'I'm so sorry to hear it,' he'd said, swinging his chair back to his desk and picking up a paperclip. 'What's—?' He stopped abruptly. What was the best way to put such a delicate question? Has he had an accident? What's he got? Is it imminent? Can anything be done? Everything seemed tactless.

A vivid picture of Geordie Blair flashed into his head. Bluff, humorous, warm-hearted, a kind of country version of his father, but physically stronger – the result of a lifetime of heaving hay bales around and hauling calves into the world instead of sitting behind a desk pushing a pen.

'You wouldn't recognise him, Adam,' Jean said, as if guessing his thoughts. 'He's just a husk. There's nothing left of him.'

Her voice had shaken slightly for the first time. Jean Blair had always been a strong woman; it didn't take much imagination to guess at the distress she must be feeling.

Adam fiddled with the paperclip, turning it round and round between his fingers. This was difficult. His father hadn't exactly forbidden him to visit George at Forgie End Farm, but he'd felt bound to take his father's side in the dispute that had opened a chasm between the two brothers. As a child, he'd adored the farm. Jean's voice had brought the rich reek of it flooding back – the unmistakable warm smell of cowpats, of hay and meadow flowers, of baking and woodsmoke. He was unprepared for the profound sense of nostalgia. He clenched his fist so hard that the paperclip bit into his palm.

'I'm so sorry.' What a bloody useless remark. 'Can I visit him? Where is he?'

'He's at home now. He's been in and out of hospital for the last eight weeks, but he refuses to go to a hospice. We're preparing for the worst with the help of a Macmillan nurse.'

'Macmillan? Isn't that cancer?'

The word had slipped out and it lay like a stone between them. Adam cursed inwardly. Couldn't he have been more tactful?

'He was diagnosed with bowel and stomach cancer three months ago. There's nothing they can do. If he'd discovered it earlier—' Her voice shook again, an almost imperceptible tremor, then it had gone and the strong Jean came back. 'I won't bore you with the details. It's all come as a bit of a shock. We haven't had much time to prepare ourselves.'

'I can imagine.' Adam hesitated. 'Do you need some legal help, Jean? I'd be very happy to make sure the paperwork is all in order. A will, for example—'

He'd felt better offering practical help. He was a lawyer: taking care of people's estates was what he did.

'Adam, we moved our business from Blair King when – when Geordie and your father had their row.'

She'd said it gently, but Adam had still cringed. The Great Family Rift. Two decades of bitterness and animosity.

'Of course. I imagine it's all taken care of. So what can I—?'

'He'd like to see you. He really wants to talk to your father, of course, but he sees this as a preliminary.'

'Right.'

'He'll be gone soon, Adam. He has a million regrets and he wants to set them to rest. And he doesn't want your father to have it all on his conscience after he's died, with no opportunity to put things right.'

'That's a generous thought.'

'Will you come out to the farm?'

Adam had dropped the paperclip onto the desk and stared unseeingly at it. His father had made his views clear hundreds of times. *I'll never see the bastard again.* He'd kept it up for years, with only two exceptions – the first at Adam and Molly's wedding, at Adam's insistence, and then at his nephew's funeral as a result of Jean's pleading. Even then, he'd not said a word to Geordie. Not one word. James Blair was made of steel.

'I'll come,' he'd said quietly, 'but I can't promise that I can persuade Dad.'

Predictably, it was Lexie who bounced out of bed first.

'Great move, coming back here,' she announced with horrible cheerfulness as she dragged back the curtains and sunshine flooded in.

Molly groaned and rolled away. The earpieces were still wedged in place. She pulled them out and slipped the iPod under her pillow, but kept her eyes firmly closed.

'Just *look* at that view! Fancy a cuppa? Or shall I order breakfast? What do you feel like?'

Lack of sleep dragged at Molly. 'Go for a walk, Lex,' she mumbled. 'Do some painting. Whatever. Come back in an hour.'

Lexie laughed. 'You're grumpy.'

Molly pulled the pillow over her head and curled up tightly. If she didn't sleep a little longer, she'd be useless all day.

Soon there was silence. The sunshine bathed her in its warmth and gently toasted her until she fell asleep again.

An hour later, she lingered by the huge picture window as Lexie finished dabbing at the red wine stain on her eau-de-nil dress and hung it up to dry. Outside, a few wispy clouds scudded across an otherwise perfect sky. There was no mirror loch this morning; a light breeze was whipping the water into ripples that weren't quite white horses. In the distance, half a dozen dinghies scudded across the blue expanse. The conjunction of rock and grass and sharply-angled mountains was spectacular.

On impulse, she called out, 'Shall we stay tonight? I'd like to stay.'

'You sure?' Lexie emerged from the bathroom. Her hair was an inch or two longer than she normally wore it, and her face a little less angular.

Molly, studying her friend, thought that pregnancy suited her. It took the edge off her restless energy, replacing it with a kind of contentment. After Jamie's death and all they'd been through, it was a welcome sight. She crossed the room and hugged her.

'How's baby Mulgrew-Gordon?'

'Active.'

Lexie reached for Molly's hand and placed it on the bulge.

'She kicked me!' Molly was shocked to feel the stirring of a response to the movement somewhere deep in her own belly.

Lexie laughed and settled her hands on the bump. 'She's going to have Patrick's dynamism. What are you thinking about breakfast?'

'We'll go down, have the full spread.'

'Really?' Lexie didn't say, *What about Adam?* but the unspoken question was there all the same.

'Really. Let's go.'

They picked their way down the stairs, Lexie clutching the handrail to protect against trips, Molly braced for the encounter in a buttocks-clenched, lips-pursed, face-of-plaster kind of way because, although she'd made up her mind to do this, there was a cost.

She was prepared to feel hostile. She was braced for insecurity, and jealousy, and guilt. What she wasn't prepared for was feeling sympathy for the woman Adam had brought with him.

They saw her at once, sitting all alone at a table in a corner of the dining room, turning a mobile phone fretfully round and round in one hand. She was an exotic bird, gloriously clad in emerald silk, but a dejected one.

'Are you on your own?' Molly said, surprising herself by stopping by her table en route to the window.

The woman looked up. 'Adam is already out on the hills.'

Memories flooded back in force. In their first year together Molly and Adam had joined a hill-walking club. Ben Lomond had been her first easy ascent. Ben More, Mull's scenic island peak, her second. Her third had been Ben Nevis, granddaddy of them all. The recollection scythed through her – Adam in his tatty trousers and red jacket, secretly carrying champagne in a backpack all the way to the top to toast her ascent of Britain's biggest mountain.

When had the romantic gestures stopped?

'I didn't think he would be up so early this morning. He was putting his boots on at six o'clock!' The woman's lips (painted pink, the colour of the rhododendrons on the driveway) were curved into a rueful smile. 'I asked him, I said, "Adam, what are you doing? Come back to bed," but he said, "Shhh, sleep, my beauty, I shall walk."

And then he was gone.'

Where had Adam found this striking woman? She was improbably perfect, an airbrushed film star. Her face was oval, her cheekbones high and prominent. Her skin was the colour of pale caramel, and flawless. She had outlined her eyes in black kohl again, and her eyelashes were mascaraed to perfection.

And there was nothing in any of this that made her right for Adam, Molly thought with a surge of belligerence.

'I'm Sunita, by the way.' The vision held out her hand. Molly spotted a large diamond – right hand, not left – and perfect claret-painted nails. 'And you're Molly.' Sunita's smile was brilliant, her dark eyes unreadable, but not hostile. 'Adam talks of you often.'

Does he? Does he really? Molly was shaken by the idea that Adam might discuss her with this woman. It seemed unlikely because he had never been much of a talker – but then, what did she know of Adam now?

'Won't you sit? Please?'

Graceful hands fluttered at empty chairs and Molly's curiosity overtook her hostility. She pulled out a chair and sat.

Sunita turned to Lexie, who had settled herself and her bump in the chair with the best view. 'And you're Alexa Gordon. I'm so pleased to meet you. Adam is such an admirer of your work. He has some large paintings – but then, you know that, of course.'

Molly wondered, Is it because she is with Adam that I don't want to like her?

'What brings you here?' Lexie asked.

'Truthfully? I organised it as a surprise. Adam needed time off. He's such a workaholic. I mean, really, he never stops. You must have found that too, Molly?'

Molly blinked. She doesn't know him well. If she knew him, she would not have brought him here. Not if she wanted his company.

'I like your top,' she blurted out, and was instantly annoyed at the inanity.

'This old thing?' Sunita squinted down at it. 'I only brought it because I know Adam adores me in emerald. You know how he is, Molly. He just loves to pay compliments all the time.'

Molly was thrown. She didn't recognise an Adam who tossed compliments around. Or did she?

She foraged in her memory banks for whispered admiration. 'I love your hair.' 'You smell delicious.' 'You look beautiful in that.' Had he once said such things and she'd just forgotten? Had there been a particular point at which he'd stopped?

'How long have you been seeing Adam?'

Sunita shrugged. 'A few months.'

Molly thought of the envelopes with the Blair King frank on the front that kept arriving at home. He'd known this woman for months, was serious enough to bring her *here*, yet the envelopes, with their nitpicking caveats, whomsoevers and whereats, were still arriving?

'Well,' she said, helping herself to a piece of Sunita's toast, 'have a great day, Sunita. I'm sure he'll be back in time for dinner.'

Chapter Five

Although the descent should have been easier than the climb, the hill was steep in places and Adam had to scramble down with care. It would not be sensible to rick an ankle – or worse – out here on his own. Because of this, it was midday when he marched into the car park at the back of the hotel, his feet smarting and his legs alarmingly weak.

Their room was locked and there was no response to his knock. He'd have to get a key from reception. Or perhaps Sunita was enjoying the sun down by the loch. Dumping his small backpack on the cedar walkway outside their room, he went back down the stairs to look for her.

There were half a dozen people down on the foreshore. Lexie Gordon, her crimson hair unmistakeable, appeared to be painting. Several children were scrambling around on the rocks while a man was stretched out in the sunshine nearby. A woman, perched on a rock, her arms round her knees, was talking on a phone.

It had to be Molly; he'd know that pale gold hair and the long back anywhere. Even the distant outline of her body excited him, just as it had years ago – only this time desire, being one-sided, hurt.

Before he could think about what he was doing, he headed for the path across the field. Lexie remained oblivious, her concentration on her task absolute. What was she painting? Even Alexa Gordon's rough sketches, these days, were worth good money; her partner Patrick Mulgrew had ensured that.

He was a dozen paces away from Molly now, and there was still no sign that she was aware of his presence.

'—I can't believe you're saying this. ... Don't you *dare* tell me that ... Listen. Shut up for one minute and just *listen,* will you?'

Molly was nettled.

'No! We will not pick another date and we will not go ahead without you. You will clear whatever it is you have in your diary, and you will make sure you come to his lunch party. You *and* Adrienne and the boys. Do you understand me, Logan?'

Adam had to stop himself smiling. Molly's brother Logan was also a partner at Blair King. He was gifted, charming and hardworking; he arrived in the office early and left late, as most of them did – but then, Molly could hardly criticise him for that because the term 'workaholic' fitted her like a sheer silk stocking.

He and Molly had played a game once, at some party: 'Describe your partner in one word'.

'Conscientious,' Molly had written on her scrap of paper.

'Driven,' Adam had scrawled.

And they'd both laughed, wryly acknowledging the truth of their descriptions.

'Right.' Irritation had crept into Molly's voice. 'Fine. Don't you worry about the arrangements, I'll manage.' There was a short pause. Adam heard only the lapping of the waves on the shingly beach and the squeals of the children playing. 'I *know* I'm an events manager. I've *said* I'll organise everything. Just be sure you turn up, and Logan—' another short pause. 'For God's sake bring a nice present. I don't know! Use your imagination!

Okay. Yes. Yes. Bye.'

It wasn't until she'd cut the call that she turned her head and became aware of him.

'Oh!'

He'd never seen her hazel eyes so wide. For a second he thought she was going to scramble up and run away from him again, but she didn't move.

He hesitated. 'May I sit? I've just staggered down from some lump over there—' he waved towards the hills, '—and my legs are telling me I'm shockingly unfit.'

Lump. It was an old joke. The first time Molly had ever climbed a mountain, she'd been surprised at the length of the trudge. 'Call that a mountain?' Adam had joked. 'That's just a lump.'

He caught a hint of a smile before she moved aside, shifting her long legs in their skinny jeans to make room for him. She was still wearing Converse hi-tops, he noticed. She'd been welded to them. He scanned the shoes more carefully. They even seemed to be the same pair, grey with white trim and a small stain by the top lace on the right shoe where she'd splashed hot oil one day.

His wife was a stranger, yet not a stranger. The purgatory of separation niggled at him.

He crossed his ankles and sank onto the rock.

'I don't know how you *do* that,' she burst out, smothering a smile again.

'Do what?'

'That sitting thing. You know, without losing your balance.'

Adam leaned back against the rock and closed his eyes. He wanted to look at her. He wanted to drink in every detail, but it was too painful.

A few yards behind him, a child yelled, 'You're *horrible*, Jason. I'm going to tell Daddy!'

'Tell Daddy what?' came a man's voice. 'No, don't bother. I have a feeling I don't want to hear. Come on now, you lot, get your things, it's time for lunch.'

'Aww.'

'Must we?'

'Can I have chips?'

Adam opened his eyes a crack and was relieved to see that Molly wasn't studying him. Instead, she was staring at the children.

She'd never wanted kids. He'd asked her one day, before they were married. They'd taken a short break to the sun and he'd come out with the question as they sat by the swimming pool at the less than luxurious hotel, surrounded by a squealing, shrieking, yelling crowd of youngsters, whining for ice cream, or pizza, or chips every few minutes.

'God no,' she'd said, frowning as a particularly large child leapt into the pool and sent splashes jetting across a dozen yards. 'Can you imagine?'

It had been an ill-chosen holiday, and if they'd found out anything about each other in those few days it was that package holidays didn't suit them. Soon they'd both been too busy scaling their respective career ladders to discuss the matter of a family again. And that had been that.

'I'm sorry we startled you last night,' he said, his voice low. 'I had no idea you were going to be here, or I would never have—'

'You don't need to explain.'

'I just wanted you to—'

'Ah, there you are!'

Another voice interrupted his explanation and Adam sat up abruptly. He didn't mean it to look like a guilty start, and the thought that Sunita might interpret it like that unsettled him.

'Hi!'

Gold sandals winked across the last few clumps of grass and wobbled up the uneven surface of the rock.

'Oh! Damn!' Sunita swayed and might have fallen if Adam hadn't sprung to his feet in one lithe movement and caught her. 'Ouch!' She reached down and rubbed her ankle.

Adam noticed Molly's frown and knew she was wondering, as he was, whether the stumble had been deliberate.

Sunita seemed oblivious.

'Thank goodness you caught me,' she said, her smile dazzling. She raised her arms and hooked them round his neck, then pressed her ruby-painted lips to his mouth. 'Have you had a wonderful morning?'

She could hardly have made the statement of possession more obvious. So it had been deliberate.

Molly stood. 'Listen, I'll leave you two. It's time for lunch, and Lexie needs to eat.'

'Maybe we'll see you at dinner?' Adam called as she leapt gracefully across the rocks.

She lifted a hand in acknowledgement, but if she replied, he didn't catch it.

'Lovely girl,' Sunita said, laying the palm of her hand on his chest. 'Now, tell me all about where you've been and what it was like. I'm dying to hear about your climb.'

Molly, hopping from rock to rock, was conscious of Adam's gaze following her and her face burned. She had not known she still felt like this.

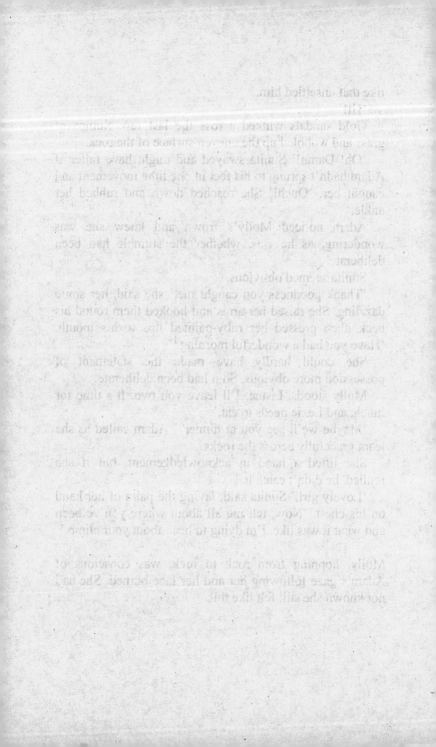

Chapter Six

Caitlyn Murray grabbed for the tin of baked beans as a boy raced down the aisle, backpack flailing behind him as he sprinted for the door.

Too late. The backpack hit the display and yanked a corner tin out of place. Cans crashed noisily onto the floor and rolled in surprising directions under the shelving.

'Kevin McQuade, I've told you before!' she yelled after the small boy.

It was no use. The thieving brat had gone already and there wasn't much any of them could do about it. The days when the local constable would have grabbed a snotty-nosed kid by the ear and dragged him terrified to his father for a ticking off were long gone. Kevin – who lived a few doors down from Caitlyn's family on the Summerfield estate – wouldn't suffer. He definitely wouldn't be told off by his parents. In fact Caitlyn suspected it was his mother who'd sent him out to steal. Angie McQuade had an exaggerated sense of what she was owed by the world at large.

'You OK, Cait?'

One of the assistants scuttled from behind the shelves, his face a picture of concern.

'It's fine, Joe. I'm fine.'

She ducked away and reached to retrieve one of the tins.

'Here, let me.'

'Thanks Joe.'

'He take anything?'

'Probably. It really bugs me. Honest folk work for a living.'

'Like you and me, yeah? Doesn't pay much though, does it?'

'Still,' she said.

It was Friday night, but Caitlyn didn't have any plans, which was just as well because she didn't get away until almost ten o'clock.

The supermarket was on the edge of Hailesbank, on the site of an old printing works. Caitlyn could remember the factory. She'd even been inside once on a school trip. She could still hear the noise of the machines and see the grimy windows, looking like no-one had cleaned them for a hundred years. Her friend Jenna said it was about time that smelly old place was pulled down and Hailesbank needed a supermarket anyway, but Caitlyn missed the factory. She liked the magic of seeing the vast sheets of paper hammering through the massive presses, building yellow upon magenta upon cyan upon black until everything came together in a perfect full-colour sheet at the end.

Everywhere had supermarkets. She didn't know where there was another print works. Still, a job was a job. She had to make up for the salary she used to earn from her job in Edinburgh and needed every penny she could get to help her mum out.

'Night, Cait!' called Joe, who was guarding the door to stop latecomers sneaking in. 'Safe home!'

'You too.'

She scurried through the car park. There were only four cars left. Earlier, she'd seen people driving round and round, searching for spaces. Shopping here was a stressful experience.

Caitlyn didn't have a car. She walked out of the car park and took the path along the river to the bridge. The bus to Summerfield left from the town hall, and she had just ten minutes to catch it or she'd have to walk the couple of miles home.

From the far side of the bridge she could see the bus, waiting at the stop. She started to run. It was uphill, and by the time she got close she was puffing. The town hall clock read ten twelve. If Dan was driving, she'd be fine. If it was Jake, he might decide to leave early.

She was fifty yards from the bus when she heard the engine start up and it pulled into the road.

'Stop!' She waved her hands frantically. 'Stop! Oh please!'

She glimpsed Jake's face, resolutely averted, as the bus trundled past her.

'*Bother* you, Jake Thorogood!'

She flopped down onto the low wall outside the police station, her feet already throbbing from long hours of walking round the store. Jake had been impossible since the time he'd made a pass at her at the pub Christmas social and she'd had to slap his face. Caitlyn despised her curves, she longed to be whippet thin so that clothes looked good on her, but it seemed her shape appealed to men like Jake. The wrong sort of men.

She stood up resolutely. She'd have to walk; sitting here wouldn't get her home. She turned towards Summerfield. It'd take her half an hour if she strode out, forty minutes at this pace. She didn't have the energy for striding, so forty minutes it'd have to be. What was bugging her most was not Jake's behaviour, nor even the fact that she'd have to walk; it was that by the time she got home there'd be no chance at all of seeing Iona May before she fell asleep.

Caitlyn's youngest half-sister was six years old and cute as a kitten, with soft, fluffy blonde hair, blue eyes as big as two moons and a little nose that turned up at the end. She didn't look much like their mother and there was no resemblance at all to Mick Boyce, the child's now-absent father – and thank heaven for that.

She passed the last house in Hailesbank and stepped into the gathering darkness where the town lights ended. At least there was a pavement the whole way. She started counting steps. It was a mile and a half now. One thousand, seven hundred and sixty yards in a mile, that made two thousand, six hundred and forty yards. She couldn't stride a whole yard though, so maybe three thousand steps till she was home. She resolved to count and got to one hundred and six before thoughts started crowding in.

Like how good it would be not to have to share a room with her other half-sister, Ailsa. Like where she'd be now if she hadn't resigned from Blair King a year ago. Like what her life would have been like if her dad hadn't died and her mum hadn't let Mick Boyce move in.

She switched to counting cars that passed instead of steps. It was easier.

Two the other way, just one going in her direction. Then a rival supermarket's delivery van. The poor driver had obviously been working late too. Behind it, a string of cars.

She lost count.

Farm Lane, where Caitlyn lived with her mother, was about as unlike a farm lane as you could imagine. There was the old Crossed Keys pub at one end of it, and maybe that had been a barn or something a long time ago, because it was built of rough stone, but the rest of the lane was council housing. It was grey and dismal, and all the houses looked identical, except that some had tidy front patches with a small square of green grass and a few flowers, others had been concreted over so that there was no work involved in keeping them tidy. Yet others were used as a dumping ground for everything that wasn't wanted in the house but no-one could be bothered to take to the tip.

She was nearing one of these, the one that belonged to Angie McQuade, whose youngest son Kevin had caused havoc in the supermarket earlier. One of the older McQuade boys was emerging from the front door, on his way for a quick pint at the pub, no doubt, having polished off whatever grub Kevin had filched. Caitlyn kept her head down and strode on, praying she'd get past before he realised who she was.

Too late.

'What's yer hurry, Cait-no-mates?'

The youth stepped out in front of her and seized her wrist with a malicious grin. It was Ricky, the eldest. Caitlyn had been at school with Ricky and knew he was a bully. She wasn't afraid of him – she knew too many of his secrets for him to be any real threat to her, but if she didn't handle him right, she'd waste more precious time before she got home and she really wasn't in the mood for a fight.

She squared her shoulders and looked him in the eye. 'You're the one in a hurry, Ricky. You're running out of drinking time.'

He released her wrist to glance at his watch. 'Shit!'

'They'll be taking last orders. You'd better run.'

He swung away. 'Another time,' he cackled. 'You and me—' He made an obscene gesture.

He made Caitlyn feel uncomfortable. She could handle

Ricky on his own, but if he was in a crowd, he might gain courage.

'Enjoy your pint,' she called after him. Never show weakness.

The Murrays lived a few doors further down. They used to have a small lawn, but after Mick left, her mum got Malcolm Milne to come and lay some slabs in the small space between the front wall and the house. 'I haven't the time to keep it nice, and that's the truth,' Joyce said when Caitlyn protested.

Caitlyn was working in Edinburgh at the time and couldn't spend hours gardening either, so she could hardly object.

At the gate, she paused. She longed to get through the door and collapse on a chair with a cuppa, but she knew it wouldn't be that simple. It never was in the Murray household.

She turned her key in the lock. It opened with a protesting creak.

'Harris has just farted, Harris has just farted,' Lewis chanted, prancing round and round her in the small hallway. The older of the Murray twins (by seven minutes) clamped two fingers over his nose. 'Pooh.'

'Have not.'

'Have sot.'

'Have *not!*'

'Stop it, you two,' Caitlyn said wearily. 'Just give it a break, huh?'

She'd hoped that the twins might be in bed, but no such luck. Lewis (bigger and more dominant) dashed past his brother, pinching him on the arm as he ran.

'Ouch! That hurt, you bastard!'

'Harris, language!'

'Well, he pinched me! Tell him off!' Harris's face was

tragic. One day, perhaps, the twins would stand together against the world, but that day could be a long way off.

'Ignore him. Come here.' She folded her arms round the boy, feeling the bones under the skinniness. Harris had always had health issues.

A shadow fell across them as Ailsa slouched out of the front room.

'They're mental.'

She pulled a strand of bleached hair in front of her eyes and examined the ends. The fluorescent pink of her nails exactly matched the colour she'd painted her lips. Ailsa was fifteen and obsessed with her looks (which would be lovely, Caitlyn thought, if only she'd let nature have its own way). She certainly wasn't much interested in her young brothers. Caitlyn worried about leaving her in charge, but if Joyce was on duty at the care home there was little choice. There wasn't enough money to pay a babysitter.

She straightened up and released Harris. 'Get your pyjamas on, boys,' she called as Lewis reappeared, tearing the wrapper off a chocolate biscuit. She tweaked it out of his hand.

'Hey! Gimme that—'

She held it above her head. 'You know you're not allowed biscuits at this time of night. Now go and get ready for bed. I'll be up in five minutes.'

His bravado collapsed in the face of her quiet authority and he stomped off muttering, 'It isn't *fair.*'

She turned to Ailsa. 'Have they behaved?'

Ailsa shrugged, tossing her head so that the blonde locks swung in a wave round her face. 'I guess.'

Caitlyn took off her jacket and hung it on a peg alongside Iona May's little pink fleece, her mother's mac and an assortment of football shirts belonging to the boys.

'Is Iona May asleep?'

'Yeah.' Ailsa's pout receded. 'Had to carry her up, she went off in the middle of her video. We hadn't even got to that bit where Shrek—'

'Ready!' came a voice from above.

'Smelly, smelly, farty!' chanted the other.

Ailsa rolled her eyes and a half-smile tugged at the corners of Caitlyn's mouth. 'Stick the kettle on, Ails, will you? I'd kill for a cup of tea.'

'What did your last servant die of?' Ailsa muttered as she swung away, but she went to the kitchen anyway.

Chapter Seven

Molly pulled back the curtains in the living room of her apartment at Fleming House and blinked as sun flooded in. A kestrel was hovering above the field beyond the formal garden, its wings barely fluttering, suspended in the vivid blue sky. Suddenly it swooped, rose and flew off down the river, and the gracefulness of the movement almost winded her.

I live here on borrowed time, she reminded herself, grabbing her jacket and handbag and heading for the door. It's not where my career should finish – and staying here would be a dead-end because there are no opportunities for promotion.

She had come here to hide, desperate to escape a grief so bound about by guilt that she could confess it to no-one, and it had proved the perfect sanctuary. The work here was not so much mentally draining as physically demanding. Each day she drove herself to the point of exhaustion, so she was sometimes able to sleep.

She blamed herself for Jamie Gordon's death and for the failure of her marriage.

Had anything she'd done been justifiable – or forgivable?

Unsettled, Molly pulled the door behind her and scuttled down the stone stairs to the oak door. Seeing Adam had disturbed her, and that was the truth of it.

No. Not just Adam. Adam with another woman.

The commute to her office in the main part of the

49

building was all of forty yards. It ended in a climb of twenty-two marble stairs before her route veered away from the ballroom, with its floor-to-ceiling windows and crystal chandeliers, towards a service corridor and a more modest room. Still, not many offices boasted views across such magnificent parkland.

The job at Fleming House had served her well for the past two years, but at last she was ready to move on. She should call a recruitment agency and start to look for something else.

She hooked her jacket over a peg on the door and booted up her computer. While it hummed and whirred, she pulled last night's list towards her and was about to slot her glasses onto her nose when the ring of the telephone on her desk made her jump.

'Molly Keir?'

'Hello?' The deep voice at the other end of the phone was familiar, she just couldn't … 'Barnaby?'

She'd worked alongside Barnaby Fletcher at Petronius Marketing in Edinburgh for years, but what had once been a working relationship that crackled with creative energy had become little more than a name in a contacts book. 'Wow! You've been so quiet I thought you must have emigrated.'

His deep-throated chuckle took Molly right back. They'd had such fun.

'Still here, just busy. What about you?'

Barnaby's brand of sunshine was invigorating.

'Oh, just running around organising everyone.'

'Nothing's changed then.'

'Are you in Edinburgh?'

'Uh huh.'

'Let me guess. Cloud Nine?' She named a computer game firm they'd worked for at Petronius. She'd heard he'd nicked the contract when he'd gone freelance.

'You haven't lost your nose, Moll, hiding away in that rotting pile, I'll say that for you.'

'Hardly a rotting pile. We've turned everything round.'

'I'm sure you've worked miracles. I have every faith in you – which brings me to why I'm calling.'

'Oh yes? So why *are* you calling? Not that I'm not pleased to hear from you,' she added. Just hearing Barnaby's voice had already made her morning feel brighter.

'You've been at Fleming House for – remind me – how long?'

'Almost two years.'

'We all thought it was an odd move.'

Molly said nothing.

'Your choice, of course. But knowing you, I can't imagine it's part of your career plan to stay there for ever.'

'Probably not,' she conceded.

'I've got a proposition for you.'

'And you a married man too!'

'I've been doing exceptionally well. This year especially, despite the difficult market conditions. I'm so busy, in fact, that I can't cope on my own, there's far too much work. I need a partner. And I'd like it to be you.'

Molly's mouth dropped open. She twisted her glasses round and round between her fingers.

'Why me?'

'We have complementary skills. I'm a strategist and a high-level planner. You deliver. You're an ideas person and a first-class events manager – and you've got a magic touch with people. We're a great team, Molly. I always thought so. I've been thinking long and hard about whom I should ask, and I keep coming back to one name –

Molly Keir. It feels right. *You* feel right. I'm just hoping that you're ready to come out of the hole you've been hiding in and take on the world with me. What do you say?'

'I'm stunned.'

It was true. Her head had begun to spin. She was dazed. Her heart had started to beat faster.

London?

As a partner?

The prospect was almost unimaginably exciting. She'd compete with the big guys, get a pop at the juicy accounts. It would bring out all her skills, demand peak performance, draw out the creativity that had been buried recently.

'It would mean a move to London,' Barnaby was saying, 'but you always used to talk about how much you'd love that if it weren't for Adam being a lawyer in Scotland. And now that you're divorced—'

'We're not divorced, actually.'

'No? I thought—'

'Nothing on paper.'

The latest envelope from Blair King was lying in front of her, still unopened. She dropped her glasses on the desk and picked it up. The first year apart from Adam had been desperately difficult. No-one would have blamed him for filing for divorce immediately once he'd found out about Jamie, yet he'd done nothing more than quibble about things that were quite unimportant. Custody of the cheese grater, the OS map collection, the *West Wing* box set.

'Never mind that,' she said, 'tell me more.'

'I said partnership, but it's probably time to go limited liability. You'd be a director. There's more than enough work, so we'll need to hire staff right away.'

'Wow. Golly.' She gulped, trying to take it in. 'Does it

have to be London?'

'Follow the money, Moll, you know that. Yes, we have to be in London, but there's plenty of work in Scotland, ripe for the picking. You could be in charge of anything that comes up there, if you want. It'll give you some reasonable chunks of time to be at home with your father; I know that would be a concern.'

'You're right,' Molly admitted reluctantly, but her duty to her father wasn't something she could walk away from – nor, despite the excitement of Barnaby's proposal, did she want to. 'Dad's getting on a bit, and he's beginning to lose his sight. Being so far away would be a worry.'

'You've got a brother, right? And it's only an hour by plane.'

'I guess so.'

'Listen, I know I've given you a lot to think about, but I'll need to know soon. You're first on my list, but there are other options. Can you make it into Edinburgh tonight? We could discuss it over dinner.'

Molly pulled her diary towards her. At a push, she could make herself free. 'I can be there.'

'Good. Make one of your famous lists. Ask me anything you need to know.'

'You bet.'

'One last thing before I go. Equity.'

'Equity?'

'I wouldn't want it to be a shock when we meet, so I'm putting it on the table now. If you're to be a director, you'll need to buy into the business. That's only reasonable. I've done all the hard graft so far, and I need recognition of that and proof of your commitment. Plus, the bank will demand working capital if we're going to move into offices and start hiring staff. My money's all tied up in cash flow and equipment.'

'How much are you looking for?'

The sum he named seemed unimaginably large. Molly swallowed.

'I'm prepared to open the company accounts to you so that you can take financial advice, but honestly, Molly, you'd never regret it. You'd get it all back, and a shedload more. I've got faith in myself and I've got faith in you. We can conquer the world! Or at least,' his deep chuckle made her smile, 'hit top spot in the world of marketing. I'm giving that target five years.'

It was impossible not to be swept away by Barnaby's enthusiasm. 'You're a silver-tongued charmer.'

'You'll join me?'

'Whoa there!' Molly fought to put the brakes on her own enthusiasm. 'It's a big decision. Let's just say I'm excited.'

'Good. I appreciate that. We'll talk tonight. Hadrian's, seven thirty.'

'See you then.'

She sat in the abrupt silence staring out to the park, where a family of deer had ventured almost up to the house and were grazing peacefully in the sunshine.

She'd been ambitious once; it was one thing Adam had loved about her.

She could remember his exact words. She'd been working as an intern in a marketing agency in Edinburgh one long not-so-lazy summer. Adam's grin had still been boyish, his face unlined. They had been sitting in the Meadows, snatching precious time on a mellow evening, enjoying an illegal barbecue in a foil container. It had left, she remembered, a scorch mark on the grass, which Adam had dabbed at guiltily and fruitlessly.

'You've got a spark. Sparkle. A sprinkle of sparkles.'

His admiration had spurred her on. Maybe now was her chance to reconnect with that sense of ambition.

She pulled out a pad of paper and checked the action list she'd made last night.

WORK

- Calm Ellen Prosser's pre-wedding nerves (and deal with her *mother*!)
- Negotiate delegate day rates for the insurance company conference
- Source peonies for Sophia di Constanza's collection launch.

PERSONAL

- Book venue for Dad's celebration
- Issue the invitations
- Find a gift.

How different might her lists be if she took up Barnaby's offer?

Chapter Eight

'I can be in the Abbotsford,' Logan said down the phone, 'by six forty-five. Any chance of you joining me?'

He caught Molly as she was closing down her computer. She clamped her phone between her shoulder and the side of her head, tucked her reading glasses into their case and dropped them into her bag.

'Tonight?' she said, picking up her handbag and grabbing her jacket from the hook on the back of the door.

'Of course tonight.'

'You're impossible, Logan!'

'Me? Why?'

'I've been trying to get hold of you for weeks and you expect me to drop everything and run at a moment's notice when you finally deign to call.'

'It's been busy here. Can you?'

Molly swallowed her irritation. 'I am heading into Edinburgh this evening, as it happens,' she admitted with great reluctance, 'but I was planning on showering and changing first. I've got an important meeting.'

'I'm sure you look presentable. You always do. If you leave now you should make it.'

'*Logan!*'

'I've got a great idea for Dad's present—' he went on, ignoring her.

'You have? What?'

'—and I'll tell you all about it when I see you. Bye.'

'No! Logan, tell me *now*—'

But he had cut the call.

She stared at her phone, fuming. He hadn't even asked her about her meeting.

Molly had taken the train from Hailesbank into Edinburgh many times since she'd moved out of the terraced house in Trinity where Adam still lived.

'Why don't you sell?' Lexie asked her on a regular basis.

But Molly was content with the arrangement. It might seem odd to outsiders, but it suited her. Her investment was still an investment and Adam was looking after it and paying the bills. She paid a nominal rent on the flat within Fleming House and she didn't have to worry about where to move or what to do with the money.

And *how* Adam would be looking after it! Molly was organised, but Adam was almost compulsively tidy. He would never drop his trousers on the floor at night; they'd always be folded and hung up, the pockets emptied. His toothbrush, toothpaste, shaving kit, deodorant and dental floss would be neatly lined up in the bathroom in just the right place. Molly would take a bet for any amount that she could walk into the kitchen right now and know exactly where the potato peeler was, the corkscrew, the paper block for making notes or writing shopping lists, the electric whisk, the ramekins that he'd probably not used since she left, or the egg poacher that he probably used every day.

She used to tease Adam about his tidiness, but the familiarity of the household arrangements was oddly comforting. In a world where everything had been shifting – was still shifting – at least one thing would always be reliably the same.

The train ambled into Musselburgh, and shortly

afterwards, green fields turned into suburbs: new estates of detached houses for the upwardly mobile, then acres of 1930s bungalows, each sitting in a pretty plot. Bungalows mutated into city streets – Victorian houses and rows of tenement buildings where families co-existed in flats sharing a common stair.

She should think about Barnaby.

She *was* thinking about Barnaby.

Still, she couldn't help her thoughts drifting back to the weekend. It had been a shock, seeing Adam there with another woman – not that he wasn't entitled after what she'd done to him. But Molly didn't believe he was in love with Sunita. Not even close. He didn't have that look in his eyes, the intensity that she knew and remembered so well.

'We're now approaching Waverley Station—'

Molly jolted upright. They were in Edinburgh already, and despite her intentions, she'd given no thought to Barnaby's proposal at all. She had been thinking instead about the picture of Adam in his parents' house, the boy in grubby shorts leading the cows on his uncle's farm in for milking, a look on his face of beaming pride.

What had happened to that radiance? Exactly where, over the years, had the happy little boy on the farm slithered into adulthood and life in a lawyerly cell?

She pulled out her mobile.

'Logan? I'll be there in five minutes.'

'I'm here already. What's your poison?'

'Just some sparkling water, thanks.'

'I'll have it set up.'

She walked up the ramp out of the station to one of the best panoramas in Europe. For some reason, the pretty jumble of the Arts and Crafts flats in Ramsay Gardens drew Molly's eye tonight, standing in such stark contrast to their brooding neighbour, the Castle. Could she bear to leave this for London?

A piper, busking on the corner of Princes Street, struck up a dirge and she smiled to herself. Sooner or later the dour side of Scottishness always surfaced.

She began to weave her way through the narrow cobbled lanes to where the Abbotsford Bar stood, almost unchanged for half a century. Logan was leaning on the burnished wood of the broad bar, drinking a pint of something dark. She hovered for a moment, studying him. He was tall, just as she was, but dark-haired. They had the same even features and clear skin, and they both had hazel eyes. They both had a long, straight nose and generous lips. There, perhaps, the resemblance ended. Molly's features were finer and more feminine; Logan was more chiselled and his cheekbones were better defined. He wore his hair short, but with some length on top, and it was thicker than Molly's and wavier.

It was obvious he'd come straight from work. Sharp suit, crisp shirt with double cuffs and gold cuff links she knew for a fact had come from Tiffany's, Church's lace-ups you could see your face in. Adam never spent money on himself, but Blair King must be doing well judging by Logan's extravagance. His two sons were at private school, Adrienne didn't work and they lived in a five-bedroomed house in smart-set suburbia. She wasn't resentful of his success, only annoyed that she'd created the mess that had caused her own career to stall.

'You're looking different,' she said. 'What's with the beard?'

Logan stroked his chin and laughed. It never seemed to matter how stressed Logan was, he always had an easy laugh. 'It's quicker than shaving. Anyway, Adrienne likes it.'

'How is Adrienne? And the boys? I haven't seen them in ages.'

'They're fine.'

She picked up her water. 'What was your idea?'

'Idea?'

She shoved his arm. 'Stop winding me up. I've only got twenty minutes.'

He drained the last of his beer and waved the empty glass towards the barman. 'What would you say to clubbing together to get Dad something special?'

'Fine. Any ideas?'

She was ready for the airy, 'Oh, I'll leave that to you, just tell me how much I need to chip in.'

Logan said, 'You know Aunt Jessica?'

'Dad's sister? In Melbourne?'

'We've only got one Aunt Jessica, I believe.'

'Don't be sarky. I was surprised, that's all.'

'There's only a year between them, so it's her seventieth next year. I thought we could get him a plane ticket.'

Molly gaped at her brother. He'd been spraying money around like champagne from a well-shaken bottle in the last couple of years so the generosity of it was no surprise, but it was unlike him to be so imaginative.

'It's a great idea.'

'Thought you'd like it. Can you afford it? Don't want to push you.'

'Of course. I'd love to do something special for Dad and I'm hardly spending any money at the moment. Let's go for it. Half and half.'

'Attagirl! Thanks, mate.' He lifted the freshly pulled pint and sipped at it appreciatively. 'So what's this meeting you're off to then?'

'Oh—' Unexpectedly, Molly felt the need to keep

Barnaby and his offer to herself. 'Nothing.'

'You always did clam up when you were planning something,' Logan said.

She grinned. Logan was right. She was deeply superstitious about sharing her schemes until they came to fruition. 'I'll tell you if it comes to anything.'

'Hmm.' He put his beer down on the counter and kissed her cheek. 'Same old Moll. Will you organise the ticket? Let me know how much I owe you.'

'You are coming to Dad's party, aren't you? You and the family?'

'Saturday evening?'

'I changed it to Sunday lunch. Don't you ever read your emails?'

She punched his chest lightly with an exasperation that was not feigned at all. 'Sun-day. Sun-day. Got it?'

'Yes, Miss.'

'Hah!'

She gave him a quick hug and headed for the door, shaking her head. Managing Logan was Adrienne's job now – for which relief, much thanks.

The moment she spotted Barnaby Fletcher in a corner of the restaurant, she knew she had to accept his offer. It wasn't just that he hadn't changed one bit (except maybe put on a few pounds), it was the surge of adrenalin she experienced at the idea of working with him again.

'You look—' he held her at arm's length and studied her face, '—exactly the same. That is to say, stunning. Here.' He pulled out a chair for her. 'Sit down. Are you all right there? This is wonderful. Terrific. It's so *good* to see you.'

He filled his expensive jacket and, where once there

might have been a little more slack round the neck of his shirt, the flesh almost bulged above it. Almost, but not quite. He was still a fine-looking man – not classically handsome, but with pleasant, open features and a warmth in his gaze that was impossible not to like.

'I won't ask about Adam,' he said when they had ordered, 'but tell me about life at Fleming House. I want to know everything that's been happening since I saw you.'

'A few lows, inevitably,' she confessed. 'Never enough people on the ground, never enough budget. But the highs have been considerable. I've built it from virtually nothing into a highly profitable venture.' She couldn't keep the pride out of her voice.

'Tell me more.'

He ate while she talked, which suited her. Her stomach was so knotted that she had no appetite. 'We honed in on the wedding trade. I persuaded Lady Fleming to make a few rooms in the house available for the bridal party and we upgraded the ballroom and its facilities. Business has been incredible. The grounds are lovely, of course, and we use top-notch caterers. But the highlight has been converting the barn into a restaurant and conference facility.'

'That sounds like a challenge.' Barnaby, finishing his steak, was watching her closely.

'It needed tight management. I brought it in before time and under budget.' Did her sense of achievement show? The conversion had been a major project and she had managed it alongside running the events.

Barnaby cleaned his plate and patted his stomach appreciatively. 'So,' he said, studying her, 'now to the big question.'

Molly's heart began to race. So here it was. Her future.

This was a negotiation, and Barnaby Fletcher was good at negotiations – but so was she. Professionalism kicked in.

She avoided Barnaby's eyes, lifted her glass and held it in front of the candle on the table between them.

'I've been thinking about it.'

'And?'

'I'm very flattered.'

Don't show him how excited you are. Play hard to get.

Barnaby leaned forward and edged the glass aside with a gentleness surprising for such a big man. The directness of his gaze was unnerving – he had a knack of making you feel he could read your thoughts.

'I hope I don't sense a "but" coming on, Molly. You know this opportunity is made for you.'

'It's a big decision.'

'I know.'

'It means moving away from all my friends. More importantly, it means moving away from Dad.'

Molly raised the glass to her lips and took a sip. It was a buttery Tokay, and very good. Barnaby had never been a man to skimp on quality in any aspect of his life. If she lived in London, she could enjoy this kind of life. If she were part of Barnaby's business, she'd be on expense accounts – and with the kind of clients they'd be pitching for, you weren't talking McDonald's.

But it was about much more than the good life. It was about stretching herself to the utmost, using her creativity and management skills at the highest level.

'You've asked for a lot of money.'

'You'd earn it back in a couple of years.'

'I'd still have to find it.'

He sat back and looked at her levelly. 'That can't be impossible. It's a good offer, Molly. I've been frank about the current contracts and the future prospects. You must have been keeping up with the industry; you know what's possible.'

'I'm not certain—'

Barnaby looked at her, one eyebrow raised. 'You have doubts about your ability to do the job?'

'No! Of course not. I'd relish the challenge.'

'I can't believe you're seriously worried about raising the cash, but I understand you'll need to talk it over with your lawyer.'

Molly winced.

'OK, not Adam, but you must have a lawyer. I do need an answer, Molly. Let's see – this is Monday. Shall we say Friday for a decision? You understand that if you turn this down I'll need to get moving on Plan B pretty quickly.'

'Give me till next Monday?'

It wasn't just about playing down her interest now. She'd have to work out how to raise the cash, and there was only one way she could think of …

Barnaby said coolly, 'There's a queue.'

'I imagine there is. But I will need to talk to a few people first. That's fair, isn't it?'

One corner of Barnaby's mouth lifted.

'I promise you'll have my answer a week today.'

'Fair enough. I'll keep my fingers crossed that it's the right one.'

They parted amiably, Molly to catch her train, Barnaby to go to his deep feathery mattress in the luxurious surroundings of the Balmoral Hotel. It had been an interesting evening.

Chapter Nine

Caitlyn, laden with carrier bags, hobbled along Farm Lane wishing she were the kind of person who could nick a supermarket trolley without so much as a blush. But, leaving aside the certainty of being sacked, stealing anything was strictly against her principles.

The potatoes in one of the bags in her left hand weighed only fractionally less than the bottle of Coke in the heaviest bag in her right. The cucumber she'd thrown into the trolley (healthy, no calories, on offer) had nicked the polythene and was starting to slide out. Harris had demanded baked beans, Lewis had insisted on spaghetti hoops. Ailsa, on a health kick, wanted a melon. Thank heavens Isla May hadn't made any demands and her mother was eating next to nothing.

When, fifty yards from number eleven, the end of the cucumber finally split the bag, everything spilled out – baked beans, spaghetti, melon and all. She came to an ungraceful halt.

'Damn!'

Crotchety with tiredness, she lurched towards a tin that was rolling towards the gutter. If Kevin McQuade came past now, the shopping would be off the pavement and into the McQuade kitchen in a blink. She rammed the contents of the split bag into the surviving carriers and prayed she could make it along the road in one piece.

Lurching lopsidedly as she struggled to bear the weight of one bulging bag now with the potatoes, the melon *and* the bottle of Coke and holding it just off the ground in case it, too, decided to split, she rounded the last bend before her house. Someone was sweeping an electric trimmer across the hedge, left to right, right to left, sending leaves tumbling to the pavement in every direction. She arrived at the gate (or rather, the space where a gate had once swung), dropped the bags inside the wall with relief and studied the legs on the ladder above her.

'Hello-o!' she shouted towards the skies, trying to make her voice heard above the noise of the trimmer.

The face that looked down at her was an ocean of freckles, topped by hair the colour of a newly pulled carrot. Malcolm Milne. That ginger had made him a target for teasing all his life.

He turned off the trimmer.

'Hi, Caitlyn.'

Malcolm, like Ricky McQuade, had been in her class at school, but where Ricky had been in the loud-mouthed gang of bullies who'd made the teachers' lives hell and failed every exam, Malcolm had been one of the victims because – as well as the ginger mop – he'd worn his heart on the outside of his threadbare burgundy blazer.

Caitlyn learned when she was very young how to defend herself. You had to, when it was just you and your mum against the world. You had to, when your mum's new partner turned out to be a spineless waste of space.

She'd never paid much attention to Malcolm Milne. Maybe she should have done more to protect him, but the first rule of school had been look out for yourself.

She studied the muscular figure in the faded denims and heavy check shirt, his sleeves rolled up to the elbows. My God, he'd changed! How had she not noticed? Malcolm Milne had been a scrawny little boy with sticky-out ears, but she saw now that his eyes were a deep sea green and were kind. He'd matured well – gardening obviously suited him.

'Still working for Ibsen Brown?'

Ibsen Brown, a Summerfield local, had moved up a gear from being a jobbing gardener and, with the help of his new partner, Kate Courtenay, had set up a gardening business, Brown Earth. She'd heard it was doing well – there was no shortage of well-heeled folk in Hailesbank and the pretty conservation village of Forgie who were desperate for help in the gardens of their comfortable homes.

Malkie clambered down the ladder and dusted his hands together. 'Aye. Ibsen's got a new contract, as a matter of fact.'

'Yeah?'

'His dad's retiring and he's taking over his work. All the formal gardens at Fleming House. The grass too. It's a big job.'

Caitlyn said, 'That's good news for Ibsen then.'

Malcolm smiled at her. She liked his smile. It was a little crooked because his teeth weren't straight, but it went all the way up to his eyes. 'Aye, it is. But I'm afraid it might make it harder for me to find time to cut your mum's hedge. Ibsen's putting me in charge up at Fleming House, you see.'

He looked so proud, and shy, and embarrassed, all at the same time, that Caitlyn leaned forward impulsively and kissed his cheek.

'Malkie, that's brilliant! He must think really highly of you.'

A wave of red infused Malkie's throat and embarked on a voyage upwards.

'Thanks.' He gazed at her awkwardly, then turned

back to the ladder. 'Best get on.'

'How's Sassy?'

Malcolm had been going out with plump little Saskia Kelly, who worked down at the baker's, for three years, ever since she'd had a pregnancy scare that turned out to be nothing.

'Oh, you know.' His grin was still there, but his eyes glazed over and he turned back to the hedge.

Caitlyn bent to gather up the tattered remnants of her shopping bags and finally made it to the front door as the whine of the hedge cutter started again. She had just located her key when the door was yanked open and Harris's grinning face appeared.

'Caitlyn's in love with Malkie, Caitlyn's in love with Malkie,' he chanted.

'No, I'm not. What are you talking about?'

She dropped her bag on the floor behind the door and shrugged off her jacket.

'We saw you chatting him up.' Lewis joined in the chorus. 'Caitlyn's in love with Malkie.'

'Don't be ridiculous, I am not. And anyway, he's with Saskia.'

The twins stared at each other and giggled. 'No he's not. Sass's brother told us they've split up.'

Isla May sidled out of the front room and hugged her knees. 'Caitlyn—' The little voice was suspiciously ingratiating.

'What?' Caitlyn said guardedly.

'You know the summer camp at school?'

Caitlyn groaned. 'Not that again, Isla May.' Her sister had been pestering her about school camp for weeks now, ever since Joyce had told her there was no spare cash for her to go. 'You know what Mum said.'

'Aww, but Caitlyn—'

Caitlyn sighed and put her hands down to release Isla May's grasp. She squatted down on her heels and looked her little sister in the eye. 'Sorry, sweetheart. You know we'd pay for it if we could, but we can't. Mum's working too hard as it is.'

'But everyone's going!'

'Don't go on about it, there's a love. We'll think of another treat for you, but the camp's out of the question.'

If Isla May had pouted, or sulked, or had a tantrum it might have been easier, but the surge of disappointment in her eyes and the way she bit her lower lip to stop it wobbling was hard to bear.

Caitlyn straightened and put on her determinedly happy voice. 'Now – cheesy pasta for supper, or fish fingers?'

Isla May was easily distracted. 'Cheesy pasta. Please.'

'Good. And you can help by setting out the forks on the table. OK?'

When she'd finally got Isla May and the twins into bed, she finished the washing up and turned her attention to the ironing. How her mother had the energy for the extra shifts she'd taken on at the care home, she had no idea, but it meant a lot of chores would be left undone unless she squared up to them herself.

There. Done. She gathered the pile of sweet-smelling, freshly pressed laundry in her arms and ran up the narrow stairs.

School shirts for Lewis and Harris. She opened their bedroom door carefully and tiptoed across to the small chest of drawers. Harris was rolled into a ball, one hand under his cheek. Lewis was sprawled across his duvet on his stomach. They always slept just so. Caitlyn studied them for a moment, a small smile playing around the corners of her mouth. If only they were always so quiet!

She hung Isla May's best dress on the hook on the back of her little sister's bedroom door. She'd grow out of it soon, then they'd have to find some money to buy her another one. There was always something.

Ailsa, plugged in to her earpieces listening to something loud, was oblivious to her entry. Caitlyn didn't bother to disturb her, she merely slipped her Oasis top, the one she'd asked for last birthday, into a drawer.

The rest of the pile belonged to her mother. She pushed open the bedroom door and walked in. Joyce had given up the double room at the front so that she and Ailsa could share. This room had a mean aspect out across the yard at the back on to the house behind it, an ill-maintained, ugly place with a broken window and another that had been boarded up, the yard full of junk and slipped slates on the roof.

She hung up her mother's spare uniform, pale blue with white trim round the collar. The fabric had been washed so many times it had almost bleached out and it seemed to drag the colour from her mother's face.

There was a photo on the chest by Joyce's narrow bed. She picked it up and studied it. Caitlyn was now twenty-two; her mother was forty-three but looked nearer fifty. Here was Joyce in her twenties, in an off-the-shoulder black sweater and stonewashed jeans. Her hair was tied back in a bouncy ponytail, and she was smiling so that the dimple on her right cheek – the one that exactly matched Caitlyn's – was in clear evidence.

When had Caitlyn last seen that dimple? When had her mother's skin started to look so sallow, her eyes lose their sparkle? She was still slim, her build lighter than Caitlyn's, but she looked gaunt rather than trim. What had happened?

Caitlyn answered her own question. Mick bloody Boyce, that's what had happened. Four more kids and precious little income. A man who'd slid from saviour to sponge in an alarmingly short time.

As she made her way back downstairs, she heard a key slide into the lock and the front door creaked open.

'Caitlyn, dear—'

Joyce's voice was slurred.

'Mum? What are you doing home?'

Joyce slumped against the doorframe, her skin grey, her eyes drooping.

'Migraine,' she mumbled.

Caitlyn leapt down the last few steps. 'Here. I'll help you.'

'Tried to—Can't—'

'Hush. Here.' Caitlyn hooked her mother's arm around her shoulders and supported her weight. Joyce Murray was nothing but skin and bone, but it took all her strength to get her mother up the stairs.

She pushed open the door to the small bedroom. 'Get your uniform off. Here's your nightie. I'll get you a drink and some pills.'

'Too late—'

'Still.'

Caitlyn was concerned. Joyce had suffered the occasional migraine for years, but recently they'd become more frequent, and the attacks were debilitating. What she needed now was complete rest – and Joyce in bed meant more responsibility for Caitlyn. She might even have to call off a couple of shifts at the supermarket, which meant their income would drop, which meant there would be more pressure on both of them to work even harder to pay the bills.

She blamed herself. The job at Blair King's smart

Edinburgh office had been her dream until she'd spotted a client file that had made her first puzzled, then deeply uneasy. She had raised the matter (tentatively because she was young and still unsure of her ground) with Agnes Buchanan, the chief cashier.

'It's fine, dear,' Agnes had said, handing the file back to Caitlyn with such matter-of-fact indifference that Caitlyn felt temporarily reassured.

But still it didn't make sense to her. The worry kept her awake until, gathering all her courage, she braved the partner concerned a few days later.

He'd had a slick answer all right, but it didn't ring true.

'There's no problem,' he'd said, smiling at her kindly. 'It was just an expedient.'

She'd had to look the word up. A stratagem, it meant, a means of doing something.

After several more worried nights, she knew she had to take it further. They'd told her at her induction that there were processes and procedures for this sort of case. She had made it all the way downstairs and was only a few yards from young Mr Blair's office when she'd met the partner again.

'Caitlyn? What are you doing down here?'

She'd blushed scarlet and stuttered.

'Not that file again? You stupid girl.'

She could still remember the sneering look on his face.

'What do you know about these things? Just do the job you're paid to do and I'll do mine.'

For a couple of weeks, Caitlyn had kept her head down and wrestled with her conscience. Should she take it further? What if her suspicions were proved wrong? She'd be kicked out or, at the very least, her life would be made a misery.

So when Mick Boyce upped off to live with his new

woman, she'd seen it as an opportunity. She'd leave Blair King and pick up a job in Hailesbank. That way she could be nearer home and she'd be able to help Joyce out more.

Only it hadn't worked out like that. She hadn't been able to get a job in Hailesbank that paid half as well as the one in Edinburgh, so there was more pressure, not less, on Joyce.

Chapter Ten

'Damn!'

Adam was half way along the track from the main road to Forgie End Farm when the underside of his car scraped rock.

He'd been driving too fast. His car wasn't built for these roads. Should he stop and see if there was any damage?

He drove a tentative few yards further. No ominous rattles, no tell-tale growling. Perhaps it would be all right. At least he wasn't driving a sports car like Logan Keir's.

How could Logan afford a car like that anyway? He shifted into second gear and edged up the speed again. It wasn't as though the partnership was doing especially well. There was so much pressure on law firms these days. There was endless red tape and you had to have a nominated money-laundering specialist in the firm, for example. Professional development seemed to cost more and more, and it was an endless struggle just to meet the monthly wage bill, not to mention the rent and rates. It was all targets, bloody targets, with endless post mortems and recriminations every month if they weren't met.

Adam's hands clenched around the steering wheel. He'd realised even before he'd qualified that he'd made the wrong career choice, but the pressure from his father had been enormous. If he'd met Molly earlier ... or later ... or if she'd been less ambitious, maybe he could have found the courage to switch career.

He bumped over another stone and grimaced.

He shouldn't blame Molly. She'd had a point to prove to her clever brother and she'd wanted to make her father proud. She never talked about it much, but losing her mother so young had definitely affected her. For his part, he'd seen the damage caused by Geordie's decision not to join the firm, and duty had taken precedence. Their pasts had shaped them both.

He smiled to himself. Targets! Everyone thought lawyers made a mint. If only they knew.

A shadow fell across his face as the track entered a small copse. In the last few days, the weather had changed and, although it was still August, the temperature had dropped appreciably. The sun had warmth, but the shade held portents of autumn.

The track took a sharp turn to the right and emerged fifty yards in front of a metal gate.

Adam slowed to a halt. There it was, only a hundred yards away – the farmhouse. A lump formed in his throat, catching him by surprise.

Forgie End Farm was solid, square and undecorated – grey granite, hewn from local quarries and designed to withstand wind and weather.

How many years was it since he'd last been here? He swung open the car door, walked slowly towards the gate, and studied the façade as if he were seeing it for the first time. The farmhouse had been built to be practical, a functional, serviceable home for a family. Three sash windows upstairs, two windows and a door on the ground floor, all neat and symmetrical, like a child's drawing. The Georgians had a fine appreciation of symmetry.

There was a small porch over the door, supported by two granite columns. The porch had obviously been intended to provide shelter from the driving rain as much as for aesthetic reasons, though these days the front door was hardly ever used – everyone entered from the yard at the side. The roof was steeply pitched to deal with rain and snow, and two large chimney stacks (one at each end) serviced the large fireplaces in the draughty living room and dining room. When had they last been used? Jean and Geordie lived in the kitchen, so far as he could remember.

Adam had a lump in his throat again. You'd think the place had been in the family for generations, the way he felt about it, but Uncle Geordie had bought it just forty years ago.

And that, Adam thought with a grimace, had been the start of the famous family feud.

He snapped open the heavy metal latch and swung the gate open. Well, it would surely soon draw to an end, because Geordie was dying. Time to stop feeling emotional about the house and go and visit the man.

'He's quite good today,' Jean said, drawing Adam into the large farm kitchen, the hub of the home. 'Eh, laddie, it's good to see you.'

She stood back and looked up at him, her skin grey with tiredness, her eyes clouded with age. How old must she be? Only in her early seventies, not old by today's standards. He hadn't seen her since the wedding, when she'd betrayed nothing of the grief that must have dragged her down after her son's death. And now here she was, dealing with yet another blow.

Impulsively, Adam put his arms round his aunt. She felt fragile in his embrace, like a small bird. She allowed herself to relax into his arms for a moment, and when she pulled back, her eyes were unnaturally bright. She jerked her head away at once, too proud to show sadness – or fear.

'The nurse has been and now he's sleeping, but he won't sleep for long. You'll have some tea?' She strode to the sink and turned on the tap. In so many ways she hadn't changed, he thought. Still the tweed skirt – he could swear it was the same one she'd worn to Hugh's funeral – still the sensible brogues. She was a farmer's wife, and she looked like one.

Best to tackle the difficult conversation head on. 'How long has he got?'

She lifted the Aga lid and set the kettle on it, then turned and leant against it, a well practised pose. She crossed her arms and looked him squarely in the eye. God, he admired Jean Blair. You had to have mettle to be a farmer, and if you didn't have it when you started, you developed it or failed in the role – and she was tough.

'You can never tell, not with cancer. It might be days, it might be weeks. It's not likely to be months.'

Adam sank onto a chair. He dealt with death every day – it was the inevitable by-product of a life spent dealing with wills and legacies – but he had not had to confront the messy, difficult process of exiting this world on a personal level since Hugh's unexpected demise.

'Oh. I hadn't thought it would be quite so—'

'So quick?' She reached behind her, lifted two mugs off a mug tree and set them down on the worktop. 'Do you know, an awful part of me prays he'll last a few months, but that's worse than selfish.'

'Is he in pain?'

'The morphine keeps it under control. Mostly. But it's not good. If I were a more generous soul I'd pray for a swift release, but there it is. I'm not.'

She pursed her lips into a tight line.

'Aunt Jean, don't ... you're not a bad person. Of course you want to have him as long as possible.'

Adam felt helpless. Molly would be good in this situation; she was terrific with people. It was one of the many traits that had attracted him to her – her brilliance was so much more than superficial gloss.

He checked his thoughts. Why was he thinking of Molly? She was no longer available to him, had not been his since the invidious, slithering descent of their marriage into – what? – indifference? No, not that, never that. Yet he'd not noticed how badly they had let things slip. He blamed her long hours. Event management sucked up time. She'd never been there for him when he'd arrived home, late himself, stressed and unhappy. They'd become strangers.

And then there'd been her affair.

The kettle boiled, its whistle emitting a thin shriek.

'Tea, Adam? Or coffee?'

'Tea. Please. Can I help?'

He jumped up. Action, any action, was better than sitting here wallowing in unpleasant memories.

'If you fancy cake, there's some in the tin over there.'

He remembered the tin. Auntie Jean's cake tin, the cream one with the pale green lid. There had always been something delicious in that tin. How many times had he and Hugh sneaked down in the middle of the night to raid it? Giggling like girls and sure their exploits would not be found out if only they were quiet enough. As if Jean would not notice that half her biscuits had disappeared, or that the cake had ragged edges!

Emptiness grabbed at him. It was a day for unexpected emotions. He'd grieved for Hugh briefly, but in the course of his busy life, he had not *missed* his cousin. Now, in this kitchen, the beating heart of Hugh's childhood home, he felt the lack of his presence with an acuteness that shocked him.

'Lemon drizzle cake?' He turned to his aunt. 'You remembered it's my favourite? I can't believe you've made time to bake. You are a wonder.'

The warmth in his voice was real, and something of his tone clearly reached his aunt. She smiled. 'Geordie still gets pleasure from it.'

'Geordie gets pleasure from what?'

Adam spun round. His uncle was standing in the doorway, upright, smiling, but so gaunt that it took all Adam's self-control to keep the shock off his face. The old collie, Caro, padded in at his feet.

'My baking.' Jean's tone was light. She dropped a hand on the dog's head. 'Hi, Caro, you all right? Dogs have never been allowed past the kitchen in this house, but—'

'—but she refuses to leave my side,' Geordie finished. 'You'd think I hadn't much time left, eh?'

Adam walked across to his uncle and took his hand, scarcely daring to shake it for fear the fragile frame would unknit and collapse in front of him.

'Here, let me help you to a chair.'

'I may be dying, but I'm not helpless yet,' Geordie said, his smile so like Adam's father's that Adam almost winced. How could two brothers look so alike and yet be so different? 'And yes, your baking does give me pleasure, Jean. I'll take a piece of that cake. How's that lovely wife of yours, Adam? No bairns yet?'

Adam sucked in his breath sharply. Had he really been so out of touch with his uncle and aunt that they didn't know about his separation? He cleared his throat.

'Erm … she's still lovely. But I'm sorry to say that the marriage didn't work out the way we thought it would. We're living apart.'

He lifted his mug. He didn't want to look at their faces,

because he didn't want to see surprise or disappointment. But his words fell into silence, so that in the end he had to look up. Jean and Geordie were not looking at him, they were looking at each other. He could not read their expression, but the intensity of the exchange caught his throat.

At last Geordie said, 'I'm sorry to hear that, lad. Don't tell me what happened. I don't want to know. And I won't lecture you about the "for better or worse" thing that we used to think was important. I imagine your mother's done that already.'

Adam stared at him miserably. He could find no words to answer his uncle.

Jean said bluntly, 'Is there someone else?'

'Not for her, not now.'

'And for you?'

'No.' The answer, out before he could consider it, surprised him. *So what of Sunita?*

Geordie lifted his sliver of cake and nibbled at it. 'Work going well?' His face was skeletal, but his eyes were still bright and his mind was clearly as active as ever.

This man, Adam thought, had the courage to do what I failed to do. Disliking the law, Geordie had defied his own father, taken out a hefty mortgage on the farm, and left the partnership to follow his dream. Easier, perhaps, with a brother – or at least, it must have seemed so at the time.

'It's a challenge,' he said, a sense of loyalty preventing him from telling the whole truth.

'Aye, I imagine it is. So's farming.'

'You've stopped the dairy?'

'Had to. The price of milk plummeted. But you'll know that, you're not daft.'

'I know. It's a shame though, I always loved the cows.'

'We miss them too. We were thinking of getting a few again,' Jean said. 'There're some farmers making more of a success of the dairy business by not selling the milk. They add value to it instead.'

'I can see how that could be done.' Adam's mind had leapt ahead of her words. 'You'd have to process it in some way, make yogurt, or cheese or butter. Premium products. Maybe organic – could you go organic here, or would that take years?'

'We've been organic for twelve years.'

'Oh. That's great. So—'

'We can't do it now, not with Geordie—' Jean gestured at her husband.

'I'll be leaving her in the lurch,' Geordie said. 'Can't be helped, but it leaves the farm—'

Jean said, 'I might have to sell it.'

Adam stared at her, aghast. 'Sell it? Sell Forgie End?'

'What other option will I have? I can't farm the place on my own, not even with help.'

'No. I suppose not. I can see that.'

He had a sudden vision of Molly in wellies and dungarees, her golden hair blowing in the wind, looking at him and laughing. *Ridiculous*. Even if they'd still been together, Molly had her own career. Ambition had always driven her, and her ambition was most certainly not to be a farmer's wife.

'Anyway, that's our problem.'

Geordie said, 'I'd like to see your father, Adam. Make my peace. Does he know I'm ill?'

An image of James Blair, his face a mask of stone, rose in front of Adam's eyes. He'd invited himself to his parents' house for supper, knowing that pleading his case would be easier with his mother there. 'He's *dying*, Dad,' he'd said.

'See him, James.' Rosemary had rallied to Adam's side. 'Don't go to your own grave with this rift on your conscience. He's your brother.'

But his father had simply turned and left the room.

'He knows,' Adam answered.

'Ah.' Geordie's smile was rueful. 'I see.'

Adam was filled by a surge of anger. It was so *stupid*. Whatever had happened between them, Geordie was dying now. Simple humanity demanded reconciliation.

'I'll get him here, I promise,' he said impulsively. 'I'll work on him.'

'Don't make promises,' Geordie said, 'that you can't keep.'

'I'll keep it,' Adam said grimly.

He left soon after, full of nostalgia and longing, anger and sadness, assuring them he would return soon and vowing to bring James. It had been a difficult morning – more difficult by far than he had anticipated – and things didn't get any easier when he finally made it back to the office.

'Shereen James is pregnant,' his father said abruptly, not even looking up. 'We'll need to get cover. Any ideas?'

Shereen James was a junior secretary, but she was smart and knew the business well.

'We could get someone from an agency.'

'That'll be expensive,' James Blair growled. 'Bloody maternity legislation.'

'Don't,' Adam said warningly. 'Prejudice is out of the ark, Dad. Women have rights, babies need their mothers. We'll just need to get on with it.'

'We should have employed a man.'

'And don't ever repeat that sentiment outside this room.' Adam, shaken by his morning's experiences, was in no mood to put up with his father's waspishness. 'This partnership has painstakingly built a reputation for fairness and gender equality and that's important for our continuing business as much as it is just and proper.'

James Blair looked up and gave a sudden smile. The smile, somewhat rare, changed his face when it came, showed a glimpse of the man Adam knew his father could be. Stress affected them all.

'Hmmph. Well – any suggestions?'

'What does Agnes think?'

Agnes Buchanan, chief cashier at Blair King, had been with the firm since she'd left school, heaven knows how long ago. Forty years? There wasn't an employee off sick or a paperclip ordered but Agnes knew about it and had calculated the effect on the balance sheet. James always referred to her as 'our rock' or, in private, and with a drink in him, as 'the rock of ages'.

'She suggested Sheila Huffing, the girl who left a couple of years ago to have a baby, but apparently she's not keen to come back to work.'

Adam had an inspiration. 'There's that girl who left last year. Caitlyn ... Caitlyn Murray? I never did understand why she moved on. Some family problem, I think.'

'Was she any good?'

'I'll check. I know people were sorry she left.'

'Fine.'

James looked down at his papers again, his tone a dismissal.

Adam stood and watched him. He looked so like his brother, or at least like the Geordie Adam remembered before the weight fell off. Was this the moment to tackle him about the visit again?

No. Not at work. There were too many distractions, too many stresses.

'I'll get on to it right away,' he said.

Chapter Eleven

Molly's father, Billy, lived in a small bungalow in the Edinburgh suburb of Fairmilehead. South of the city centre, high on a slope just below the Pentland Hills, it had been an ideal home for the two of them after her mother Susan died. Logan had been twenty-one and already at university, Molly just fourteen. At first she'd moaned about leaving Hailesbank, but it was more convenient for Billy's work and she'd soon adapted to the change.

Molly drew up outside and turned off the ignition. Billy kept the place neat. He had been a watch and clock repairer and was by nature meticulous. Precision was his hallmark. He had been forced to learn other skills after Susan died. Cooking – well, he'd never quite mastered that because multi-tasking was not his forte. The carrots would be perfect, but fifteen minutes before the potatoes were soft enough and a full half hour before the meat was ready. He'd managed the laundry. The ironing took him ages, but Molly's school shirts had always looked brand new. And, to her surprise because she'd thought he'd dislike the inevitable dirt, Billy had really taken to gardening.

She surveyed his work. Neat stone steps up to the front door, three shallow terraces on each side of the path, planted out with alpines and heathers, their colour split by strips of perfectly mown grass. How long would he be able to go on gardening? Or cooking or ironing, for that matter? He was only seventy today – not old by any means, but all those years of close work had taken their toll. Billy's sight was failing and he'd been told that total loss of vision was probable.

Molly opened the car door and stepped out. They were due at the restaurant by one and she wanted a chat with her father first.

'Happy birthday, Dad! You're looking terrific!'

Billy Keir grinned at his daughter, his eyes huge behind his thick lenses. 'Thanks, love. You don't look so bad yourself.'

Molly examined him. He'd always dressed neatly, though in recent months she had begun to notice small signs of neglect – a spot on his shirt front, a loose thread on his cuff, tell-tale evidence that worried her. Today, though, he had clearly made a supreme effort. He had donned his best suit, his white shirt looked as though it was straight out of the packet (it probably was) and the burgundy and dark green diagonal-striped tie he'd picked, though on the dull side for Molly's taste, was knotted perfectly.

'Logan and I have got you a present,' Molly said, stooping to kiss his cheek – her father was a good six inches shorter than she was, 'but we'll give it to you at lunchtime, if that's OK.'

'Very mysterious.' Billy beamed at her. 'I hope you haven't gone to too much expense. I'm an old man, you know. I don't need anything.'

'Maybe you don't *need* anything,' Molly said, taking his hand and leading him through to his kitchen, 'but you *deserve* to be spoilt. And today, spoilt is what you're going to be. Coffee? I wanted a chat before we leave.'

'That sounds ominous.'

'Not ominous. Just something I need to sound you out about.'

'Spit it out, love, forget the coffee. It'll only make me want to pee,' Billy said, lowering himself stiffly onto one of the tall stools by the breakfast bar.

Molly sat.

'I've been offered a job,' she said. 'Well, more than a job really, a chance to have a stake in a marketing company. Become a director.'

'Molly Keir! That's wonderful!' Billy's hand shot out and he grasped her arm. 'My little girl, a company director. Heavens to Murgatroyd. Who would ever have thought it?'

Molly's heart swelled at his reaction. She'd known he'd be proud of her. The next bit was harder.

'I haven't accepted the offer yet. There are a couple of problems.'

The magnified eyes gazed at her questioningly. 'Oh yes?'

She sipped the steaming coffee. It was too hot and she blew across the surface to cool it down. Here goes.

'The first thing is investment. Barnaby wants me to put money into the business.'

'I can lend you some. How much do you need?'

'Oh, Dad.' Molly smiled at her father. If he knew just how much Barnaby wanted, he'd probably keel over. It was probably as much as the bungalow was worth, certainly considerably more than any savings he was likely to have. 'A lot. It's really kind of you, but I'll have to look elsewhere. There's my share of the house—'

Her voice tailed away. If she was going to accept Barnaby's offer, talking to Adam about releasing equity from the house was the only real option.

Billy's expression darkened, and Molly knew what he

91

was thinking. Her father had always liked Adam, right from the first day she'd brought him home.

'Nice lad you've got yourself.' She could remember his words, spoken in this very room. 'Sensible. Straightforward. Steady.'

She'd thought that too, hadn't she? Until he'd become more and more tied up at work, and mounting stress had made him ill tempered.

Her father said, 'I wish you and Adam would ... I thought maybe—'

'I know.' She tried to make it as gentle as she could. 'But it's not going to happen, Dad. He's got someone else. I met her last weekend. She's absolutely gorgeous, another lawyer, I think, so she'll be perfect for him.'

They can talk divorces together, she thought bitterly.

'Anyway,' she went on, 'I'll have to talk to him.'

'You said there were two things.'

'What?' Molly's mind was full of what talking to Adam might entail. They'd agreed he would live in the house until they decided what to do. He'd been good about it, but the arrangement suited both of them. Now she was going to change that, how would he react?

'The other thing?' She cleared her throat. 'The company's based in London.'

She watched him carefully. His reaction would tell her everything she needed to know, however much he might try to hide it.

'Yes, well, it was bound to be, wasn't it? I mean, that's where all the money is.'

His eyes flickered, the movement magnified by the lenses. So he did mind.

'If you hate the idea, I won't go.'

She didn't want him to know how much it cost her to utter those words.

'You don't need to worry about me.'

'But I do, Dad. Of course I do.'

'I'm not useless, my darling. I can take care of myself.'

Molly looked at the huge eyes, then down at his hands. They were getting arthritic, but he never complained.

'Barnaby says I can take care of any work we get in Scotland. I can be here quite a lot. Maybe I could even park myself back in my old room a couple of nights a week.'

'Stop, love.' He held up one of his hands. 'You don't need to justify your decision. Go. Follow your dream. I'm proud of you. And I'll be fine.'

Molly slipped off the high stool and moved round the breakfast bar to hug him.

'Thanks, Dad. I'll let you know how it all goes. Come on.' She held out one hand and helped him off his stool. 'We'd better get going. It's all very well to make a grand entrance, but we don't want to keep people waiting too long for your own party, do we?'

When Molly and Adam had bought their house together, they had chosen to live in Edinburgh's north suburbs near the Forth estuary. The house had needed gutting to strip out old wiring, antiquated plumbing and damp plaster And it had been even more work than they'd anticipated, but they'd done it. They had drawn up a plan of action together, made lists (Molly), gathered competitive tenders (Adam) and managed the transformation from rundown, dilapidated dump into smart contemporary-but-classic home.

Our forever home Adam had said. But then things had started to change.

The rows had begun gradually. They hadn't even

argued; a lot of the time, there had just been silences. Awful, mean little silences, born of a determination not to snap at each other perhaps, but somehow the lack of words had been worse.

Could she blame Adam for it all?

Molly, only half listening to her father as she negotiated her car through the busy Edinburgh streets, wondered why in heaven's name she was thinking about all this now. Today of all days.

'I can't even remember the last time I saw your Aunt Mima,' her father was saying.

'It must have been my thirtieth,' Molly answered, her brain on automatic.

Of course – that was what had brought Adam into her head. The last family party had been her big three-o. A pig roast and a ceilidh at that school with the gorgeous garden. All their friends had been there, laughing and dancing – and Adam, being Adam, had presented her with a smart new backpack with slots for walking poles, zipped pockets for a phone and maps, hooks for keys or crampons or a whistle. And a voucher, she remembered, for a weekend at the Loch Melfort Hotel.

Had they ever used that voucher? She could not remember going. Perhaps it was still sitting in its envelope somewhere, tucked behind the sculpture on the mantelpiece in the living room, overlooked by both of them when she'd moved out.

An awful thought struck her – he hadn't used it last weekend, had he? Spent the voucher – *her* voucher – on that Sunita woman?

'The lights have changed.'

'What? Oh, sorry.' She indicated left and moved forward.

'Where are we going? Are you going to reveal it yet?'

'Patience, Dad,' she said, teasing. 'It's a surprise, remember.'

A surprise? The real surprise had been her thirty-first birthday. No pig roast that year, no ceilidh band, no dance, just the promise of a dinner for two somewhere special.

A promise betrayed.

Molly would never forget that morning – the frisson of excitement, waiting for the birthday gift, the one that never appeared. The disappointment when there was no birthday greeting, not even a card. He'll make up for it later, she told herself all day. But he hadn't. She'd gone to work, gone home, waited. Nothing. Just a brief muttered call – 'I'll be late, Moll. Sorry. See you later. Don't wait up' – terminated abruptly. He'd been in a meeting, that much was clear. And he'd forgotten her birthday, that was even clearer.

Then Lexie had rung, cheerful and full of congratulations.

'Is Adam taking you out? Where are you going?'

'No. He's at work.' Trying to sound nonchalant.

'He's not! What a rat! Are you going tomorrow instead?'

Molly, determined to be cool, not to betray anything of the deep hurt and disappointment she was feeling – *it's only a birthday* – had burst into tears.

Lexie had been filled with protective indignation. 'Listen, I'm about to head into town with Jamie. He's at a loose end tonight and I'm doing nothing special, so we thought we'd treat ourselves to a nice meal. Now we can treat you too. Even better!'

Molly had known Jamie Gordon since primary school. She'd sat across the supper table from him at Lexie's house more times than she could count, but she couldn't remember the last time they'd met.

'Sure you don't mind me gatecrashing?'

'He's my *brother*,' Lexie had said, laughing.

It had been a memorable evening. Molly's mood had edged from self-pity to gratitude, and from there to genuine enjoyment. She'd forgotten how uncomplicated Jamie Gordon was. He was cheerful, funny and very physically attractive. He turned heads. She'd watched, amused, as first one girl found an excuse to brush past him at the bar and stop to apologise breathlessly, then another. Jamie was oblivious to their attentions. He appeared to be without vanity, which had made him all the sexier.

'Lights, Molly. Stop!'

She braked and they were both thrown forward.

'Sorry!'

'What on earth are you thinking about, lass? I'd quite like to get to my party in one piece.'

'Sorry,' she said again. She really must concentrate; she'd almost shot the lights and it was a busy junction, but the past had slid into her head and she couldn't shift it.

That was how it had begun. As she had become slowly estranged from Adam, she had found herself turning more and more to Jamie for companionship.

That's all it is, she'd excused herself. Surely Adam could not begrudge her some fun when he was working? These days, he seemed to spend every weekend that he wasn't in the office out on the hills and she'd increasingly found excuses not to join him. The dry humour she'd once liked so much had turned acerbic. Jamie, by contrast, was straightforward. He laughed a lot, took her to the ten-pin bowling alley, insisted she make up a team for the quiz night at the pub in town, or invited her to keep him company at some movie or other.

I'll tell Adam soon, Molly had promised herself again and again. When he's got time to listen.

One night, mildly drunk, Jamie had leapfrogged over a cast-iron bollard, misjudged it and fallen, clutching his groin and roaring with laughter, onto the cobbled street. She'd gripped his hand and pulled him up, anticipating that she'd have to support him all the way to the station and manhandle him somehow on to the train back to Hailesbank. But she had underestimated Jamie's fitness and, before she realised what was happening, he was on his feet and his arms were around her.

The sudden closeness took them both by surprise, and then his mouth was on hers, his kiss hungry, and she was kissing him back, as if desperate to slake a thirst she had not known even existed.

'I'm sorry,' he said, his voice hoarse, when at last he pulled back an inch and looked into her eyes. 'I shouldn't have—'

'Shut up.' She hooked her hands around the back of his head and pulled him towards her again.

I'll tell Adam, she said in her head. Soon.

But she hadn't told him, and in the end he had found out in the worst possible way.

'Here we are,' she said to Billy, spotting a parking space in Heriot Row and pulling the car smartly into it. 'It's not far now.'

The beginning of something new always promises joy. Endings are more complicated.

The mistakes we make, she thought, can sometimes destroy us.

Chapter Twelve

Now that she had negotiated the streets of Edinburgh successfully, if a little raggedly, Molly was looking forward to the party she had arranged.

They were late, but only by a few minutes, and that was the birthday guest's prerogative.

'Here they are!'

'They're here!'

'All together everybody!'

'Happy Birthday to you, Happy Birthday dear Billy—'

Billy sniffed. Laughing tenderly, Molly unhooked her arm from her father's and pulled out a handkerchief. 'Here. I knew you'd need it!'

'Silly!'

Billy waved her away, embarrassed, but he took the hankie, removed his glasses, blew his nose loudly, then set off on a round of greetings.

'Hello, Mima! Hello, Frank! And Joe! Good to see you, mate.'

Molly stood and watched affectionately. Dear Dad. He'd been so brave since Mum died. He'd never remarried ('no-one could ever match your mum') and he'd borne the burden of bringing her up with uncomplaining good cheer. She owed him so much.

'You've done well, Molly.'

She turned at the voice. Adrienne was by her side, her neat brown bob immaculate, her nails a perfect glossy purple, her Armani suit probably straight off the racks in Harvey Nicks.

'Thank you.' Molly stooped for the obligatory air kiss.

She had little in common with Adrienne. Logan's wife had been cabin crew with British Airways, but she'd conceived Alastair soon after the wedding (neatly planned, Molly judged) and had given up working at once. And it was work, not children, that defined Molly.

She said, 'I'm just so pleased we're all here. We are all here, aren't we? I can't see Logan.'

Adrienne wrinkled her small nose in what Molly took to be a token of apology. 'He said he might be a bit late – but he is coming. He promised,' she added hastily as Molly's eyes darkened.

'Really! He is impossible!'

'Tell me about it.' Adrienne shifted her clutch bag from under one arm to under the other and reached for a glass of champagne offered by a passing waiter. 'I swear he's got worse recently. Sorry,' she said, this time with a moue, 'not the day to complain.'

Molly was surprised. She'd never heard Adrienne sound anything other than effervescent, confident of her status in life and bolstered by the expensiveness of the possessions with which she surrounded herself.

'Don't worry,' she found herself consoling Adrienne, 'there's time enough.' She looked at her watch. 'We can enjoy drinks for another ten or fifteen minutes. Have you called him?'

'His phone's off.'

'Ah. Don't Alastair and Ian look smart!' Molly changed the subject with practised adroitness. She'd dealt with enough crises in her time to be skilled in smoothing things over.

'They're great.' Adrienne's face softened as she looked across the room to her children, and maternal pride replaced tension. 'At least we're all getting a holiday soon. Logan has promised to take ten days off work and we're heading off to Botswana for a safari at half term. One of the luxury experiences, of course, glamping in Africa.'

'Sounds wonderful.' And another extortionate expense. Logan *was* doing well. But at what cost to family life? Surely no hastily snatched holiday could compensate for the lack of his day-to-day presence? 'How old's Alastair now?'

'Eleven.'

'Golly, how quickly they grow up,' Molly said with a flash of guilt. She should get to know her nephews better. She studied Alastair from across the room – tousle-headed, a little overweight, and all his attention firmly on some game he was playing on his mobile phone – and the recollection of Barnaby Fletcher's offer flooded back again. She still hadn't given him her reply – but if she accepted, there'd be even less chance of becoming a proper auntie to these two boys.

Near her, she sensed a small commotion, a swirling and moving of people, an opening up of a space, and she saw that Logan had arrived.

'Happy Birthday, Dad!'

Molly surveyed her brother with the familiar mix of affection and exasperation. He had such easy charm. He'd always found everything so easy. He was naturally gifted, sailed through school and university, and was made a partner at the firm within five years of starting there – but recently, he'd changed. With the growing trappings of wealth had come something else: tension.

Logan hooked an arm round his father and said proudly to the room at large, 'Isn't he wonderful? He doesn't look a day over eighty,' causing a ripple of laughter and sparking a gleam in Billy's eyes that brought a lump to Molly's throat all over again.

Damn! She was emotional today.

Molly was used to stress. She knew it could lodge in your neck, or your spine, or your guts, and send you into a downward spiral. Stress could tear you apart; it could freeze you so that your capacity to make decisions was destroyed. But it could also be a positive and Molly had always thrived on low-level stress. She made more lists, became more efficient, got more done.

'Great to see you, my boy. Great to see you. I'm so glad you were able to spare the time to make it to your old man's little celebration.'

Molly swung away with a frown. She couldn't watch. Why should he be praised just for turning up, when she had spent so much time organising everything? Chiding herself for her pettiness, she headed for the kitchens to give the signal to start service.

A low voice near her said, 'Is there room for another at table? If not, I'll leave right now.'

She hadn't noticed the lean figure standing awkwardly near the door. 'Adam! What are you doing here?'

'I dropped by the office and Logan insisted I should come along. I didn't realise it was a special family occasion—'

Molly gaped at him.

'Listen, I'll go.'

She tried frantically to deal with the situation. How dare Logan ask *Adam* to her father's lunch? And yet – he looked so miserable. His shoulders sagged and he was biting his lip. Logan had put them both in an impossible position.

'No. Don't go.'

He lifted his head.

'It's not your fault, it's Logan's. He's got about as

much sensitivity as a rhinoceros. You can stay. We can be civil to each other, can't we? And Dad will be so pleased. He was saying just this morning how fond he was of you.'

'I don't want to embarrass you.'

She knew every crease of his face. The tiny scar under his chin where he'd fallen off his bike, years ago. The small vertical line between his eyes that deepened when he was worried, but these days didn't entirely fade. The fine laughter lines at the corners of his eyes were more firmly etched than they used to be.

The small changes touched her. She said, 'I know you don't. You're not. Here—' she lunged at a glass of champagne, the last on a passing tray, and handed it to him. 'Drink this,' she took his elbow, 'and come and chat to Joe. You remember Joe? Dad used to work with him. I'll just go and organise another place at table. Joe, here's Adam, do you remember my husband? Isn't it lovely he's been able to come and help us celebrate?'

And so, with a glittering smile that masked her discomfort, she left the guests and got on with what she was best at – organising.

'How could you?' she hissed at Logan as he passed.

'How could I what?'

Molly nodded her head towards Adam, who was standing alone amid the guests, out of place. *No longer family*. But then her younger nephew jumped up at him out of nowhere and she saw his mouth crack into a warm smile. He studied the game on the phone he was handed, bent and put an arm around Ian's shoulders and conferred with great seriousness. After a minute, Ian walked off, content, his problem solved.

'Ask Adam to the party.'

'He was at a loose end. Why not?'

'I can think of a hundred reasons why my brother should not have asked my soon-to-be-ex-husband to a family celebration.'

'Dad adores him,' Logan said blithely. 'He's thrilled that he's here.'

How could she argue with that? But Adam's appearance might raise hopes of a reconciliation where there could be none, and she could do without the strain of having to be polite all meal.

She gave up.

'Please,' she said to Adam, indicating the chair next to her, 'be seated.'

'Molly, are you sure—'

'Sit, Adam.'

He sat. But it was as she had feared. The conversation steered a jaggy course through a field of thistles.

'How's Lexie? When is she due?' (Easy, neutral.)

'Did you enjoy the weekend at Loch Melfort?' (Careful, more dangerous.)

'You?'

'How is work?' (Damnably predictable.)

'Your father's looking well.' (Ditto.)

On and on, the exchanges painfully civil. It was an unexpected development in the long journey they were making. Later, she might evaluate it, but right now, it was impossible.

'Got the envelope?' Logan hissed under cover of applause. Joe Spall, Billy's long-time work companion, had been on his feet for eight minutes, his tribute warm and funny.

'What?'

'Dad's present. The ticket. You did get it, didn't you?'

Of course she had it. What she had not been able to do was discuss with Logan exactly how and when they would present it.

He held out his hand. She hesitated.

'Quick!' His fingers furled and unfurled rapidly, beckoning.

She located the envelope in her bag and held it out. 'Shouldn't we—?'

But he was on his feet, and speaking.

'Before you all get back to drinking—' he paused for the laugh, '—there's just one more thing to do.' He flourished the envelope aloft. 'Give Dad his present. It's from Molly as well, of course,' he turned briefly to where Molly sat, her face scarlet. 'And it's a very special gift for a very special person. A ticket—' he waved the envelope again, '—to Melbourne! You're going to visit your sister!'

He handed the envelope to Billy as applause erupted. Molly sat very upright in a supreme effort at containing her feelings, her hands clenching her knees under the white damask tablecloth. She sensed Adam moving and the next moment he had laid one hand over hers. She clung on to it, squeezing his hand with all her strength.

He did not flinch.

Logan sat down, flushed with the success of his surprise.

'He can be such an arse,' Adam said, his voice just loud enough for her to catch.

Her eyes flickered towards him. What did she expect to read in his expression? Sympathy? Anger on her behalf? *Love?* Whatever she expected, it was not amusement, but Adam's eyes were brimming over with barely controlled laughter.

It was exactly the right response. She giggled and her tension dissipated. Adam knew how to handle her; he always had, until …

Molly withdrew her hand.

'Thank you,' she said quietly.

'Excuse me,' Logan said a few minutes later, pushing his chair back, 'just got to check something.'

'He's chained,' Adrienne said loudly, 'to his damn phone.'

He'd miss the cake. Molly's moment, if there was a particular moment in this day of her arranging.

Well then, he would miss it. Molly gave a discreet signal, the lights dimmed, the kitchen door opened and there was a flickering golden light. Dozens of candles – how many? – had been lit and seven small fireworks sent showers of stars spiralling upwards.

'Oh, wow!'

'Look at that!'

It was the small touches that made an event memorable. The carefully chosen colour scheme, the table flowers to match the mood, the photos of bride or groom as toddlers scattered on the tables. And the cake.

The cake, Molly considered, should be the highlight of any occasion. Over the years she had commissioned dozens of traditional wedding cakes as well as many humorous ones, clever cakes for special birthdays, and sophisticated cakes in the shape of company logos, designed to impress corporate guests.

Billy's seventieth cake was in the shape of a clock. Not just any clock, but a faithful copy of the grandfather clock that stood in the hall at home, the family heirloom that had inspired her father to take up his profession aged sixteen.

The clock face was a transfer print of a wedding photograph, Billy and Susan holding hands and gazing at each other out of the past. The hands were at seven and twelve – 7.00, the closest Molly could get to seventy.

Across the table, her father looked at her and beamed. It was all she needed. He knew how much thought she had put into it, and he appreciated it. It was reward enough.

Afterwards, Adam melted away as quietly as he had arrived.

'Thank you,' he said, 'for allowing me to share your special family day.'

'No problem,' Molly said, and watched as he collected his coat and left.

But there was a problem. Soon she was going to have to call Adam and ask him to sell the house. She would be setting in motion a train of events that would be irreversible.

Chapter Thirteen

'Carry yer bag home for yer?'

Caitlyn grinned. It was like being back at school, when such an embarrassed offer was the accepted preliminary to an awkward date.

'Hi, Malkie. Good to see you.' She handed him two carrier bags with relief. 'How did you know I was coming off shift?'

'H-hm.' Malkie cleared his throat. 'Tell you the truth, I nipped round to your house. Harris said you were due to finish around now.'

He'd cheered her up. It was some time since a guy she liked had made any kind of effort.

They reached his battered old van just as the first few drops of rain began to fall. 'Here, get in.' He held open the door and Caitlyn slithered inside. It smelled of damp earth. She liked the smell. It was like Malkie: honest and real.

He opened the doors at the back and placed her shopping carefully inside.

'Finished work today then?' she asked as he jumped into the driver's seat, slammed the door closed and turned on the ignition.

'Aye.' He never had been a great one for chat.

'No more grass to cut?'

He put the van into reverse and backed out of the space as the raindrops turned into a deluge. 'Grass was finished yesterday. There're always jobs to do, you know, in a garden, but with the rain coming … Anyway, Ibsen said to go home.'

'But you came for me instead.' She watched, a smile tugging at the corners of her mouth, as he blushed.

'Aye.' His glance was short, but the intensity of feeling in his deep green eyes took her by surprise.

'Tell me about Saskia,' Caitlyn said as they left Hailesbank and started along the short road to Summerfield. Short if you were in a van – a long way if you had to hike it, as she'd had to the other night.

'Sass?'

'If we're going to start dating, Malcolm Milne, I need to know where you stand.'

His laugh was infectious.

'What? What are you laughing at?' she said, smiling.

'Who said we were going to start dating?'

'Isn't that what this is about?' she said, suddenly uncertain.

He negotiated a bend just as a lorry came in the opposite direction, throwing a fountain of water up across their windscreen. Half blinded, he drove on for another dozen yards, then pulled into a layby.

'Might as well give this rain a chance to stop.' He leaned forward and peered out of the windscreen, where what seemed like a waterfall was gushing down to the bonnet.

'I like it, Caitlyn.'

'What?'

'Your directness. I can't tell you how refreshing it is after Sass.' He reached across and took her hand. 'If we do start seeing each other, can we always be like this, do you think? Honest, I mean. Can we make a pact?'

Caitlyn was startled. 'I'm guessing that honesty wasn't Saskia's style?'

He dropped her hand and rubbed his face. 'You could say that. Right from the first, I guess. You heard about—'

'She told you she was pregnant is how I heard it,' Caitlyn said gently, 'but that turned out not to be true.'

'She knew what buttons to press. Things were never great with us, and in the end she found a better option. That's about it.'

'You stayed with her a while.'

'Three years. I was lazy. Maybe not lazy, more like a wee dormouse who'd gone to sleep for the winter and didn't feel warm enough to wake up again.'

Caitlyn smiled at the image. 'So what changed?'

He shrugged. 'I got up one day and she'd propped a note against the teapot. "Gone with Vernon," she wrote. "Bye".'

'That was it?'

'She wasn't so bad to me. She'd only taken her clothes. One of my mates, his girl cleaned him out. He was left with a change of underpants and a burnt saucepan.'

'Generous.'

'Aye, well. I was lucky. Vernon's a builder. Cash trade. He's minted. Sass didn't want our old rubbish.'

'And you, Malkie? How do you feel?'

'God's honest truth? Relieved as hell.'

The rain had stopped. Cars sped past on the narrow road, sun glinting off damp paintwork. A hundred yards further along, one flashed through a puddle and sent spray to the top of the hedge. Each time, briefly, a rainbow flashed. There was beauty in everything, if you just looked.

'So.' Caitlyn wriggled round in her seat so that she could look at Malkie square on. '*Am* I next in line? Or is this just a courtesy taxi for a poor exhausted lass?'

'Do you want to be? Next in line?'

'We could give it a try, maybe. See where we go.'

'Seems fair.'

He looked at her.

She looked at him.

It was nice.

After a while she stopped looking and smiling, and said, 'Maybe I should be getting home.'

He turned on the ignition and the engine spluttered into life.

'That's settled then,' he said.

Joyce's migraine lasted two days and left her weak. She lost two shifts, while Caitlyn gave up two of hers to look after the family.

Isla May hadn't mentioned the school camp again, but she'd brought home a leaflet about it and left it next to the kettle in the kitchen.

The boys needed new shoes. And new shoes meant they needed new football boots too. They kept growing.

Ailsa moaned because she never had any spending money, and having to do her share of minding the little ones meant she couldn't get a job to earn any cash of her own.

Caitlyn didn't mind living on next to nothing. She didn't mind not having many new clothes. She managed to survive on very little, and heaven knows Joyce was just the same. But she did find it hard that, despite all their efforts, they *still* couldn't manage.

So when her mobile rang one morning as she walked to work and she realised that it was Blair King's number, she hesitated only for a moment before she decided to answer it.

'Hello? Caitlyn Murray speaking.'

'Caitlyn? This is Adam Blair.'

The boss's son! She'd thought it might be Agnes Buchanan, who'd been so helpful to her when she'd started at Blair King, or Deirdre, who'd had the desk next to hers. But Adam Blair? What did Adam Blair want? Was it to do with …

Fear grabbed her.

'Caitlyn? Are you still there?'

She cleared her throat. 'Yes, I'm here.'

'How are you? What are you up to these days? We were so sorry you decided to leave us.'

Caitlyn swallowed. She still lived in dread of having to explain things. She should have faced up to the situation immediately, and she hadn't been brave enough. The trouble was, leaving Blair King had been no solution. Every day she'd thought about what she'd seen and every day she grew more and more angry with herself for not having had the courage to take her worries further. Mr Blair was nice. What would he have done to her? Nothing, probably. Even if she'd been wrong, she would have been following the correct procedures.

He was still speaking. 'We were wondering if you might be free to come back and help us out for a few months.'

She blinked in disbelief. 'I beg your pardon?'

'Sorry, is this a bad connection?' He said it again, more slowly this time. 'We were wondering – I was wondering – whether, by any chance, you might be free from work commitments at the moment. Do you remember Shereen James?'

Shereen James? Had she seen something too? Wrapped up in her obsession, Caitlyn couldn't make sense of Mr Blair's words. 'I remember her, yes,' she muttered cautiously.

'Shereen's taking maternity leave and we're going to need cover. We could go to an agency, of course, but I remembered you and wondered if—'

'You want me to come back to Blair King?'

'Just for a few months. You know the ropes, you were highly thought of. It would be a terrific solution for us.'

When she didn't answer, he said, 'But I expect you're nicely sorted out somewhere else. It was a bit of a long shot.'

'No, I—' Caitlyn had no idea how to answer him. She'd earn good money at Blair King. She might even be able to negotiate a higher temporary rate than the salary she'd been on – but on the other hand, she could be thrown right back into the situation she had fled.

Need drove her.

'When would you want me to start?'

A sudden gust of wind caught her hair and flapped it in front of her eyes. Behind her, a lorry thundered across the bridge so that she lost Mr Blair's next words.

'Sorry, I couldn't hear that.' She clawed back her hair and tried to concentrate.

'I said: could you start in a couple of weeks? It would be good if you could overlap with Shereen for a week so that she could show you the ropes.'

Inside Caitlyn, excitement began to stir. Maybe she could skirt round the problem for the few months she'd be there. Maybe she wouldn't have to face up to anything – and more money coming in would take the pressure off her mother. Ailsa was old enough now to take a bit more responsibility.

Then again …

'When do you need to know?' she temporised.

'Tomorrow? Sorry to push you, but I can go to the agency to find someone and I do need to get this sorted. I just thought it would be worth trying you. If you can't come, just say and—'

'I didn't say I couldn't come,' Caitlyn said hastily. 'I need to sort something out, that's all. I'd like to come. In principle.'

'You would? Excellent. Can you call back tomorrow, before the end of the day? Does that give you enough time to sort whatever it is out?'

'Yes. Yes it does. I'll call tomorrow then, promise.'

'Fine. Goodbye for now.'

'Bye.'

The sun was trying to burn through the mist and the day felt more hopeful. In front of her, the traffic was rumbling across the bridge, into Hailesbank, out of Hailesbank. People going about their business, intent on making a living, meeting a friend, enjoying life. Going back to Blair King could mean a new beginning for her – if she could face it.

'I know it's only been a few days,' Caitlyn said when she managed to snatch a ten-minute break around lunchtime to call Malkie, 'and you might be busy tonight, but if you're not, can you meet me for a drink? There's something I need to talk about and you're the only person I really trust.'

'Want me to pick you up at the supermarket?'

'No. Thanks. If we can meet in the Duke of Atholl I can walk. It's not far and I'll need to clear my head.'

'I'll drop you home after.'

'Now that,' she said, 'is exactly what I wanted to hear.'

But she needed to hear more from Malkie. She wasn't ready to tell him everything, but she wanted to see his reaction. It would be like flipping a coin – you didn't know what you wanted to do, but when you called 'heads' and it came down 'tails' and you were disappointed, you knew then.

They'd only been out once. He'd walked her along to the skittles alley at the back of The Crossed Keys and they'd had a hilarious time. Caitlyn had played carefully and with better judgement than skill, while Malkie had been over enthusiastic, but had had luck on his side. He'd let her win. At her front door, there'd been a tentative kiss and a hug, then he'd strolled off with a wave and a 'See you soon!' and she'd wondered how slow he'd take it.

His affection was not in doubt this evening – as soon as she walked through the door of the Duke of Atholl, he was by her side and she was in his arms, and the hug felt solid and safe.

'Wow,' she grinned as soon as she could breathe, 'that was enthusiastic.'

'I thought you wanted support.'

'Did I sound that needy?'

'Just a wee bit wobbly. What's yours?' He gestured towards the bar.

'Have you got a drink?'

'Just arrived. I'll have one pint, no more cos I'm driving.'

'I'll have a half, then.'

She found a table in a corner and sank down onto the over-stuffed banquette. The Duke of Atholl had once been a smart hotel, but over the years it had become tired. It wasn't the best pub in Hailesbank, but she'd chosen it because it didn't have music blaring out so loud you couldn't hear yourself talk.

'Here you go.' Malkie took a long slug of his pint and slid in beside her.

'Thanks for meeting me.'

'I'll never say no to seeing you.'

She managed a weak smile. The tension that had kept a knot in her stomach ever since Mr Blair's phone call eased a fraction.

'So what's it all about?'

Caitlyn took a deep breath, and explained.

'So you see,' she finished, just as she got to the last sip of her beer, 'I've got to make a decision.'

She didn't expect Malkie to understand the ins and outs of her story, but she did trust his instincts.

'Right.' He leant forwards, his elbows on the table, deep in thought. 'So you saw something you didn't think was right?'

'Yes.'

'You challenged the guy, and he had an explanation?'

'Yes.'

'But you still thought it was wrong?'

'Yes.'

'You didn't think anyone would believe you, you were just a wee junior and he was a boss.'

'One of the partners. Yes.'

'So you left.'

'It was when Mick Boyce walked out,' Caitlyn said. 'It all happened around the same time.' She crumpled. 'I funked it, Malkie, that's the truth of it. I kidded myself that I'd be helping Mum, but it was a huge mistake.'

Malkie was frowning with concentration. He was more used to making decisions about whether a rose was ready for deadheading than following the ins and outs of office procedures.

'I've got it. But I don't see the problem. You didn't do anything wrong. You don't know for sure he did. You've been asked back. It's great money. All you have to do is keep your head down and do your job. It's a no-brainer, isn't it?'

'You think it's that simple?'

He took her hand. 'Sweetheart.'

Caitlyn's heart swelled at the endearment.

'You need the money. Your mum needs help. You're great at the work. It is that simple.'

'What if I find something else when I get there?'

'You don't know you will. The guy's explanation might have been true. You don't need to look for trouble. Just do the job.'

'But if I—'

'Look at me.'

She looked. Malkie's feelings had always been transparent. When he'd been a boy, that had led him into all sorts of trouble with the bullies, but now he was a man, she loved him for it. Right now, his expression was earnest.

'If you do come across something dodgy, the first thing is you tell me. The second is we discuss it. The third is we do whatever we decide is right. You're not going to get into trouble, sweetheart. The worst that can happen is that you lose your job again. Isn't it?'

Caitlyn laughed. 'Put like that, it doesn't seem so bad.'

'That's my girl.' He pulled her close and gave her a cuddle.

'Is that what I am, Malkie? Truly? Your girl?'

'Oh yes,' he said. And this time he kissed her properly.

The corner they were sitting in was gloomy, but it wasn't dark. 'Hey,' someone called after a minute, 'why don't you two get a room?'

They broke apart, giggling like teenagers.

'Come on,' Malkie said. 'I'll take you home.'

Chapter Fourteen

Adam was resolute.

'You have to come with me, Dad. Your brother is dying. I don't think he has long. Don't let him carry your grudge to the grave.'

'The situation was not of my making,' James Blair said stiffly. He was standing at the window of his office on the main floor in Blair King's Queen Street premises. The street had turned into an urban race track ever since vehicles had been barred from Princes Street. Buses, lorries, cars, bicycles all fought for space and played catch-me-if-you-can with the traffic lights – but there were compensations. They were high enough above the traffic not to notice the noise, and beyond the road were grand gardens with trees that could not mask the views to the north, across the Firth of Forth. It was a small recompense, thought Adam, for enforced imprisonment in this place.

'No,' Adam said, 'and it wasn't Geordie's either. It was my grandfather's scheme.' He took a deep breath. 'Was it really so terrible?'

James swung round, his bushy eyebrows knitted. 'He got all the money.'

'You got the shares in the firm,' Adam reminded him, 'and they've yielded you a good income over the years. All Geordie got was an advance on his inheritance.'

'He got it then and he got it unconditionally. I've had to slave here for forty years, and I haven't been able to release any capital.'

It was an old argument, although they hadn't aired it for a long time. Adam hadn't dared. Now he gritted his teeth and ploughed on.

'He got cash because he needed the money to buy the farm – and he's been slaving away too. He's not exactly a rich man, Dad. Farming's no sinecure.'

Silence. James had swung back to the view, his shoulders hunched.

Adam crossed the floor and laid a hand on his father's shoulder. 'It's over, Dad. It has been over for years, admit it. The settlement was fair in some ways, unfair in others. In the end, what does it matter? He's dying. He can't take it with him. He's lost his son. Don't let him lose his brother too.'

His father was breathing heavily, but he hadn't refused.

Sensing a weakening, Adam pressed on. 'I'm going out to see him after work today. Come with me.'

Silence.

At last James said, 'We'll see. Have you found a replacement for Shereen yet?'

Adam swung away, the smallest of smiles playing on his lips. It hadn't been a 'yes', but it was better than a 'no'.

'Caitlyn Murray has just called back.' His smile broadened. 'She's no fool, that girl. Can you believe it, she asked for a hefty pay rise, and when I quibbled, she said she'd checked the agency fees and I was still getting a bargain.' A low chuckle from somewhere near the window told him his father's mood was lifting. 'She's willing to come for six months.'

'Good. I like spirit.'

James turned and pulled his chair out from under his desk. The meeting was at an end.

'There's a lady here to see you.'

Puzzled, Adam glanced at his diary. It was empty. He frowned. He'd been on the point of nipping out for a sandwich.

'Did she give a name?' he asked the duty clerk on reception. He shouldn't have to ask.

There was a muffled conversation.

'Miss Ghosh, she says.'

Sunita?

'Tell her I'll be there in five minutes.'

It had been two weeks since the difficult weekend at Loch Melfort. Adam hadn't seen Sunita since they'd arrived back in Edinburgh full of false protestations of 'Wasn't that great?' and 'How clever you are to arrange my favourite hotel for me.'

That was bad of him. She'd meant well; it hadn't been her fault that Molly had been there, dampening his enthusiasm. Nor had it been her fault that he'd allowed Logan to tempt him along to Billy's seventieth birthday party last Sunday, but, wrung out, he'd called her and cancelled their evening date.

He set his desk in order, pulled his jacket off the hanger on the back of the door, ran his hands through his hair, and headed for the stairs.

'Hi, darling. What a nice surprise.' He took both her hands, pulled her from her seat and kissed her cheek. 'You're looking exceptionally smart today.'

The hair that sometimes hung so heavily to her shoulders was neatly coiled and swept to the back into some sort of bun arrangement. 'Bun', Adam thought, was perhaps not the right word – it smacked of spinsterhood. This was elegant. The coiled hair hung low to her collar, thick and shiny, and showed off her long neck.

He took her arm and turned her half round. 'It's nice. I haven't seen you wear it like that. It makes you look very businesslike. Are you in court?'

She shook her head. 'Just meetings. Have you time for lunch?'

'Only if we can grab a sandwich somewhere. Sorry, but I'm quite pushed for time today. I have to go out later.' He steered her outside and down the wide stone steps that swept down to the busy pavement.

'That new deli, then? The girls at the office were saying they make great sandwiches to order, and the coffee's good.'

'Perfect.'

She tucked her arm through the crook of his elbow and they strolled along the street. I couldn't ask for a better partner, Adam thought. Her figure was stunning; she was clever, and fun to be with. On an impulse, he stooped to kiss her cheek. It was smooth as a polished pebble and the colour of light toffee.

'What was that for?'

'Couldn't resist. You're looking so beautiful.'

'Flattery,' she laughed, 'might get you a long way. Here we are.'

Over toasted focaccia stuffed with goat's cheese and rocket, the reason for her presence became clear.

'My auntie,' she announced, 'is getting married. Will you come with me to the wedding?'

'Sure. When is it?'

'Oh, not till next April.' She bit prettily into her sandwich, her creamy white teeth leaving a precise scalloped edge in the thick bread.

'Fine. I'm sure I'll be able to arrange time off.'

'It's in Kolkata.'

Adam, chewing, choked inelegantly, crumbs spraying

onto the table and wedging themselves somewhere deep in his throat.

'Are you all right?'

Kolkata! She'd sprung that one on him. Adam's mind raced ahead. Popping down the road to Leith to attend a Hindu wedding was one thing. Travelling half way across the world to Kolkata was quite another. It was a statement. Her family would see him as a fixture in her life – the man she cared for enough to bring all that way, to introduce to her nearest and dearest. It was, if you thought about it that way, a kind of trap. And he had just walked right into it.

'You will see my grandfather's house,' Sunita said when he had recovered. 'He made money. He bought a house in Alipore. It's a very beautiful place. Once it belonged to the British, of course – all the property in that part of the city belonged to the British. White Calcutta, they called it. But now everything has changed.'

Across the room a girl had just come in, tall and blonde, just Molly's build, and his mind switched instantly. There'd been such anguish on her face during Logan's speech and he couldn't miss the subtle shifts in her expression as her cake was carried in, until at last he could see the pain ebb away. He loved that he could read her so well. Even at the lowest point of their relationship, that skill had never deserted him.

But it wasn't difficult to read someone's expression when you had your hand raised to strike her.

He winced.

'Are you all right, Adam?' Sunita asked, noticing.

'Sure, sure.' He picked up his focaccia but his appetite had deserted him and he dropped it back onto his plate.

He would never forget that night, not for as long as he lived. And nor, he guessed, would Molly. How could you forget the moment you discovered that your wife had been seeing someone else? Offering her body to someone else – her beautiful, familiar limbs entwined with his; her mouth shaping words of endearment that had always been murmured to *you*? How could you forget the writhing pangs of jealousy, or their lightning transformation into anger?

No, he would not forget, nor could he ever forgive himself. And even if Molly could find it in her heart to pardon his behaviour, he was sure that there was no way she could ever trust herself with him again. One moment, one terrible, uncontrolled moment, and he had messed up everything.

'It's big, and it's white, and there are verandahs on two sides, towards the garden. You should see the garden, Adam! There are fire trees and mangoes, and a beautiful big tamarind. The mangoes are so sweet and juicy! They never taste the same over here. And there are figs and a jacaranda, and laburnum. And curry leaves, of course, for the cook.'

'Sounds idyllic.'

'It is.'

'And very big.'

'He is rich. He will love to meet you, Adam. I know he will.'

'April, you said.' Already his mind was racing. He knew he didn't want to go, but how could he get out of it without hurting Sunita? Damn it, he wasn't very good at this.

'April. But we need to check some things. You must have at least six months on your passport, you know. Perhaps you should check this? And you must apply for a visa. We can combine the visit with a small tour, perhaps? Along the Hooghly river? That is very beautiful. Or perhaps to Rajasthan? To the famous palaces? To Agra. You must see the Taj Mahal, Adam. It's so beautiful. So romantic.'

If he'd been in love with her, the smile that accompanied this statement would have been something to treasure.

James Blair sat in silence, his large frame hunched down into his jacket as though he could pretend he wasn't really there at all, as Adam drove to Forgie End Farm. He kept his face averted from Adam, looking out of the side window. Every part of his body spoke of discomfort.

Adam knew better than to try to make conversation. What would they talk about, anyway? He'd had enough of work for the day, small talk was out of the question, and a discussion about what would meet them at the farm would be ill advised.

When they drove through the copse and stopped at the gate, there was a pause. Adam was just thinking he would have to get out and open his father's door himself when his father did so. At once, a chill wind blasted in, bringing a couple of papery beech leaves with it. Autumn was here, with a bleak message. Time was marching on, and his uncle might not live to see another year.

At least, Adam thought as he watched his father put a hand on the gate, he'd managed to get him here. What was he thinking? Was he nursing the smouldering embers of resentment, or battling with his darkest feelings? Adam held his breath. Don't stop now, he thought, don't do that to me, or to Geordie.

His father reached out and unhooked the chain.

Adam let out his breath. It was going to work.

He'd reckoned on an hour and had prepared himself for

half that. What he'd never considered for a minute was that they would still be at Jean and Geordie's farm almost two hours later – or that he would hear laughter coming from the room next to the kitchen, where Geordie's bed had been set up.

He looked at his aunt, the small vertical line between his eyes the measure of his puzzlement.

'Was that—?'

Her face, a mask of exhaustion, relaxed a fraction and a faint smile played at the corners of her mouth.

'Oh Adam, lovey. It's more than I hoped for. That's a sound I haven't heard in here for a long time.'

Adam rubbed his hands up and down the sides of his nose. 'Good,' he said. 'It's good.'

Jean leaned forward, her gaze direct. Adam had an inkling he knew what was coming.

'About Molly.'

He didn't want to talk about Molly.

'What happened?' Jean Blair had never been less than challenging and old age hadn't changed that.

'It—' Adam searched for a way to answer her. 'It didn't work.'

Jean's look was scathing. 'Don't give me that. You two had been together for years. I've never seen anyone happier. You don't just let a marriage go. Especially not someone like *you*, Adam.'

Adam shifted on his chair, leaned back, crossed one leg over the other, then uncrossed and re-crossed it. Restless was a normal state for him, but pressure of this kind exaggerated the feeling.

'You two were perfect for each other. That wedding of yours was one of the best I can ever remember, and not just because you kept it simple. Molly could no doubt have called in a truckload of favours to have the most ostentatious wedding of the century, but she didn't. I liked that. I felt it was right for you. *She* was right for you.'

Adam swallowed. He found it hard to think about the day he and Molly had married. 'We're getting married outside,' they'd announced on the invitation, 'whatever the weather does. So come prepared!'

The minister had agreed, the guests had arrived dressed in kilts, smart suits or sparkly or floaty dresses – and every one of them had worn walking boots.

He shuffled on the chair. However hard he tried to put that day out of his mind, he would never forget it.

They hadn't been married ten minutes when Molly, surveying the assorted range of wellies, hiking boots, winter boots and hefty shoes, had said, 'It's great to see everyone listened to the instructions.'

'Except the bride.' Adam had smiled, looking down at the ground-length ivory silk of her wedding gown. Friends teased Molly that if her career in marketing ever stalled, she could always turn to being a model, and she had never looked more beautiful than she looked that day.

'What do you mean, except the bride?'

'Well – not under that, I imagine.'

'I am so wearing boots!'

'I don't believe you. Lift up your skirt!'

'Really Adam! In front of our guests?' Long tendrils of blonde hair had escaped from her elaborate French braid and were wafting in the brisk breeze. Her face had been aglow with happiness.

Adam had captured a stray frond and tucked it behind her ear. He hadn't been able to resist kissing her neck, just below where a fat pearl hung from her lobe, creamy and gleaming in the sunshine.

'I don't believe you're wearing boots,' he'd challenged. 'Prove it.'

'OK, I will!'

She'd grabbed fistfuls of silk and hoisted her dress upwards to reveal her hiking boots, scrubbed to look as good as new, specially polished to a high sheen and laced with scarlet ribbon.

Cameras snapped and flashed, and the laughter of the guests had echoed down the valley and startled a flock of crows.

'That's bad luck,' someone had muttered, staring down river.

'Rubbish. Stupid old superstition,' another had retorted.

'Six crows. They say it means a death.'

'Shut up, Angus, don't be such an old killjoy.'

Adam, still laughing at Molly's boots, had fleetingly thought the comment macabre and then forgotten it. Oddly, the words came back to him now. There had been a death. Jamie Gordon had died, and with his death any chance of saving Adam's marriage seemed to have died as well.

He said to his aunt, 'I thought she was right for me too. Sadly, Molly thought otherwise.'

It was boorish to blame her and he regretted his words immediately.

A door somewhere opened, creaking on old hinges.

Jean put a hand over his and said, before his father could arrive and interrupt their conversation, 'Fight for her, Adam. She's worth it.'

Chapter Fifteen

'You're on.'

'I beg your pardon?'

'It's Molly. I said "you're on".'

There was a whoop at the other end of the line.

'I'm delighted, Molly, really I am,' Barnaby Fletcher crowed. 'This is the beginning of something great!'

'Me too. I can't *tell* you how excited I am!'

The job at Fleming House had been a godsend, but it wasn't what Molly wanted to do indefinitely. She had so much more to offer than pandering to bridezillas or sweet-talking low-level corporate types who thought their booking was God's gift. And with Adam having a new woman in his life …

Well, that was it. The end of a marriage she should probably have insisted on winding up some time ago, and the beginning of a new life on her own. At last she'd started along the motorway of arrangements and rearrangements that would end in London.

'Your timing was impeccable,' she told Barnaby. 'I'm ready for a new challenge.'

'And Fletcher Keir is ready for you.'

'Keir Fletcher.'

'Sorry?'

'It sounds better. Say it, Barnaby. Keir Fletcher. Keir Fletcher. Keir Fletcher. It has a fantastic ring to it.'

'But it—' There was a silence at the other end of the line.

'Oh God,' Molly said, 'I know what you're thinking. It gives me more prominence. But that wasn't it at all. It was just … Forget it. It's your business.'

'Actually,' Barnaby said, 'once your money goes in, we'll be equal owners.'

'Well, whatever. We could call it Peach. Or Indigo Peach. We could call it Random Feather. Or Jubilee Monday. We can call it anything we want!'

This was heady stuff. A business to play with! No, not 'a' business – *her* business.

Barnaby laughed, the whole-body chuckle that never failed to lift her spirits. 'You've just underlined exactly why you're the best person to join me, Molly. You're so sparky and creative. I love it. Now – to the nitty gritty. Can you fly down to London? Even just a day would do. We should meet and talk everything over. I'll get the legal papers drafted, you need to get them checked and, of course, you need to get the capital lined up. How soon can that be organised?'

Molly's heart sank. She'd considered every possible alternative, gone down every avenue, and all exploration led back to the same inescapable conclusion – the sale of the house was the only way of financing her new venture.

'I'll call Adam today. It might take a month or two to get the cash through. I suppose I could talk to the bank and see if they'll give me a bridging loan.'

'Bridging loan? You'll be lucky, these days. Listen, I'll talk to my people and see what they say. A legally binding promissory note might be enough in the short term, but it would have to be short term. The business needs the capital injection.'

'Got it. Don't worry, Barnaby – I bet the house sells within a week.'

An hour later, she put the phone down and scanned the

list she'd been making as they talked.

- Talk to Adam
- Hand in my notice
- Alert lawyer and bank.

Amazingly short for such a big step, but she'd already told her father and Lexie knew, and those two people were the most important in her life. She didn't suppose Logan would miss her much and the only impact on Adam would be the sale of the house. As for friends, she'd hidden away here for so long that most of them had given up on her, apart from Lexie. Still, London was going to be a new start, and she was ready for it.

Her mobile rang. Lexie – perfect timing.

'Hi. I was just thinking about you. I've accepted the job in Lon—'

'Molly! Help me!'

Molly corkscrewed round in her chair and sat bolt upright. 'What is it? Have you fallen? What's wrong?'

Lexie groaned. The sound started low and built in volume until it was more of a howl than a moan.

Molly shot to her feet. 'Christ Almighty, what's happened?'

The scream subsided into ragged panting. 'I've gone into labour!'

'But you're not due for another month.'

'Tell the baby!'

'Where are you? Where's Patrick? Have you called the hospital?'

There was another groan.

'Speak to me, Lex. Where are you?'

'I'm … in … the … cottage.'

Molly shoved the phone into her pocket and ran. A

minute later, she was hammering on the front door of the gardener's cottage. Damn it! Why was the thing locked? Lexie never locked it, unless she was sleeping here – a rare event these days.

'Lexie! It's me! Let me in!'

From somewhere inside she could hear the unearthly moaning again.

'Lexie! Can you get to the door?'

'Wait! C-coming.'

There was a heart-stopping pause, then the sound of dragging footsteps. The key grated in the lock and Molly was able to push the door open.

'Thank God! Are you OK?'

Lexie's skin was pallid against the crimson of her hair. Sweat gleamed on her face, the unhealthy, oily slick of the unwell.

'It's started.'

Molly put one arm around her waist and the other across her shoulders. 'Come on. Let's get you somewhere more comfortable. Where's Patrick?'

'Tokyo.'

'Shit. No point in calling him, then.'

Unexpectedly, Lexie laughed. 'Typical man, huh? Never there when you need them.'

'Have you called an ambulance?'

Lexie started walking up and down the corridor. She turned by the front door and strode back to the studio door, turned and came back to the front door. It was a short corridor, only a dozen feet, hardly the place for a walk. At the front door she paused for a moment, turned again, paced the length of the corridor, turned the handle of the studio door and flung it open. Light flooded in.

The cottage was tiny, just a bedroom, kitchen and bathroom, but its outstanding feature was the large living room with its three floor-to-ceiling French windows leading into the mansion's old walled garden. Autumn, Molly noticed as she followed Lexie into the bright space, was here. The tall beech tree in the far corner of the garden was turning to gold and leaves were already whipping free and swirling to the ground in the brisk morning breeze. It was secluded and pretty, but above all, it faced north and threw flat light into the room – which was why Lexie had made this space her studio. Large canvases were stacked against the wall and an easel stood near the far window, the last painting for her exhibition awaiting final touches.

Not today though. It seemed as if today was going to be the day when something – *someone* – quite different would be clamouring for attention.

Lexie, striding determinedly round the perimeter of the room, said, 'God, no. You can't call an ambulance unless it's an emergency and they don't consider being in labour an emergency. Oh Molly!' She came to an abrupt halt, her eyes huge and dark against the pasty white skin. 'What if there's something wrong? She shouldn't be coming yet – aahh!'

She doubled up again as a contraction wracked her body.

'Let's not panic,' said Molly, panicking. She was used to coping with crises. A sick chef, a hungover band, no wine – such things were the stuff of day-to-day event management emergencies. But a baby?

She watched helplessly. Patrick would be better at this than she was. He was always calm and in control. On the other hand – this was his baby too, and he was totally in love with Lexie. How would he cope with watching her suffer?

'Right,' she said decisively. 'I'd better get you to

hospital. This is the real thing, you reckon? Not just one of those false labour whatnots?'

Lexie gritted her teeth. 'Molly. My waters have broken, the contractions are less than ten minutes apart. It may be unusual to go into labour so quickly with a first baby, but yes, believe me, this is the real thing.'

'OK. I'll get the car round.'

'I don't know if I can sit in it.'

'What d'you mean?'

'I don't know if I can sit at all.'

'What am I meant to do then?'

'Listen, get the car, we'll figure it out. Hurry!'

Molly fled. All thoughts of London, of Barnaby, of having to face Adam were gone. The only thing that mattered now was Lexie, and getting the baby delivered safely. The enormity of the task hit her. This was about a new life. Please let everything be all right, she prayed, and felt like adding, childlike, if you make everything all right, I promise to be good. Whatever that meant.

Lexie stared at the back of the car, where Molly had thrown half a dozen towels seized from her bathroom.

'Towels? Why towels?'

Molly shrugged. 'I dunno. Anything you ever read about birth seems to involve boiling water and lots of towels. I managed the second bit.'

'Well, I sincerely hope we don't need them. How am I meant to get in?'

Molly stared at the back door of her car, which she was holding wide open.

'It's a Volvo, Lex, not a Mini.'

'I can't sit down.'

'Then kneel. Whatever, I dunno, but unless you want

to have this baby on the grass, you're going to have to do something.'

Lexie clambered in. 'These towels might be useful after all,' she muttered, arranging them around her as she half lay, half knelt along the back seat.

'Ready?'

'Just go!'

Molly shot into reverse. Pebbles sprayed left and right as she threw the car into a turn and headed for the drive.

'Jeez!'

'OK in the back?' Molly called anxiously over her shoulder.

'If this baby doesn't finish me off, your driving will.'

'I thought you wanted to get to the hospital.'

'Alive.'

Molly, glancing in the rear-view mirror, saw Lexie fling out an arm to brace herself against the back seat as she braked at the bottom of the drive.

'Fast? Or safe? Which?' she demanded irritably.

For answer there was only another moan. She sped up. It was three miles to the main road, but at least the hospital was on the right side of Edinburgh. All she had to do was hit the city bypass and it would be plain sailing.

'Damn!'

She stopped.

'What? What is it?' came a voice from the back.

'Nothing. There's a queue at the roundabout.'

'Shit.'

'Won't take long,' Molly said, much more confidently than she felt.

For a few minutes there was silence. Then Lexie said, 'Soon I'll be a mother.'

'Have you only just realised that?'

'It's becoming more concrete. It's been more about

being pregnant till now. Soon the baby will be real. I wonder what it will be like.'

'What? The birth? The baby? Or being a mother?'

'Being a mother.'

'Endless,' Molly said dryly. The queue began to inch forwards. She could see the roundabout half a mile away.

Lexie went on as though she hadn't heard. 'No more quick weekends away. No more peaceful nights. No more special time just with Patrick.'

'It's what you wanted.'

'It was Patrick who wanted it. He had such a shitty time with his own father back in Ireland, I think he's got the urge to prove he could do better.'

'He'll be a great dad.' Molly rolled forward again. With luck, she might make the next change of lights.

'Aargh!'

'You all right?' Molly asked anxiously, wondering whether there was any way she could nose the Volvo between the lines of traffic. It wouldn't make her popular.

Behind her, Lexie had started panting heavily. 'Fine,' came through gritted teeth. 'I could run a marathon. What do you think?'

'I think we're off,' Molly answered thankfully, whisking through the lights at the roundabout just as they turned red. A car, fast off the mark from her right, beeped furiously. She ignored the angry face of the young male driver. He'd change that expression fast enough if he had to stop and help deliver a baby. 'Five minutes. Can you hang on?'

'Sure. I'll just tell baby not to be impatient.'

Molly grinned.

Seven minutes later, she pulled up outside the maternity wing of the Edinburgh Royal Infirmary. The back door swung open and Lexie tumbled out, staggered the few yards to the large glass doors, and sank onto her hands and knees.

'I'll have to park the car,' Molly called. 'You OK for a minute?'

Already the doors were swinging open and Molly could see a porter wheeling a chair across to where Lexie was kneeling. She was in the hands of professionals.

Thank goodness.

But for all the strength of the early contractions, the baby wasn't keen on emerging. The hospital wanted to send Lexie home, but her blood pressure was rising. Molly had never imagined that giving birth could be such an extended process. Lexie was determined to have a natural birth, but as she grew tired, her fears grew.

'What if something's not right?' she cried, squeezing Molly's hand until it hurt. 'What if there's something wrong with her?'

'She'll be fine,' Molly said, trying not to wince at the pressure on her fingers. If she could help Lexie through childbirth, a sore hand was a small price to pay. Still, watching her friend sweat and cry out only to fall back onto her pillows in a state of utter exhaustion confirmed one thing absolutely: she was never going to put herself through this.

'What if she isn't though?'

'Then you and Patrick will deal with it,' Molly said quietly, smiling steadily at Lexie.

'Patrick! Oh my God, I haven't told him! Have you called?'

Molly said soothingly, 'I've left a message. I'm sure he'll call back as soon as he can.'

But Patrick's phone had been switched off and she had no idea whether he'd pick up the message.

As the day drew on and the soft grey of evening melted into the blackness of night, Molly wondered whether it would ever end. At some point Lexie's mother, Martha, appeared and Molly was able to sneak away to the canteen for some refreshment, although it was hard to concentrate on eating.

It was almost six in the morning when Lexie finally gave birth. Molly had been sitting in the hard chair by the side of the rumpled bed for more hours than she could count.

'I can't go on,' Lexie said, flopping back tiredly against the pillows. 'I can't do this any more.'

She looked weary to the bone. Her scarlet hair, usually a jaunty crown atop her head, was flattened and plastered down with sweat. Her chocolate brown eyes were dull with fatigue and she had pale blue smudges in the hollows underneath them.

Molly hadn't dared look in a mirror to check her own appearance. She longed to sleep. She'd already cajoled Lexie through several crises, and was beginning to lack the stamina to talk her through another when the midwife said suddenly, 'Give me your hand.'

'What?'

'Your hand.'

The midwife looked excited. When Lexie reluctantly extended one arm, she took hold of Lexie's hand and guided it down between her legs. 'Feel it?'

The transformation on Lexie's face was astonishing. Molly, almost too tired to follow what was happening, sat up.

'What? What is it?' she cried.

'It's the head,' Lexie whispered, awed. 'Oh Molly, it's the baby's head. She's coming!'

'When I tell you to push, push,' said the midwife.

This time Lexie didn't say, 'I can't,' or whimper exhaustedly. She was like a new woman. She leaned forward, and pushed.

The door of the birthing room swung open.

'I'm not too late, am I?'

'Patrick!'

Patrick Mulgrew, more dishevelled than Molly had ever seen him, strode to the bed. Lexie took one look at him and gave one last magnificent heave. The baby slithered out, red and protesting, her head covered in fine black down. Lexie started laughing and crying at the same time. Molly, slipping out of Patrick's way, stood at the foot of the bed and took in this newly minted family. Lexie was soon cradling the baby and looking up at Patrick, who had encircled his lover and his child in a protective embrace.

Molly watched as Patrick extended tentative fingers towards the slippery skin of his newborn child. He could have held her in just one of his strong hands.

Tears welled up in Molly's eyes.

I didn't think I'd feel like this.

It had taken seventeen long hours and she had not known she was on a journey, but in these last few seconds, her universe had spun and everything she thought she wanted had been tossed into the air and landed in a jumbled mess around her feet.

A baby. So perfect, so tiny, so wanted.

A loving family.

Molly fished in her pocket and found a tissue. Turning away, she blew her nose surreptitiously.

She had turned her back on her chances, and now she might never find this kind of happiness.

Chapter Sixteen

On her tenth birthday Molly's mother gave her a heavy glass paperweight. The top of the glass was clear, with a few perfectly round little bubbles trapped inside. A flower grew up from the bottom, surrounded by fresh green leaves, its petals a pretty pink. One bubble, a little larger than the rest, nestled on the surface of one of these like a drop of rain after a shower.

The paperweight fascinated Molly. She loved to stroke its smooth roundness and look at the patterns on her carpet as the sun's rays hit the convex surface of the ball. If you looked through the glass at the garden, suddenly the grass was in the sky and the sky had plummeted to the ground. Everything was upside down.

A few years later, in science lessons, she learned the reason this happened. It took some of the mystery away, but not the fascination. As she stepped inside the front door of her old home in Trinity, this same disorientation engulfed her. Carpet became ceiling, walls swivelled. She stuck out a hand to steady herself.

She had walked into a topsy-turvy world.

'Are you all right?' Molly shrank back from Adam's steadying hand. If he touched her …

Molly saw a flicker of hurt in his eyes and cursed herself for her reaction. It wasn't that she found him unattractive, quite the opposite, although she couldn't tell him that. And anyway, why should he care if she found him repugnant these days? He had Sunita Ghosh to love him.

'Yes. I'm fine.'

She looked around. He hadn't done anything to the place. The hallway was the same traditional shade of heritage paint as it had been the day she'd left. Adam turned and started walking towards the kitchen, always the hub of the home. It had been the room she had found hardest to leave and still missed most.

'Come in,' he called over his shoulder. 'Coffee? Or wine?'

'Just water is fine,' Molly said. She wasn't sure she could swallow anything right now. Her throat felt as dry as paper and nerves were unsettling her stomach.

'Sure? I'm going to have a glass of wine.'

'Quite sure.'

She looked round the kitchen. He'd taken down the photograph that used to hang on the wall above the table, the one of her and Adam and Jamie Gordon, taken by Lexie at Tantallon Castle. It was hardly surprising. The picture hook that had once supported it hung forlornly untenanted, and she thought it strange that he hadn't had the urge to at least stick a calendar on it.

'You sounded rather serious on the phone,' Adam was saying as he turned the tap on to let the water flow cold. 'I've been bracing myself all day.'

'Have you? I'm sorry. I felt I had to warn you. I didn't want to just turn up and—'

'—and what?' Adam said, filling one of the heavy-bottomed glasses that had been a wedding present and handing it to her. 'Give me my notice?'

Molly gulped.

He had opened the fridge door to look for wine, but there must have been something in her silence that alerted him because he paused and turned.

'Ah. So that *is* it.'

Molly sank onto a chair. He'd always been too good at reading her. 'I'm sorry, Adam. I know you like living here.'

'What is it? You're seeing someone else and you're going to move in together – is that why you need the money?'

'No!' Contrition flared into anger. 'You're a fine one to talk! You and that Sunita woman—'

'Sunita woman? Isn't that a bit patronising? She's not just "some woman", she's an extremely smart lawyer, and she deserves some respect.'

'I didn't mean it like that. It's just … I didn't know you were seeing anyone. That night at Loch Melfort took me by surprise.'

Adam lifted a glass down from a cupboard and filled it with wine. When he turned back, he was more composed. 'We have to move on, Molly. I guess that's what you're doing and it's what I'm trying to do too.'

'Yes. You're right. And I guess you don't need to inform me of everything that's happening in your life. We're free agents.'

Adam swallowed half the wine in one quick draught. 'Exactly. So—' his glass hit the table so hard that some of the wine splashed onto the wood, where it glistened under the overhead spotlight.

Molly waited for him to find a cloth and mop up the drops. The Adam she knew would have done that straight away, and the fact that he did not signalled how distracted he must be. She pulled a tissue out of her pocket and wiped them herself.

When she looked up, Adam's glare had softened into something she could not quite describe. He'd always been so much better at understanding what she was thinking than she'd been at interpreting his expressions.

'So, I'll shut up,' he said quietly, 'and listen to what you have to say.'

'Thank you.'

Across the room, something caught her eye. On the stainless steel fridge freezer was the magnet she'd given him one Christmas, a tiny red heart, a silly stocking filler that he'd scoffed at, then placed precisely in his careful way.

It was still there.

The magnet slipped if you banged the door. The easy thing would have been to take it off and bin it, because Adam needed to have everything just so – but he had kept it, and that had to have been a matter of choice. He'd taken a conscious decision.

She stared at the spot of scarlet. What was she to make of it? That he couldn't let a habit go? Was that it? Had Sunita seen it? Would she have challenged its presence? Had Adam defended it? Or did she not come here? Judging by the level of intimacy displayed at Loch Melfort, that seemed unlikely.

'Well?'

She whipped her head back. 'Sorry. It's a bit strange being back here.' She took a deep breath. 'I'm not seeing anyone else, Adam.' She didn't have to give him the satisfaction of knowing that she hadn't dated a single man since Jamie had died. 'I'm moving to London.'

If she'd thought that would provoke a reaction, she was wrong. Adam sat like stone.

'Do you remember Barnaby Fletcher? He's offered me a partnership in a brand new marketing business. A co-directorship, to be precise.'

Adam said quietly, 'That's very well deserved.'

She glanced at him sharply. Was he being sarcastic? His face was deadpan, his look inscrutable.

'Thank you. Naturally, I am expected to put capital into the business. Barnaby has already spent a great deal of money building it up to the point where it's ready to take off—'

'You had everything checked by a lawyer, I hope?'

'Of course,' said Molly, who hadn't yet. 'And I've tried very hard, Adam, but it's a great deal of money and there's only one way I can lay my hands on such a substantial amount.'

'I can see that.' He stood up and started to pace around the kitchen. Adam never had been able to sit still for long.

'I'm sorry, Adam. If there was another way—'

'It's your house too.'

'I know, but—'

'Don't apologise.' He stopped in front of her and rested a hand on the back of a chair. He'd taken his jacket off. His shirt, she noticed, was crisply ironed and fresh. Adam was fastidious in his habits, but he had never done the laundry, or the ironing. In the split of chores, he had been 'head of waste management and vacuuming', she had been 'laundry maid and chief duster and polisher'. It had never been something they'd discussed or argued over, it had just fallen that way.

Who did the dusting now? Who lifted the ornaments on the mantelpiece in the front room and rubbed beeswax into the beautiful oak?

Adam said, 'Maybe it's the catalyst we've been needing, Molly. We've allowed things to drift, but we can't go on like this, can we? Of course you'll have your money. And I'll start divorce proceedings.' His gaze was frank. 'I have to suggest you find a different law firm to represent you. I'd like you to believe that I only want what's fair, but you need to be sure of that. Have you got someone?'

'I—'

Molly blinked. She should have foreseen this. It was the obvious consequence of her demand. Their relationship had entered a maze long ago, and neither of them had been able to find either an exit or a meeting place among the dark hedges of the labyrinth. Adam might have found a path through to sunlight, but she was still blundering into dead ends and being forced to turn back.

Not any more. London was her exit. No more dead ends.

'Yes,' she said. 'That would be best.'

Chapter Seventeen

Ricky McQuade was drunk. Nothing new there. Caitlyn, sitting near the back of the bus from Hailesbank to Summerfield after a long shift, slunk down in her seat in the hope that he wouldn't see her, but, inevitably, he did.

The smell of stale perspiration, mixed revoltingly with nicotine and alcohol, wafted under her nose as he swung himself down onto the seat next to her. His hands were surprisingly elegant, with long, slim fingers, but they looked grubby and the nails were jagged and embedded with grime. Caitlyn tried hard not to wrinkle her nose.

'Hey, Caitlyn, aren't you goin' tae say hello?'

'Hello, Ricky.'

''S better. Nice tae be polite, eh?'

He pulled out a packet of cigarettes and glanced sideways at Caitlyn.

She crossed her arms and looked out of the window at the darkness. He wouldn't light up. Even if he did, it was the driver's problem, not hers.

''S awright.' His grin was toothy. ''S awright, doll, just windin' you up. Where've you been, eh?'

She counted the lights of cars as they flashed by and tried to work out how she was going to evade him once they got to Summerfield.

'Dinnae tell me you've got a boyfriend. I wouldnae like that, darlin'. But no,' he swung half out into the passageway so that he could swivel towards her and leer. 'Yer savin' yerself for me, naw?'

He cackled wheezily, a smoker's rasp.

'You and me,' he swung close and nudged her, 'we're gonna be great, eh?'

Everyone on the bus must be listening. Embarrassed, Caitlyn said, 'Cut it out, Ricky. You're drunk.'

'Gie's a break, doll. I'm no' that drunk. 'S nice, eh?' Aggrieved, Ricky started addressing the other passengers. 'Try tae be friendly and that's what you get, eh?' He sniggered and flung a heavy arm across Caitlyn's shoulders. 'She loves me really.'

The beer breath was repulsive and a wave of nausea swept over her. She wriggled out from his embrace.

'Stop it, McQuade.'

The authority in her voice was enough to check him and he subsided sulkily.

'You always were a bossy bint,' he muttered, slumping back in his own seat and pulling his baseball cap down over his eyes. 'Stew, then.'

At Summerfield, half a dozen people climbed off the bus. Caitlyn, recognising a friend of her mother's, sent her a pleading look.

'Ricky McQuade been on the booze again?' the woman said, smiling.

'You noticed?'

'Hah! Come on then, Caitlyn, we'll get a wiggle on. He's in no state to keep up.'

She was right. By the time they reached the first corner, Ricky McQuade was doubled up and spewing into the gutter fifty yards behind them.

It had been Caitlyn's last shift at the supermarket – tomorrow she was going to start back at Blair King. She was hoping to come home to peace and a timely retreat to bed, but as soon as she pushed open the front door she realised that Ailsa was still up. Music was blaring from the front room. She could hear its heavy beat even through the closed door.

Instinctively, Caitlyn glanced upstairs. Could the little ones really be sleeping through that? She listened for a moment but there was no noise from above, so she dropped her bag in the hall and shoved open the door to the living room.

'Ailsa?' she burst out, more astonished than shocked.

One fair head and one shaven head jerked apart and Ailsa's face turned towards her above the back of the sofa.

'Hi, Caits, you home then?'

'No, I'm still at the supermarket. Who's this?'

The man stood up. He was at least six foot two and well-muscled – at least, that was the impression Caitlyn got, although the intricate tattoos displayed from wrist to shoulder made tracing the outline of the muscles in his arms a tricky task.

'Hi.' A large hand shot towards her. 'I'm Wallace.'

Caitlyn did a quick calculation. With a name like Wallace it was more than likely he'd been born soon after the film *Braveheart* had been released, which would make him around twenty. Too old to be snogging her sister.

'Ailsa is only fifteen,' she said coolly, ignoring the hand.

Out of the corner of her eye she saw Ailsa flush crimson. 'Caitlyn,' she hissed, clearly mortified.

To give him some credit, Wallace didn't flinch.

'I ken. I'll treat her fine.'

There was something in the steadiness and directness of his gaze that Caitlyn couldn't help admiring, but the scar above his left eyebrow was cause for concern. He looked like a man who liked a fight. She reserved judgement.

'Go away, Caits,' Ailsa said, sliding a slim arm round Wallace's powerful shoulders and glaring at her, unabashed. 'You're not my mother.'

Wallace bent down to the sofa and picked up a leather jacket. 'You're all right, Ailsa. I'd better be off anyway, got work in the morning, eh?' He grinned and stooped to kiss Ailsa's cheek.

Beauty and the Beast, thought Caitlyn – although she had to admit, despite her reservations, that there was something oddly attractive about this Beast.

'I'll call you, babes.'

When the front door clicked behind him, Ailsa raged.

'That was *so* humiliating, Caits. You made me look like a naughty kid.'

'Where's Mum? I take it she's not back yet?'

'No,' Ailsa said in a defiant tone. 'So?'

Caitlyn sighed. 'We haven't met Wallace yet, Ailsa. It's not really appropriate for me to come home late at night to find you two in a clinch on the sofa.'

'Appropriate? You sound like my stupid teacher.'

'Well, maybe there's a reason for that. I just think you should have told us about Wallace, brought him round to meet Mum.'

'Christ!' Ailsa muttered. 'What century are you living in?'

Caitlyn put a hand on Ailsa's shoulder. A little to her surprise, her sister didn't immediately shake it off.

'We just care about you, love, that's all.'

Ailsa's glare lasted about ten seconds, then faded. She shrugged.

'Whatever. You've met him now.'

She flicked her long hair back across her shoulders and marched to the stairs. 'I'm going to bed.'

'I'll be up in a minute.'

Caitlyn watched her sister's slim legs disappear up the stairs. She looked a lot older than she was, that was the problem – and besides, she was a pretty girl. Wallace, no doubt, would be the first of many young men who came panting after Ailsa Murray.

As she emerged from Waverley Station in Edinburgh the next morning Caitlyn realised she had probably overreacted to her sister's new boyfriend. She was trembling with nerves, and she realised that the nervousness must have been building for days. She'd kidded herself she was just being protective of her sister, but maybe she'd subconsciously been finding a vent for her own tension. Now that she was in Edinburgh, only minutes away from the office, she could fool herself no longer. The truth was she was not looking forward to starting back at Blair King one little bit.

When she reached Waverley Bridge, she lifted her face to the grey skies. There was a smirr of rain in the air. Typical. She'd been so filled with apprehension that she hadn't thought about the weather. She should have prepared herself properly for her first day back at the law firm. It wasn't like her to be disorganised. Normally, she would have had everything laid out on her bed or packed in her bag, ready for her early start. Easy to blame Ailsa for distracting her, but she knew she'd been exhausted last night. A long shift at the supermarket had left her tired enough. Dealing with Ricky McQuade's drunken advances, and then the unexpected presence of Wallace – what *was* his other name? – had just about finished her off.

Perhaps the rain would hold off long enough for her to get to the office, she thought, more in hope than expectation. It was little more than a damp mist at the moment.

She turned up the collar of her scarlet jacket, put her head down, and started marching towards Princes Street. The walk would take twelve minutes; surely it would hold off that long?

Six minutes later, she passed a deli. Already, a small queue of early-morning commuters had formed. Caitlyn knew that she should line her stomach with a roll or a banana, or at the very least a latte, but she couldn't face the thought of food. Maybe by lunchtime she'd be hungry. Right now, her stomach was churning.

The rain started in earnest just as she neared the corner of Hanover Street and Queen Street. Caitlyn started to run. Blair King's door was less than a minute away. If she could just get there before she was soaked ...

At the top of the steps, two cast iron braziers flanked the entrance. When the office had last been refurbished, the gas had been lit and an impressive jet of flickering flame had made the approach to the building spectacular. Guests arriving for the party to mark the opening some years ago had stopped to admire the spectacle, but Caitlyn doubted very much if they'd been lit again since then. Conspicuous consumption of gas was hardly a great message. This morning, only the rain framed the entrance as she scuttled inside.

'Can I help you?'

The girl on reception was new since Caitlyn had last worked here, and was clearly trying to mask a look of disdain as she surveyed Caitlyn's bedraggled figure. Caitlyn could hardly blame her. The rain had flattened her hair and was running down the back of her neck. The sudden downpour had drenched the front of her blouse so that the thin cotton had become almost transparent and her bra was showing through.

She pulled the edges of her jacket together, ran a hand

through her hair and said, as bravely as she could, 'I'm Caitlyn Murray. I'm starting work today.'

Behind her, a voice said incredulously, 'Caitlyn Murray?'

She swung round to see a face that was indelibly imprinted on her memory and realised with a sinking feeling that she'd already run into the one person she'd hoped she could avoid.

'Morning.'

It emerged as a croak, but Malkie's words spun back into her mind. *You didn't do anything wrong. You don't know that he did.* She plucked courage from somewhere down near her rain-sodden shoes, cleared her throat and tried again. 'Morning, Mr Keir.'

Logan Keir's hair had been longer when she'd last seen him. Now it was short and slick with rain. The wet look suited him. He had chiselled cheekbones and generously curved lips, framed by short, carefully trimmed stubble. But it was his eyes Caitlyn remembered most – the way they stared at you, defying challenge, and the pretty, dark lashes which softened the aggression. It was an unsettling combination.

Logan said, 'Have you come in for an appointment?'

'Not an appointment, no. I'm starting back today.'

Was that a flicker of alarm in his eyes? If it was, he recovered quickly.

'Welcome back.'

She watched as he turned and headed for the lift. Behind her, the receptionist said, 'Mr Blair is ready to see you. His office is in the basement. You can take the lift, or the stairs are over there.'

Caitlyn glanced across to the lift, where Logan was still waiting. She turned in the other direction and headed for the stairs. One encounter was enough – the idea of being trapped in a lift with the man was unbearable.

'Maybe we can catch a coffee later,' the receptionist called as she moved away. Recognition by a partner and a meeting with the boss's son had obviously given her street cred.

She smiled. 'That would be nice,' she said. 'Thanks.'

At the bottom of the stairs she nipped in to the ladies' cloakroom. Two minutes wouldn't make a difference and she could dry her hair off a bit under the hand drier. She took off her jacket and yanked her blouse over her head. The hand drier roared into action and she watched as the damp patches receded. Thank goodness it was an efficient drier.

Dry enough. She pulled the blouse back on and doubled over so that she could stick her head under the warm blast of air.

'What *are* you doing?'

Caitlyn shot up, hit her head on the drier and spun round, wincing.

'I was just trying to – oh, it's you.'

In front of her was Agnes Buchanan, Blair King's chief cashier, a woman so unassuming and helpful that you couldn't help but like her. On Caitlyn's very first day at Blair King, Agnes had taken her aside and said, 'It can be a bit strange at first, a new place, but if there's anything you need, or are worried about, don't hesitate to ask me.'

She hadn't, of course. Despite the offer of help, Agnes seemed to Caitlyn to be more like a partner than office staff. She knew everything and everybody, and her long years at the firm gave her unrivalled status. And for all she'd been friendly, she was a private person. She ate neat sandwiches out of Tupperware and favoured a specific combination each day of the week. Mondays were cold beef and Tuesdays cheese and pickle. Fridays, Caitlyn seemed to remember, were vegetarian, but the other combinations escaped her.

'She lives alone,' Deirdre had told her. 'I think she's quite set in her ways.'

Agnes also liked art. The only time she ever became really animated was when describing some exhibition she'd been to at the weekend. Her hobby – if you could call it a hobby, thought Caitlyn – was travelling around the country just to catch a glimpse of a Dürer or a Titian. Holidays were spent tramping round the big galleries in London, or Paris, or Madrid.

She gathered her thoughts rapidly.

'I'm due in to see Mr Blair, but I got caught in the rain.' Thank heavens she'd at least got her blouse back on. 'I just wanted to give my hair a quick dry, look a bit more presentable. Have you seen any good exhibitions recently?'

'Oh, you remembered!' Agnes exclaimed with a smile that transformed her pinched little face into something almost attractive. 'How kind. I'm just back from a couple of weeks in Prague, as it happens. The Art Nouveau is quite outstanding. The Secessionists were—' She broke off. 'Anyway, I don't suppose you're interested. Are you – I don't mean to pry, of course, but may I ask if you are seeing Mr Blair about a private matter, or—?'

'He's asked me to come back to cover for someone,' Caitlyn said, thinking it odd that the omniscient Agnes didn't already know this.

'Oh! Oh I see.' A small frown had appeared below her neat fringe, then it disappeared as quickly as it had arrived. 'Of course, he must have fixed it while I was away. I'm just back this morning. I haven't even started up my computer yet.'

Caitlyn dragged her brush quickly through her hair and examined her reflection. Hardly perfect, but it would do for now.

'I'd love to hear about your holiday,' she lied, leaning nearer the mirror to apply some pale lip gloss.

She was rewarded with another smile. 'At lunchtime then? If you're sure.'

'Sure I'm sure. See you later.'

You never knew, Caitlyn thought, when unselfishness might pay off. There might come a time when she needed an ally.

Chapter Eighteen

Adam was with Sunita at her favourite Indian restaurant in Leith when his aunt called him. Sunita had been planning an evening out for ages, and the moment his phone rang, a small frown appeared on her smooth forehead. He glanced at the caller ID, then eyed the lamb nawabi that had just been placed in front of him with regret.

'Sorry,' he said, not waiting for the inevitable protests. 'I have to take this. I'll be back in a minute.'

He strode past the large glass window, beyond the kitchens where earlier they'd stood to watch the chefs preparing the naan breads in the tandoori oven and smoking salmon on the sigri, knowing, before he pressed the green button, that it must be bad news.

'Adam?'

'Hello, Jean.'

'Geordie passed away today at quarter past three,' she said without preamble. 'I wanted you to know.'

Adam had reached the door of the restaurant. He said, 'I'm so sorry,' as he emerged into the cool of the evening and the subtle aroma of spices was exchanged for a blast of briny sea air. 'How are *you*?'

'Fine at the moment.'

He leant against the wall, and pictured his aunt standing in the farmhouse kitchen in her flat brogue shoes, tweed skirt and pearls. She'd have her small chin tilted upwards, postponing the inevitable lacerations of grief with a whirlwind of activity. His throat constricted.

'Was he – I mean, was it bad? You should have let me know. Maybe I could have come to be with you.'

'It was quick at the end, Adam. He was doped up with morphine, of course, and he was here, thank God. He'd always been very clear that he wanted to die at home, and I'm so glad we managed that.'

Adam wiped the back of his hand across his eyes. When had he last cried? Aged six, perhaps? He pressed his left hand against the wall behind him and felt the cold roughness against his skin. Somehow, it steadied him.

'Does Dad know?'

'I've just come off the phone to him.'

There was a cotton handkerchief in his pocket. Fumbling for it, he held the phone away from his face so that his aunt wouldn't hear him blowing his nose.

'How did he take it?' he asked cautiously, stuffing the crumpled square back into his pocket.

'He didn't say much, but there was a hell of a lot in his silence, I thought.'

She was perceptive. A couple of months ago Adam would never have believed that his father would display any kind of emotion over his brother's death, but after their visit to the farm, he'd noticed subtle changes in him, an almost indefinable softening round the edges of his behaviour. There'd been a new willingness to leave the office early, for example, as though the proximity of death brought home to him the preciousness of life and the importance of family.

He said, 'Can I do anything? Can I help with the arrangements?'

'Thank you, Adam, but you're busy enough with work. Your mother's going to help.'

'Really?' He hadn't known that his mother had even

been in touch with Jean recently.

'Don't be so surprised. Your mother has been visiting us for a couple of years.'

'*Mum* has?'

'We bumped into each other in Jenners in Edinburgh one day and decided that even if our menfolk weren't talking, that was no reason why we shouldn't be friends.'

'You're quite right. How sensible,' Adam said, wondering why his mother had never mentioned it. 'You won't know when the funeral is yet, I suppose?'

'One of us will let you know as soon as we can. I just wanted to tell you about Geordie myself.'

'Thank you, I appreciate that. I'll come out and see you sometime in the next couple of days. I'm sure there must be something I can do.'

Adam ended the call and stood for a moment in the soft evening light, filled with memories. His uncle as a younger man, fit and strong, taking the cows in for milking. Geordie hauling his large frame up onto the tractor to start work in some distant field. The tractor had seemed so huge – or perhaps Adam had just been small. He smiled, remembering. How he'd wanted to drive the thing! 'One day. When you're old enough,' Geordie had promised.

But he never had driven it. By the time he'd been old enough, there'd been the great falling out.

'Everything all right?' Sunita asked, looking up from her mobile.

'Sorry to be so long.' He took hold of her shoulders as he passed behind her chair and dropped a light kiss on the top of her head. 'Bad news, I'm afraid. My uncle has died.'

'The one with the farm?'

'That's right.'

A waiter arrived and uncovered a plate.

'They asked if they could keep your food warm,' Sunita said.

'Thank you.' He flashed a smile at the waiter and tucked into the remnants of his supper. News of the death hadn't diminished his appetite.

'When's the funeral?'

'Next week sometime, I imagine.'

'If I can, I'll come with you.'

Adam looked up. 'Oh. That's kind of you, Sunita, but there's no need. Really. It will be quite a small affair, just family.'

'That's why I'd like to support you.'

Adam yanked the pillow out from under his head and tossed it onto the floor. He lay straight and stiff with his head on the mattress and his eyes wide open, staring upwards in the dim light filtering in from the street. Above him, the ceiling had developed a fine crack. It had appeared after the wall had been demolished downstairs to form the open-plan kitchen diner. 'It's perfectly safe,' the structural engineer had informed them. 'There's been a little settlement, that's all. The RSJ beam is more than adequate support.' But Molly had worried.

Adam's gaze tracked the line of the crack, from near the corner almost to the centre of the room. He should get the ceiling replastered, but what was the point? Amid the pressures of daily life, it came low on his list of priorities – and anyway, he was going to have to sell the place now.

This house was full of memories of Molly. Maybe that's why he'd clung on here when common sense told him he should have sold up. This place had been so much their joint dream that he couldn't bear to let it go.

He rolled onto his stomach and closed his eyes, willing sleep to come, but his mind was still churning.

He'd set the divorce in action tomorrow. And he'd get someone round to do a valuation on the house.

The thought of Molly moving to London tore at his heart.

I don't want her to go.

There. He'd acknowledged it. And he'd figured something else out as well. He didn't want Sunita to come to a family funeral because Sunita wasn't Molly.

But he couldn't have Molly either.

Basically, he was a mess.

Fight for her, Adam. She's worth it, his aunt had urged.

But it was too late.

He woke the next morning full of resolve. He had to do three things: set the divorce in motion, put the house on the market, and break off his relationship with Sunita Ghosh. The first two were not tasks he wished to do, but they were straightforward. The third was something he really wanted to achieve, but would be thorny.

These thoughts tugged at his mind as he threaded his way in and out of the early-morning traffic on his bike. It was uphill most of the way from Trinity into town, but the exercise pumped blood to his brain and energised him for the day ahead.

It started with the monthly partnership meeting. Adam sat over a coffee as everyone settled around the boardroom table and scanned the accounts. Cash flow looked bad again. He couldn't understand it. They'd been incredibly busy, the fees were coming in, and Agnes Buchanan kept an eagle eye on office costs.

He raised it at the meeting.

'Should settle down soon,' his father said.

Adam probed, but James Blair was clearly not inclined to delve further today. 'Agnes assures me she has everything in hand.'

Uneasy, Adam left it at that. Was the old man losing interest? Maybe it was time he thought of retiring. Adam would have a quiet word with his mother, see what her thoughts were. At least it looked as though he'd managed to solve the problem of Shereen James's maternity cover. Caitlyn Murray had only been back for a couple of weeks, but already he was getting reports of how good she was.

Across the table, Adam saw Logan Keir shifting in his seat as the meeting dragged on. He picked up a pen, doodled something on the pad in front of him, and laid it down again. He took out a handkerchief and wiped it across his forehead, then stuffed the hankie away. He shoved his chair back and crossed his legs, then crossed his arms in front of him too. It wasn't like Logan to be so restless. Adam hoped he wasn't sickening for something – there'd been an unseasonal bout of flu doing the rounds. One of their key clients had a big acquisition coming up; he couldn't afford for Logan to be ill.

'Are you all right?'

'I'm fine.'

Logan uncrossed his legs and arms and cleared his throat. He pulled his chair back in to the table and looked down at his pad, frowning. He hunched his shoulders, picked up his pen and started doodling again. Across the table, Adam could see the scribbles – heavy, dark shapes, like thunderbolts, and little figures prancing around. And did they have horns on their heads? From here, they looked like little devils cavorting in the midst of a massive lightning storm.

When the meeting wound to a close, he drew Logan aside. 'Are you sure you're all right? You don't seem quite yourself.'

'Absolutely fine.'

He didn't look fine. He looked pale and there was a faint sheen of sweat on his face. He pulled the handkerchief out of his pocket again and rubbed at his face.

'You don't look so hot.'

'Really, Adam, you don't have to worry about me.' Logan's gaze flickered towards the door, then back to Adam. 'There's a lot going on at home, you know, with the new term starting and Alastair going up to secondary.'

'Not having problems, is he?'

'He's not settling in as well as we'd hoped and Adrienne's a bit uptight about it. You know what it's like. If the wife's not happy, there are always repercussions, eh?'

'Is there anything I can do?'

'Nope. Not a thing. Thanks for offering though. Can we get together later to go over that acquisition? There are quite a few points we need to discuss.'

After the meeting, Adam cornered the partner in charge of conveyancing and arranged for him to call round on Friday to do a valuation. He spent some time fruitlessly prevaricating about the divorce proceedings – should he do it all himself or would that be a bad idea? After tossing the matter around in his head, he gave up and turned to the third item on his action list – what he should do about Sunita. He'd have to see her; he couldn't dump her by text or email like some gauche teenager, but he wasn't in any mood to talk to her either.

Instead of facing his problems, he ducked them. He

collected his bike and cycled all the way out to Forgie End Farm, where he found his mother cooking.

'That smells good.' He hugged her slight frame. 'Any chance of sneaking a bit?'

Rosemary Blair had been a nurse before he'd been born and had enough natural compassion for the whole family. She'd given up working years ago, but compensated by giving her life over to charitable causes. She was a talented fundraiser and organiser and was such a natural with everyone, from the elderly or sick to children or businessmen, that she was a gift to any charity she chose to support.

Today, the full focus of her efficiency and compassion was clearly Jean Blair.

'There's enough for a small army, so I guess the answer's yes. Are you just here to give your condolences or have you a mission?'

'I wanted to do something, if I can. Where's Jean?'

'Somewhere out on the land.'

'Do you know where? Maybe I can give her a hand.'

Before Rosemary could answer, the kitchen door opened and Jean arrived, carrying a basket of eggs. 'They're laying all right, thank goodness. One thing less to worry myself about. Oh, hello, Adam.'

'Jean, I'm so, so sorry.' Adam took the basket from her and laid it on the table, then folded his aunt in his arms.

'He was ready. I thought I was too, but you can never quite be—' her voice caught, but she broke out of his hug and smiled bravely. 'Well, that's life, I suppose. Death is the inevitable conclusion. We have to deal with it.'

'I wish I could help you here.'

'You're busy.'

'I know.' Adam grinned. 'But I'd swap it all in a

164

minute for this—' He swept an expressive hand towards the window and the farmland beyond.

'Really?'

'You bet.'

His mother said, 'I expect your father would have something to say about that.'

'Yes.' Adam subsided into a chair and picked up an egg. 'I expect he would.'

The egg felt like a small miracle – smooth and still warm, the most perfectly packaged food in existence. He held it against his cheek and thought about Jean's chickens.

Chapter Nineteen

'She's acting strangely,' Caitlyn confided to Malkie on Saturday as they strolled round the Thomson Memorial Park in Hailesbank watching Isla May kick up leaves with her friend Mariella. Isla May's blonde curls gleamed in the autumn sunshine, while her friend's russet ponytail bounced and bobbed as they ran with extraordinary energy in and out of the trees that bordered the perimeter.

'She doesn't look strange, just like a normal kid,' Malkie said, putting an arm around her waist and pulling her close.

It felt so natural being here with Malcolm Milne, like they'd been an item for ages rather than just a couple of months. Everything seemed to be falling into place all at once.

'Hmm. She's stopped pestering me about the school summer camp, which is odd. And sometimes, when I get home at night, she looks kind of furtive. Her and Ailsa, now that I come to think of it.'

'Furtive?'

'In that kind of really innocent "Who, me?" way, when I haven't accused her of anything.'

'Maybe she's been trying your make-up while you're out. My kid sister used to do that.' Malkie laughed. 'She made me try it as well once. What a sight! Ginger hair and scarlet lipstick, with a good dose of blue eyeshadow.'

Caitlyn giggled. 'Don't tell me you secretly liked it?'

Malkie groaned. 'Couldn't get it off quick enough. Just

imagine if Ricky McQuade or one of his gang had called at the door.'

'You'd have been dead meat.' Caitlyn pulled a face at Isla May as she peeped round a tree trunk, then disappeared again quickly. It was good to see that she hadn't completely grown out of the delights of peekaboo. 'I suppose she might be using my make-up. Or maybe dressing up, or practising walking in heels. Though I've only got one pair of high heels, and I can't walk in them for more than a few yards myself.'

'Well, I don't suppose it's anything serious, or you'd know.'

They stopped by a bench. The sun was already dropping in the sky, the rapidly cooling air a whisper that winter was approaching. Joyce had taken Harris and Lewis to their school football match and Ailsa was out somewhere with Wallace Ford. Caitlyn still had reservations about Wallace. He seemed too old for Ailsa, too knowing about the world. Ailsa was still at school, and for all she liked to project an air of sophistication, she was still a child, untutored in matters of the heart and innocent about all the ways the wrong man could damage her. Wallace was too experienced. Her sister should be with someone who was exploring the meaning of romance, not someone who'd almost certainly broken a few hearts already. He might be preparing to break Ailsa's heart too, even if unintentionally.

Malkie glanced at her. 'You've got that look again.'

'What look?'

'The one that tells me you've got the weight of the world on your shoulders.'

Caitlyn laughed. 'Am I so transparent?'

'To me.' Malkie put a finger under her chin, tipped her face up towards him and started to kiss her.

'Oh yeugh!'

They broke apart, laughing, as Isla May and Mariella skipped away, pulling faces of disgust.

Caitlyn said, 'Malkie? This is good. I like it. I like *you*. But I'm not like Saskia, and to be honest, I'm not sure I'm quite ready for a full-on live in relationship.'

'Was I suggesting it?'

'No. Sorry, I didn't mean to – Listen, all I meant was can we just take this slowly?'

Malkie jumped up and hauled her to her feet.

'Take what slowly?' he said grinning. 'Race you to the fountain.'

And he was off, sprinting in and around the rose bushes and into the formal garden with its box hedges and half-dead summer plantings to where a monstrous gilded dolphin spewed water into a giant seashell.

'Come back!' Caitlyn called, puffing in his wake.

When she finally caught up with him, he scooped her up in his arms and threatened to drop her into the chilly water, encouraged by two very excited little girls who had found a shortcut.

'Don't you dare!' Caitlyn cried, laughing and squirming.

Malkie had a knack of getting it right. Impulsively, she kissed his cheek.

'What was that for?' he asked, smiling.

'For understanding.'

Even after almost ten weeks of commuting, Caitlyn was still finding the long days tiring, especially now that the clocks had changed and the days were getting shorter. She left home in the dark and got back home in the dark. If she didn't manage to get out for a walk at lunchtime, which happened if they were very busy or the weather was too foul, she felt like a mole.

Still, she had settled in well at Blair King. Loads of people she knew still worked there. She'd been given a desk next to Deirdre Shaw again, so coming back hadn't felt strange at all. Deirdre – kind, round-faced and unashamedly overweight – had a new boyfriend and they'd been out a couple of times as a foursome.

One Friday shortly before Christmas, Agnes Buchanan put her head round the door of their office and announced, 'I have to leave early, girls. I have an invitation to a private view at one of the galleries in Dundas Street. They've got a special Christmas exhibition on. There's nothing I need to know about before I head off, is there?'

'No, Agnes.'

'Nothing,' they chimed in response.

'Very well then. I imagine that one of the partners will be last to leave, but you both know how to lock up, don't you?'

'Yes, Agnes,' they chorused dutifully – then burst into giggles as soon as she was out of earshot.

'"Invitation to a private view",' snorted Deirdre. 'Makes it sound like she's important.'

'Those galleries are really expensive,' Caitlyn said. 'I took my mum into one once – she'd seen a picture in the window she liked. She thought it'd be about fifty quid but it turned out there were a few noughts on the end.'

'Guess Agnes has been hanging around for so long they give her a free glass of wine now and then. Makes the place look busy.'

'Well, good luck to her,' Caitlyn said charitably. 'I don't suppose she has a lot of excitement in her life. What're you up to this weekend?'

'Kev and me, we're catching the train to Glenrothes to visit his gran tonight, but he's at the footie tomorrow. I've made him promise to come Christmas shopping with me on Sunday to make up. You?'

'The usual. Get the twins to football in the morning. Isla May's got a sleepover with her friend. Heaven knows what Ailsa will be up to. I'm seeing Malkie tonight. Might have to babysit tomorrow, I can't remember what shifts Mum's on.'

'Jeez,' Deirdre said suddenly, catching sight of the clock. 'Is that the time? Hell!'

'Problem?'

'Yeah, Kev'll be waiting for me outside, and Mr Keir's left this whole stack of papers here. He must have forgotten to pick them up when he shot off to his meeting this afternoon. It's not like him. He's usually so careful. He hates anything left lying around. I ought to do it for him, but—'

'I'll do it,' Caitlyn volunteered.

'Are you sure? I was hoping you might say that but I didn't like to ask. What about Malkie? Thought you were seeing him tonight.'

'I'm sure it won't take long. Anyway, it's the least I can do, you've been such a help to me since I started back.'

Deirdre obviously wasn't about to argue. She pulled a small set of keys out of her pocket before Caitlyn had even finished speaking. 'Well, ta, I won't say no. His door's open, I checked it a few minutes ago, but lock it before you go. He goes mental if you don't. You're an angel.'

'I know.'

'I'll pay you back sometime, honest.'

She dropped the keys onto the stack of papers. 'Them's his spare keys for the filing cabinet. Stick them back in his desk drawer after, will you? You have a good weekend, now.' She opened the door, paused on the threshold and said, grinning, 'Don't do anything I wouldn't do, ha ha. Bye!'

She winked, and was gone.

Caitlyn smiled at the empty space. Making proper friends had been one of the best things about coming back here. There'd been nobody at the supermarket she'd felt any kind of bond with.

She stood and stretched. Almost quarter to six already – no wonder Deirdre had been so keen to get away. Still, this wouldn't take long, twenty minutes or so at the most. She'd have to watch her time herself – she was heading for the cinema in Hailesbank with Malkie this evening. A Brad Pitt film didn't sound her kind of thing, but Malkie wanted to go, and she liked to keep him happy. Anyway, looking at Brad Pitt for a couple of hours would be no hardship.

There was no-one on Logan Keir's floor. Everywhere was in darkness. She knocked on his door, just in case, but there was no reply, so she went in, flicking the light on.

He kept his room very tidy. Some of the partners were real squirrels – they liked to hoard everything. Mr Keir had always been one of the tidy ones, but now that he was compliance partner for the business, he obviously took security very seriously, because there wasn't a scrap of paper to be seen anywhere in his office. No wonder Deirdre was keen to get this filing done.

Caitlyn inserted one of the keys into the lock on the filing cabinet and turned it. Compliance partner – that meant making sure that all the regulations were kept properly. It must be a complicated job, she thought as she picked up the first letter, because there were so many regulations these days. Back in the old days, Deirdre had told her, people just went to a lawyer and he acted for them. Nowadays, you had to take heaven knows what along with you if you were a new client – utility bills, passports, anything that was recognised as official identification with your address on it – to prove you were who you said you were. Something to do with money laundering, apparently.

She smiled to herself. She used to think money laundering was when you forgot to take a fiver out of your jeans before you washed them. Well, she knew better now.

She started to work through the pile systematically.

L for Leishman.

B for Brown. There were quite a few Browns.

E for Edwards.

She rifled through the files, but couldn't locate a Michael Edwards. She checked again. There was no sign of the file. She scanned the documents she was holding once more. There was a form on the top, and the papers had been fastened together with a paperclip. The heading on the form on the top read, 'New client introduction'. She'd have to open a new file.

She examined the form again and felt a wave of dizziness.

Not again!

A vein started pulsing at Caitlyn's temple and her skin felt cold. *Introduced by ...*

She forced herself to look at the name again.

There was no mistake. She wanted to drop the papers and run, out of Logan Keir's office, out of the building, to be anywhere but here.

Her head was spinning. Her breath came in short, ragged bursts and she clutched at the first thing that came to hand – the hard ridges inside the filing drawer that was open in front of her. The sharpness of the metal forced her to look down.

This was real.

Think, Caitlyn. Think.

The introduction form needed lots of information. The person's name, of course. Where they lived and who had introduced them to the firm. And finally, the signature of the partner who was taking them on, and the signature of another partner.

A year ago, one of Logan Keir's forms had become mixed up with a sheaf of documents sent by a couple of other partners for filing. She hadn't really been reading them, but a name on the document had leapt out at her, stopping her in her tracks. She'd looked at it again, then at the date.

New client: Agatha Franckzac.

Introduced by: Graham Robertson.

Signatories: Logan Keir and John Masters.

She thought that was a bit odd – if Mr Robertson had introduced Agatha Franckzac, why hadn't he signed the form?

And even odder – John Masters, the partner whose name appeared on the form, had died two weeks before the date shown.

It must be a mistake. Maybe just the date?

She'd gone to Mr Keir and asked.

'It was merely an expedient,' Logan Keir had said, his eyes smiling less than his mouth. 'No-one was around at the time and it needed to be done quickly.'

'Oh. I thought maybe … Well, what should I do? Will you change the date, or what?'

To her astonishment, instead of giving her an instruction, he'd turned vicious. 'You're a silly child. Just do your job, and if you can't do your job, find another one.'

And he'd snatched the form out of her hands and marched away.

She'd been cowed. Maybe she was a silly child – she certainly felt like one. He was a partner, and she was way down the ladder.

The episode left her feeling deeply uneasy. What should she do – let it pass? Tell one of the senior partners about it? Inform the Law Society? Maybe she could do that anonymously, then she could stay on at Blair King.

She agonised over what she'd seen. An expedient, he'd said. But he'd lied on the form, hadn't he? There were lies and there were lies, but she knew that this one must be very wrong because the regulations were so strict.

If it was a mistake, surely he could just have explained to Mr Robertson, destroyed the form and filled in another one with the right dates and signatures.

It didn't make sense to her, but she lacked the courage to talk to anyone else. If she told a senior partner and was wrong, they'd definitely think she was stupid – or, worse, a troublemaker. If she tipped off the Law Society, Mr Keir would know quickly enough who'd done it, and what would her life at the firm be like then?

She started tossing and turning all night. She lost her appetite. The small edifice of confidence she'd been carefully constructing crumbled. In the end, she couldn't stand it any more and she handed in her notice.

The day she left, Mr Keir had stopped her in a corridor, blocking her way. 'Don't forget,' he'd said in a low voice, 'that you signed a confidentiality agreement when you joined Blair King. I expect you to adhere to that.'

And he'd brushed past her, leaving only the faint smell of aftershave and the lingering hiss of the threat.

In the half darkness of Mr Keir's office, Caitlyn

shivered. She'd made her decision, and she'd thought about it endlessly over the towers of cans and mountains of sugar. As time had passed and she hadn't found a job that paid nearly half as well, she'd revisited the matter endlessly. Had she really just been a stupid child?

Paralysed with fear, she looked down again at the form she was holding.

New client: Michael Robert Edwards.
Date of Birth: 16:09:1954.
Address: Moray Place, Edinburgh.
Introduced by: ...

Introduced by: Caitlyn Murray.

Chapter Twenty

'I really don't know what to do,' Molly said to Lexie as her friend peeled a damp nappy off the baby, folded it and dropped it into a poly bag. 'Here, give me that.'

She knotted the bag then dropped it in the nappy bin.

'About what?' Lexie cooed at the baby, who gurgled. 'Do you think that was a smile? Look, Molly.'

Molly glanced across to where the baby lay on the changing mat. 'Isn't she a bit young to be smiling?'

'She's obviously a very quick developer,' Lexie retorted.

Maternity suited her, Molly thought, watching as her friend played with the baby. And what a surprise that was – it was not much more than a year since Lexie had been submerged in grief for Jamie, unable to lift a paintbrush and completely at odds with Patrick.

'Now look at you—' she murmured.

Lexie looked across at her. 'What's that?'

'Oh sorry, did I speak out loud? I was just thinking how quickly all this has happened. You and Patrick, I mean, and the baby.'

Lexie gathered the baby – still unnamed – in her arms and sank onto a low chair. The slanting rays of the afternoon light caught the back of her head and formed a halo – Madonna and child, a timeless image. An indefinable feeling of sadness settled around Molly and she struggled to banish it. How can you feel loss when you have never had something?

Lexie was absorbed in feeding. The baby, her eyes closed, raised one tiny hand to her mother's breast, let go of the nipple and gave a little sigh of contentment. Molly marvelled at the miracle of life. The fingers were so small, yet so perfect; the skin pure and soft, unblemished by age or weather. If she and Adam had revisited the issue of children, might they still be together? Might they have avoided the sad descent into neglect and anger that had led to her infidelity and torn them apart?

At length the baby's head fell back and her snuffle turned into a soft snore. Lexie, rousing herself from her own half-stupor, covered herself and laid the child in her cot. 'Tea?' she murmured, her gaze filled with languorous contentment.

'Thought you'd never ask.'

In the kitchen, they debated the thorny matter of names.

'We've only got a few days left to register her,' Lexie said, fidgeting with her mug. 'Patrick wants something Irish, like Aoife or Fionnoula. I'm with him on the poetic, but I'd like something easier to spell.'

'So not Guinevere or Amarantha then?'

'Definitely not. Nor Calliope or Zuleika.'

'You've considered Zuleika?' Molly asked incredulously.

'What do you think?'

Molly reached for a biscuit, then put it back. She wasn't hungry. She quite often found she wasn't hungry these days. 'Lexie—' she started.

'Yes?'

'Oh – nothing.'

'Come on, Molly, what's eating you?'

'I saw a notice in the paper. Adam's uncle has died.'

'I didn't remember that he had an uncle.'

'We didn't see much of them – George and Adam's father fell out years ago. But they came to our wedding, and I really liked them. Jean, his aunt's called.'

'So?'

'I was wondering whether I should go to the funeral.'

Lexie put her mug down, frowning. 'Why? You barely knew him and he's not a relative any more.'

'Well, strictly speaking, he is still a relative.'

'And when are you going to address that, by the way?'

The matter of her divorce was a recurring theme, and as usual, Molly changed the subject instead of answering. 'I think I'd feel better if I went. I could just slip in at the back.'

'You could.'

'Arrive late and leave early.'

'If you want.'

'Yes.' Molly shoved her mug away and stood up. 'That's what I'll do.'

'That's sorted then,' Lexie said, looking amused. 'Delighted to be able to help you make up your mind.'

The irony was lost on Molly. 'Yes. Thanks, sweetie.' She hugged Lexie. 'Must dash, lots to do. See you later. Oh—' she turned at the door, '—if I think of a name I'll let you know.'

'Yes,' said Lexie, shaking her head and smiling, 'you do that.'

Forgie Church sat on a hill so that, although small, it dominated the village. Built in the eighteenth century, it was typically Scottish – plain, airy and unadorned except for a magnificent stained glass window depicting the bush burning in the desert. A dark oak pulpit rose forbiddingly above the congregation, who had to sit on uncomfortably upright pews arranged in neat rows.

They'd visited this church, she and Adam, when they'd been planning their wedding.

'Too traditional,' Adam had said.

'Too stuffy,' had been Molly's verdict, and they had settled, instead, on having their wedding in the hills.

She could see the top of Adam's head from where she stood. From here he looked just like his father – slim and upright, the tilt of the head just so.

The King of love my Shepherd is—

How appropriate for Geordie Blair. Molly remembered him as bluff and hearty, a real man of the land. Adam's type of man, really. A shepherd of sheep, literally.

—streams of living water flow—

—verdant pastures grow—

How clever of Jean to choose this hymn.

She was still looking at Adam, and now she glimpsed a whisk of white. He was blowing his nose. Molly felt the tears flood into her eyes in sympathy and wished she could be beside him.

The church was full. George Blair must have been a popular man. She looked around, recognised a face here and there, and wondered if perhaps Logan had come.

She would slip out after the last hymn. She didn't want to risk bumping into Adam nor, for that matter, into his parents. She had only seen James Blair once since she and Adam had separated, and though she'd made herself respond to a couple of invitations from Rosemary, she'd found Adam's mother's kindness and bottomless understanding ridiculously hard to bear.

There was a tribute by some cousin – not by James, the brother, which was interesting. The minister spoke, but Molly only half listened. Weighed down by an emotion that had hooked itself somehow to the funeral but didn't really belong to it, she felt sapped of energy.

—Take from our souls the strain and stress/And let our ordered lives confess/The beauty of thy peace—

How lovely those words were. *The beauty of thy peace.* Molly sat back and closed her eyes. Wouldn't it be nice to find peace? It had been so long since she had felt at one with herself, and with the world.

Around her, people swayed and sat, the music faded and rose again, dark clothing swirled and heels clicked on the marble floor, but in the warmth of the church, Molly, exhausted, had fallen asleep.

'Molly? Is it you?'

She woke with a start. Above her, a familiar face was surveying her with some concern.

'Rosemary?' she muttered, still drowsy. 'Oh, goodness!'

She leapt to her feet and looked around. The church was almost empty. The family must have exited down the central aisle, so – thank heavens – she would have been hidden by the congregation. Blood flooded to her cheeks. How had Rosemary …?

'I came back in for my order of service,' Rosemary Blair said, smiling, 'and spotted someone here at the back. I didn't realise it was you until … How are you, Molly dear? It's good of you to come.'

'I'm well. I – I must get going.'

But there was no escape. James Blair, returning to look for his wife, appeared at the end of the pew so that both of them now blocked her way.

'I wondered where you … Oh. Molly. Hello.'

Adam's father hadn't known how to treat her since the separation. She'd only met him once, when he'd come to a corporate dinner at Fleming House, not realising she worked there. That encounter had been stiff, and this looked as though it would be no different.

'I'm well, thank you. Nice to see you. I really must get going.'

'Adam's outside,' Rosemary said, smiling and extending an arm for Molly to hook hers through. 'He'll be pleased to see you.'

She was trapped.

He was standing alone near the gate, a pile of russet leaves whisking round his feet in the breeze. She wasn't used to seeing him in black. There was something so still about him – as if this death had undermined his equilibrium and he needed to expend all his concentration just to remain upright – that Molly's throat caught all over again.

'Adam!' Rosemary called, her arm tightening its grip.

Adam looked around. Rosemary quickened her pace. And from the opposite direction, Molly was conscious of a slender figure striding purposefully towards her husband. High heels, sharp suit, long dark hair billowing in the wind.

Sunita Ghosh.

Molly tried to stop, but Rosemary was unrelenting.

'No, I—' Molly tried to say, but already Rosemary was calling, 'Adam, look who I found hiding in the church.'

They arrived beside Adam at precisely the same time as Sunita.

Rosemary has engineered this, Molly thought. But why?

'You all right, darling?' Sunita murmured, insinuating herself as close to Adam as she could get.

Rosemary said, 'Wasn't it kind of Molly to come?'

And Molly and Adam stared at each other, entwined in mutual anguish and embarrassment.

She stopped at The Gables to unburden herself. Once, this place had been just another big house overlooking the Thomson Memorial Park, owned by someone with a shedload of cash. Now it was where Lexie lived with Patrick Mulgrew, and Molly was in here just about as often as she was in her own flat at Fleming House. She loved every inch of it. Patrick, a man of great taste, had made the place into something straight out of *World of Interiors*, and the paintings on the walls must be worth a small fortune, but somehow it still felt homely.

She heard a distinct snuffle and glanced towards a small speaker above one of the kitchen cabinets.

'Baby?'

'Don't worry, she'll sleep for a bit longer,' Lexie said. 'Was it awful?'

'You can't imagine,' Molly groaned.

They were sitting on stylish chrome and leather bar stools in the kitchen. Usually, she would be drinking in the atmosphere of the place, comparing everything to her own makeshift arrangement in her flat, wishing she could be sitting once more in the kitchen she loved so much in her house in Trinity. Now, she was in no state to admire Lexie's kitchen or dream about her own. She propped her elbows on the granite counter in front of her and buried her head in her hands.

'You're being kind,' she groaned. 'Why are you being kind? You told me I was stupid to go and you were right.'

'That doesn't mean I'm pleased about it,' Lexie said. 'Tell me.'

'What?' The word was muffled.

'Are you still in love with him?'

Molly's head came up. 'No!'

'Are you sure?'

She stared at Lexie, the blood rushing to her cheeks. 'Of course not.'

'I think you are. And I think Rosemary Blair would like you and Adam to be together again.'

'No! Impossible. After what I ...? No. And anyway, Adam has moved on. And,' Molly finished with determination, 'I'm moving on too. London is waiting!'

Lexie nodded and looked at her speculatively. 'If you say so.'

She should not have come here. Lexie's probing, after the trauma of the afternoon, was brutal.

'I'd better go.'

'You could stay for something to eat. Patrick will be home shortly.'

'No, thanks.' She slid off the stool. 'Tell Patrick I'll catch up some other time.' All Molly wanted to do was have a hot bath and slink into bed. 'Oh, by the way,' she said as she reached the door, 'I've had a thought.'

'About?'

'Baby. Her name.'

'Try me.'

'Keira. It means "dark haired",' Molly explained as Lexie stared at her.

'It does? Wow.' She looked at the huge black-and-white photograph of the baby in pride of place on the wall next to the table. The baby still hadn't lost the down-soft black mop she'd been born with. Lexie smiled – a huge, beaming smile. 'It's Irish. It's pretty. And it describes her perfectly. Thank you, Molly, it's absolutely right.'

Chapter Twenty One

It took Caitlyn almost two hours to sift through all the client documentation in Mr Keir's files, and for every second of that time her heart thumped in her chest. What if he came back? What if he caught her in his room? What if he ...?

Despite her terror, she took care to be methodical. Most of the documents could be refiled immediately after she looked at them. Anything more than a couple of years old seemed fine. Anything, that meant, from the period that Mr Robertson had been in charge of compliance. She looked more carefully at every piece of paper dated within the last couple of years.

She found the form that had been the cause of all her problems a year ago, still exactly as she'd seen it last time with the post-dated signature. He never had changed it.

To her horror, she also found more than a dozen forms attributing new client introductions to her. Stilling her shaking fingers with an effort of will, she examined the supporting documentation for each form. There were photocopies of exactly four passports. Each had been used three or four times and the names looked as though they had been deliberately blurred. Most of the second signatures were those of Hugo McPartlin, the youngest partner in the firm. Caitlyn only knew him by sight – an earnest young man with heavy black-rimmed spectacles and a constant frown, as though he were having to concentrate to keep up.

Either Mr McPartlin was part of whatever scam Mr Keir had set up, or he was completely ignorant of it. Caitlyn was inclined to believe the latter.

After a further fifteen minutes, she found a form that had been completed by Hugo himself, and countersigned by Adam Blair. Name of client: Lord Whitmuir. Hmm, very grand. She wondered whether he was a relative of Hugo's, or maybe a family friend. Mr McPartlin looked like the kind of bloke who'd know posh people. She compared the signature on this form with the ones on the documents Mr Keir had filled in. They were quite similar, but something looked subtly different. If she had to describe it, she'd say that on Mr Keir's forms, Hugo's signature looked more … careful.

By the time she'd been through every file in the new-clients section, she had found eighteen suspicious forms. Now what?

Caitlyn thought carefully. Her name was on many of the forms – what would anyone else finding these documents think? That she was part of the scam, whatever it was?

She had to act. This time, saying nothing was not an option.

Agnes Buchanan was the obvious first port of call, and a bit less daunting to approach than the partners. She knew everything about everything in Blair King and, if there was something amiss, surely she'd know best how to handle it. But Agnes shared an office with the two cashiers who worked under her and there was nowhere secure Caitlyn could think of to put the evidence.

Her mind raced. Young Mr Blair was the obvious person to go to. After all, he was the person who'd asked her to come back. He'd been warm and welcoming on her first day. She didn't find him as scary as some of the other partners, even though he was the boss's son.

She glanced at the clock on the wall. Quarter to eight. Malkie must be wondering where the hell she was – she'd been meant to meet him at seven-thirty. But she couldn't stop now – she had to do something quickly, in case Mr Keir came back.

She picked up all the documents she was sure were falsified and ran to the nearest photocopier. Please don't come back, she thought as she raced along the corridor. Please don't come back, her brain repeated as the machine whirred and clicked its way through the papers. It seemed so slow!

The words hammered in her head – please don't come back, please don't come back, please, please, pleeeease – until at last she copied the final form, gathered everything together, found a large envelope and pushed all the copies into it. Her heart still pounding, she sealed it, addressed it and ran down the two flights of stairs to where Mr Blair's office was. The door was locked. Damn! Now what? The carpet almost blocked the gap under the door.

She shoved at it desperately. Once she'd managed to get one edge in, it wasn't so difficult – the envelope was bulky, but its bulk made it relatively rigid. She gave it one last thrust, and it disappeared from view.

Caitlyn straightened up and heaved a huge sigh of relief. She hurried back to Mr Keir's office. All she had to do now was file everything again, and wait for developments.

It took endless minutes to drop the eighteen forms back in their places. Finally, she opened the small drawer in his desk and laid the keys inside, turned out the light in his office and ran down the stairs back to her own room. In a frantic flurry of movement, she jerked on her coat, picked up her bag and rushed to the door. Her mobile showed that Malkie had rung three times, but she couldn't wait to listen to the messages, not now. If she ran, she might just make the next train. She could call him back then.

At last she pushed open the door to the street – and found herself staring right into the eyes of Mr Keir himself.

She jerked back, shocked. 'Oh!'

'Still here?' He looked almost as taken aback as she was.

Caitlyn swallowed hard and croaked, 'Just leaving. Must run. Have a good weekend,' darted past him and leapt down the stone steps to the pavement. Was he staring after her? She didn't wait to look.

They never did get to see the Brad Pitt film. Still shaking when the train pulled in at Hailesbank, Caitlyn sank into Malkie's welcoming arms and burst into tears.

'Hey,' he said gently when the sobs began to subside, 'he's not worth it, you know.'

'What? Who?'

Caitlyn was bewildered. How could Malkie know about Mr Keir?

'Brad Pitt. We've missed the beginning, but if you're that desperate to see him, we'll go anyway. Or we can see the whole film tomorrow maybe?'

Despite herself, Caitlyn giggled. It sounded shaky, but it was a giggle nevertheless.

'It's not Brad.'

'I hope you haven't stood me up for some other bloke?'

He had adopted an expression of mock severity. She shook her head violently.

'Then it's nothing that can't be sorted.'

If only, she thought, but his calmness was soothing.

'Let's go somewhere quiet and you can tell me what's up.'

Finding somewhere quiet wasn't so easy. The Murray household would be pandemonium. Malkie was living with two mates, who'd both invited their girlfriends round for a takeaway.

'And the rest,' Malkie said, grinning.

'What about Besalù?'

'Mm, I could fancy some tapas, but it's Friday. It'll be heaving.'

'Then no-one will be able to hear us. It'll be too noisy.'

'True. I suppose we could try.'

They were in luck.

'We've just had a cancellation,' said Carlotta Wood, Besalù's diminutive but fiery Spanish owner. 'It's that table in the alcove, if you don't mind being a bit out of the way.'

By the time the crispy deep fried *calamares* arrived, Caitlyn found that her earlier adrenalin had translated into genuine hunger.

''S good,' she announced, munching the succulent, garlicky squid.

Malkie grinned. 'Didn't you have lunch?'

'That was ages ago.'

Twice she tried to embark on her story, and each time Malkie stopped her.

'You can tell me when we're done with eating. This is too good to spoil.'

They finished their favourites – Manchego cheese with orange marmalade, *calamares*, tortilla, *patatas bravas* and chargrilled ribs – and a carafe of house red. Caitlyn sat back with a sigh.

'You're a miracle, Malkie Milne, do you know that?'

Caitlyn reached out and laid a hand over the large one gripping his wine glass. He let go of the stem and curled his fingers round hers. 'Ready?'

She nodded. For a moment, the panic threatened to return, but she took strength from his steadiness and drew a deep breath.

'This is what happened this evening,' she started.

It took fifteen minutes to outline it all. She spoke carefully, and went back over the ground if he wasn't following her. Around them, the restaurant buzzed with happy conversation. It felt as if all of Hailesbank was out enjoying itself tonight. The walls of the alcove screened them from the worst of the noise. There was no chance anyone else would be able to hear what they were saying.

'I had to do it, Malkie. I had to get the evidence into Mr Blair's office, because if I hadn't, Mr Keir might have come back, guessed what I'd been doing and got rid of the documents.' She could feel herself starting to tremble again. 'And he did come back, Malkie.'

She was getting emotional. Everything was just beginning to sink in – what she had found, what she had done, the possible consequences ...

Had Mr Keir found out already? Everything was in order, but he'd see as soon as he looked in the cabinet that the documents he'd left on Deirdre's desk earlier had been filed.

Deirdre could have filed them, of course. Would she have noticed the same discrepancies? Deirdre was lovely, but she was always a bit slapdash. If there was a shortcut, she'd find it, and probably Mr Keir knew that.

On the other hand, Caitlyn was the one who'd been working late. What else could she have been doing?

'He saw me. He might guess.'

Malkie squeezed her hand. 'But you've done nothing wrong. He's the one who's guilty. What do you think he'd do? Come after you with a gun?'

He tried to make light of it, but Caitlyn shivered. 'I don't suppose so. I don't know.' She bit her lip. She was beginning to regret eating so much. 'What am I going to do?'

Malkie said, 'You're going to do nothing. Not this weekend. On Monday morning, you're going to go straight to Mr Blair's office and you're going to wait until you can see him. Does he go in early?'

'I expect so. Most of the partners are in really early.'

'Then go in an hour earlier than usual and wait.'

'What if *he's* there too?'

'Mr Keir? Well, so what? Blair King's offices'll be safe.'

'Should I go to the police, do you think?'

'Do you?'

She thought about it for some time. In the end she shook her head.

'No. I don't think it's my place. I don't have much experience, but I remember someone talking about some bent solicitor in some other office, and they weren't talking about the cops, they just talked about what the Law Society would do.'

'Fine. So wait till Monday and see Mr Blair. It should be his decision. The evidence is safe in his office, is it?'

'I don't think they have keys to each other's rooms. At least, maybe Mr Blair does, or his father, but I don't think—' a thought struck her and she clapped her hand over her mouth. 'Oh my God! The cleaners! They have master keys.'

'What time do they start?'

'Half past six, I think.'

'Best be there by six thirty then. I'll drive you in.'

'But,' Caitlyn said hopefully, 'he'll have the evidence already. Do I really have to go and see him as well?'

Malkie thought this through in his usual slow, thorough way. 'I think you do,' he said. 'Your name is on a lot of those papers, isn't it? That's going to take some explaining.'

Caitlyn groaned. 'I should never have gone back to Blair King.'

'Don't say that.' Malkie reached out for her other hand and took hold of it, bracing her. 'You might be in bigger trouble if you didn't know your name was in there. Anyway, you've done a good thing. A brave thing. They'll see that, and be grateful.'

'You think?'

The weekend that stretched ahead was going to be a long one. She might just have to beg him to take her to see Brad Pitt after all.

Chapter Twenty-Two

Adam stared at the envelope lying on the carpet just inside his office door. It hadn't been there when he'd left on Friday. Curious, he bent and picked it up.

FAO: MR BLAIR.

The block capitals had been scrawled in thick marker pen. He didn't recognise the writing. He turned the envelope over and pushed a finger under the flap to rip it open.

Papers. Photocopies, by the look of it.

He turned them over. Client introduction forms. Why had these been bundled up for him like this? He stared at the top one.

New client: Michael Robert Edwards.
Date of Birth: 16/09/1954.
Address: Moray Place, Edinburgh.
Introduced by: Caitlyn Murray.

Against the name Caitlyn Murray, someone had scrawled NO!! in marker pen. Adam's eyes widened with alarm. He slid the paper aside and examined the next one. A blurry copy of a passport. The name had been fudged. Somebody Edwards – but what did that first name say? Not Michael. Maybe Matthew? It was hard to tell.

He looked at the next form.

New client: Jane McManus.
Date of Birth: 24/11/1968.
Introduced by: Caitlyn Murray.

And again, there was a scrawled NO!!, a blurry copy

of a passport photograph and a name that had clearly been changed. Joan McM – something.

Adam scrabbled through the rest of the papers. Many of the forms had the NO!! scrawl, and in every case there was a blurry photocopied passport. Several of the copies had the same photograph.

He checked the name of the partner who had allegedly introduced each person. It was always Logan Keir. He found, to his dismay, that a number of the forms appeared to have been co-signed by Adam Blair. You didn't have to be smart to know that something was very wrong indeed.

Adam threw the papers onto his desk. It was Sunday evening and he had only dropped into the office to ensure that he had the documents ready and to hand for an important meeting in the morning. It was meant to be a routine visit – the last thing he had expected was a crisis.

He pressed his forehead against the window. The glass felt cold on his skin. Outside, it was already dark. Ever since the clocks had changed, the days had been getting shorter and shorter. It was early November, autumn going on winter. He shivered – but not from cold. What had he uncovered? Correction – what had Caitlyn Murray uncovered? For surely, it had to be Caitlyn who had pushed the copies under his door. She'd be anxious not to be implicated in whatever Logan Keir had been up to.

This was grave. Fabricating client introductions was a criminal offence in itself – but Logan must have done this for a reason, and it was this implication that really worried Adam. His mind raced through the possibilities. False accounting. Theft of client funds. Money laundering. Each scenario was worse than the last.

Outside, the moonlight illuminated the small carpark with a ghostly light. It bounced off the stained white tiles on the wall opposite the window. All of a sudden, his office felt like a prison cell.

Adam turned away from the bleak scene outside and surveyed the neat room. A small lamp on the desk illuminated the sheaf of papers Caitlyn had thrust into his office. They were under the spotlight, in all senses.

First Geordie's death, and now this. Adam had no doubts that there had been wrongdoing, it was only a matter of the scale of whatever scheme Logan had cooked up.

He's Molly's brother.

Adam had almost begun to wonder, in recent weeks, whether there might be a glimmer of hope for himself and Molly. They'd definitely connected at Billy's birthday party, and at Geordie's funeral …

He winced, remembering the moment that his mother had arrived with Molly in tow, and Sunita had barrelled up from the other direction. The look on Molly's face had been … What?

Embarrassed, certainly. But more than that, surely? There had been a change in her expression, sudden and subtle. He'd thought about that expression often, but still could not decide what it revealed.

He thumped his fist down on the desk. Damn, damn, damn! Why did this have to happen?

Adam reached across the desk for the phone. He had three calls to make before he thought too much more about it, and not one of them was to Molly.

Caitlyn must have been half hoping he would call. That was clear from the way she said, 'Mr Blair?' when she picked up – not surprised, merely anxious.

'I'm in the office.'

'I guessed that.'

He liked her steadiness. That must be costing her,

because the fact that her name was on the forms implicated her in Logan's wrongdoing.

She said, 'I found the forms when I was doing some filing for Deirdre on Friday evening. You have to believe that this was nothing to do with me.'

'The dates on them—'

'—were all when I wasn't even at Blair King.'

Adam changed tack. 'It must have taken some doing.'

'What?'

He'd meant to unsettle her. He didn't believe for one moment that this girl was guilty of anything, but he had to explore all possibilities.

'You must have been looking for something, Caitlyn. These documents didn't just fall out of Logan's filing cabinet and into your hands.'

'No.'

Adam wished she were in the room with him; he would have liked to be able to see her expression, but he needed to act quickly. A more detailed interview could take place tomorrow.

'So, did you think Mr Keir had done something wrong? What prompted you to go looking?'

He heard her gulp and clear her throat. 'Last year ... when I left ... I found something—' She faltered, but when Adam said nothing, she managed to go on. 'I saw an introduction form, signed by Mr Keir. It was countersigned by Mr Masters.'

'So?'

'It was dated a few weeks after Mr Masters died.'

Outside, a cloud slipped across the moon and the world went dark. Blackness seemed to engulf Adam, even though a desk light was casting its bright beams across the tooled leather of its surface. *After Mr Masters died.*

'I didn't do anything wrong,' Caitlyn was saying, her

voice defensive. 'I went to Mr Keir and showed him the form. I asked him about it. At first he said it was all right, that he'd just done it because no-one was around and it needed to be done quickly. I thought about it that night, but it didn't feel right, so the next morning I asked him about it again. He got really stroppy with me, told me I was a silly little girl and that if I couldn't get on with my job, I should go and find another one.'

Logan had said that? Logan Keir, his colleague and friend, his wife's brother, had lied to this girl and bullied her into silence?

Adam thought of the sports car, and of Logan's children at their expensive private school. He thought of the places Logan had taken his family in the last year – to Florida and New York; on a ski trip to Verbier at Christmas that must have cost a fortune. He thought of Adrienne, Logan's wife. At Billy Keir's birthday party she'd been immaculate in a suit that was clearly by some top fashion designer.

He began to feel very sick.

'Mr Blair? Are you still there?'

His mouth set in a hard line and he could feel the tension in his jaw.

'So you left?'

'Yes. But this time—' He heard her swallow again. 'I knew I had to do the right thing. I knew I had to let you know something was happening.'

'Because your name was on a lot of these forms,' Adam said dryly, trying not to be judgmental, but thinking about just how much damage Logan might have done in the past year.

'Yes. It looks as though I'm part of the scheme. Whatever it is,' Caitlyn added hastily. 'But I'm not, honestly I'm not. Your name is on some of them too.'

Adam glanced down at the top document. Countersigned by Adam Blair. Only it wasn't.

'So I copied the documents and shoved them through your door.'

He said, 'Caitlyn, I'm sorry, but you know this will not be the end of this. I'll need to talk to you again tomorrow. We'll need to get a statement from you.'

'I know.'

'I'll be talking to Mr Keir, of course. There may be a perfectly good explanation for all of this.'

Silence. She wasn't stupid.

'In the meantime, you are not to say anything about this to anyone. Do you understand me?'

'Of course.'

'We'll talk tomorrow. Don't be frightened.'

'All right.'

'And Caitlyn?'

'Yes, Mr Blair?'

'Well done. You've done the right thing telling me about this now.'

He thought Logan was going to refuse to come in to the office.

He said severely into the phone, 'I don't think you are in any position to say no.' He glanced at the old mahogany clock on the wall. The time was a quarter past seven. 'If you're not here by eight o'clock, I will call the police. Which is it to be?'

There was a long silence. Then Logan said, 'I'll be there.'

The final call was to his father.

'I have bad news. The worst.'

'Tell me.'

When he'd finished outlining what had happened, his father said, 'You're right. This is bad.' James Blair was known for his quick temper and Adam had expected an explosion. His father's restraint was almost more unnerving. 'What are your thoughts?'

'I've spoken to the girl who fed me the information, Caitlyn Murray. She's a bright kid. I've impressed on her that she's not to talk to anyone.'

'And will she?'

'I don't think so. Her name is on some of these documents, so she's heavily implicated, though I don't believe she's culpable. Logan has promised to come in.'

'Now?'

'Yes. By eight. We need to confront him this evening, while the office is quiet and before he has a chance to cook up some kind of story. Can you be here?'

'I'm on my way. Your mother won't be happy – the roast is almost ready, but it can wait. This can't.'

'Thanks, Dad. And Dad?'

'Yes?'

'I'm sorry.'

Adam didn't know why he was apologising; this mess was not of his making, but he felt the disapproval of his forebears weighing heavily on his shoulders. The Blair King partnership had been founded by Adam's great-grandfather more than a hundred years ago, and had been a family business ever since. He thought of those Victorian lawyers with their starched collars and heavy black coats, and of the succession of Blairs who had sat in these offices. He thought of his colleagues, and the families who depended on them – not just the partners, but the support staff who worked for the firm as well. Agnes Buchanan who'd been with the firm for forty years and whose loyalty was invaluable. Ellen McNaughton, one of the cashiers who worked with her, who had just announced her engagement, amid great excitement and the usual ritual of cakes. If they lost their jobs ...

And there was Molly. Molly needed her money for the business in London she had set her heart on. Adam still had no idea of how bad the situation was. He sat very still, trying to think it all through. The firm had limited liability, but the equity partners – all twelve of them – had taken out bank loans to cover cash flow difficulties and secured them against their mortgages.

At the time no-one had thought there would be any problem – the difficulty had been short term, a small downturn that could be attributed to the recession. But the recession had gone on, and on, and the difficulties had increased.

His eyes narrowed. Cash flow difficulties? Could they have been entirely down to the recession?

The more he thought about it, the worse it got.

The limited liability would only cover them for certain things. If they couldn't cover any money Logan had drawn on the falsified accounts, the bank would call in its security and they could all lose their homes. Perhaps worst of all, the Law Society of Scotland would probably suspend some of the partners' licences while they investigated the situation – and the investigation could take some time. Clients would walk. Staff worried about the future of the firm would start looking for other positions. Even the partners would salvage what they could, in any way they could. However you looked at it, the future for Blair King looked desperate.

Adam buried his face in his hands.

It took precisely two hours for him to realise that Logan's promise was likely to be a hollow one. That's how long he waited with his father for Logan to turn up. They sat in tetchy silence, watching as the minutes ticked by. When the hands on the clock reached ten, James stood up.

'Logan Keir was never going to come,' he said. 'And in any case, we never did have any choice.'

Chapter Twenty-Three

Adam stood next to James on the steps in front of the Law Society of Scotland, facing his fate. They gazed at the imposing entrance to the tall stone building with its air of implacable authority, then looked at each other, each trying to make courage outshine apprehension in their expressions.

'I never thought,' said James, 'that I would walk through these doors on an errand like this.'

'No.'

'It has to be faced.'

'Yes,' Adam said, drawing breath. 'Let's get it over with.'

Of course, it was not a matter of 'getting it over with'. Discussions with the Law Society were the start of a process, not its end. In a surprisingly ordinary office with walls painted a dull cream and lit by harsh fluorescent lights, they recounted what they knew.

'The police will be informed immediately,' said the official. 'Their prime concern will be to apprehend Mr Keir, wherever he might be. If necessary, they will issue a European Arrest Warrant and work with other authorities around the world to find him.'

'Yes, I see,' said James.

'In the meantime, we will send in a team of investigators and begin the work of interviewing partners and staff.'

'Of course. We understand.'

'All partners' licences will be suspended while the work proceeds.'

'All of them?' Adam burst out. 'Why? How will we be able to work?'

The official placed his elbows on his desk, folded his hands together as if in prayer, and said in a reedy voice that was already becoming irritating, 'If, within a few weeks, Mr Blair, you are found not to have been a party to any deception, we may see fit to restore a restricted practising certificate. In the meantime, as I explained, we must suspend the certificates of all partners in the firm.'

'I haven't done anything wrong. I've reported this, for heavens' sake! The others haven't done anything wrong either.' Adam tried to steady his hands.

'Mr Blair,' said the official with elaborate patience, 'at this point we have no idea who might be implicated in the deception. There has to be a full investigation. We will send in a team of auditors who will interview everyone, including all the partners and, naturally, the cashier and delegated cash-room partner. It will take some time, although we will endeavour to be as speedy as we can with our investigations in order to minimise the impact on clients.'

'On *clients*? What about our staff?'

The set of the man's jaw said everything. Some hours later, it was agreed that James Blair would retain his licence in order to facilitate the investigations and keep the firm operating with a skeleton staff.

It was the first of many hammer blows.

'Where is Agnes?' James asked, glancing around the room.

People glanced at each other, then blankly back at him. There were murmurs, but no clear response. They were uneasy. The atmosphere in the boardroom was troubled. No meeting of all staff had ever been called in this way without notice. Everyone was present, from the most junior secretary to the most senior partner. Adam spotted Caitlyn Murray near the window. She was leaning against the shutters, gripping the corner of the wall with one hand as if to steady herself, and her skin was white. He tried to catch her eye, hoping a calm look from him might help her, but she was staring at the ground.

'Has she phoned in?' James was asking the room at large.

There were shrugs and vacant stares.

Adam, still trying to process everything that had happened, felt a chill in his stomach.

Agnes Buchanan. Chief Cashier.

Surely not. Agnes, 'rock of ages', who had been with them for forty years. Impossible. She could not be implicated in this.

And yet ... He glanced at James, but his father was drawing breath to speak.

If Logan Keir had been siphoning money out of the firm into false accounts, surely he would need help. The partners might all have failed to spot the missing money by clever book-keeping, but Agnes could not have missed it. Agnes knew where every penny went in Blair King, right down to the drawing pins used to hold up notices in the staffroom.

As soon as James had made his stark announcement and the meeting had broken up, Adam said to his father, 'Agnes.'

He didn't need to say more. There was a flash of understanding swiftly followed by something much stronger.

'I'll phone,' Adam said. 'And if she doesn't pick up,

I'll go to her house. If she's not there—' His lips tightened. 'It's the police, I suppose.'

Agnes Buchanan lived in a neat little bungalow in a row of neat little bungalows in the middle of a 1940s estate. Each had a small front garden, most laid to grass with shrubs round the edges. Some had been bricked over to make driveways for cars, and Agnes's silver Nissan was parked in her drive.

Adam locked his car and studied the house. The garden was bounded by a low stone wall. A magnolia tree near the front window had been preserved when the drive had been laid and a couple of bushes afforded privacy from the bungalow next door. Some of the houses had been extended to accommodate young families. Agnes's home was unchanged. She had taken care of it, however; that was clear. The window frames were pristine and white-painted and the door, which looked original, gleamed from its paint to its brass knocker.

How long had she lived here? Adam had a dim memory of a funeral – Agnes's mother? – a number of years ago, and it came to him that perhaps she had lived here all her life.

What else did he know of Agnes Buchanan? Come to that, what did anyone know? She had worked for Blair King since she left school, aged sixteen. Forty years. When had that milestone been reached? Had they marked it in any way, celebrated her loyalty? Not, Adam realised, that he knew of. Had that rankled with the woman? Did she feel taken for granted, undervalued? She had never betrayed discontent.

People liked Agnes. She was calm, efficient, pleasant, and if she kept her private life private, well, who were they to pry?

He lifted the knocker and let it fall with a heavy thud.

He waited, listening.

Nothing.

He tried again.

Thud.

Nothing.

He pushed at the flap of the letterbox and stooped to peer inside. Beyond the hall a door opened at the back into what might be the kitchen.

'Hello? Agnes? It's Adam Blair.'

Silence.

'Trying to get Miss Buchanan, are you?'

He swung round. On the pavement was an elderly man, his collar turned up against the chill air, a tweed cap pulled down over his eyes. A spaniel tugged at the lead he was holding.

'Yes. Her car's here. Do you know if she's in? Are you a neighbour?'

'That's right. Next door. I haven't seen her in a couple of days. Are you family?'

Adam walked across the drive to the low wall. 'I'm Adam Blair,' he said, extending a hand, 'her employer. She hasn't come in today. It's so unlike her, we were worried.'

'Never takes a day off, that one, she told me so herself,' the man said, yanking at the lead. 'Here, Jack.'

'Do you think she might be ill? You don't happen to have a key, do you?'

'Aye, I keep a key.' The man looked doubtful. 'Never been inside, mind. I just keep it in case of emergency.'

Adam pursed his lips. 'Maybe this is the time to dig it out.'

'You think?'

'She could have fallen. She could be in bed, needing a

doctor. Anything. We could take a look, just make sure.'

'Well, if you think so. Maybe—'

Adam waited, hopeful.

'Or maybe we shouldn't. She likes to keep herself to herself. She's never asked me in.'

'Mr—?'

'Robertson. Jim Robertson.'

'Mr Robertson, she may need help.' Adam tried to keep his voice level. 'I think we should go in. If she's not there, or if she's fine, we can leave. I'll explain to her why we did it, if necessary. But if she's ill and needs help, and we do nothing—'

Mr Robertson took a decision. 'You're right. Come on then, lad.'

They left Jack, protesting, in the kitchen at number forty, and returned a few minutes later with the key to Agnes's front door.

'Here goes.'

'Agnes?' Adam called again as soon as the door opened. 'It's Adam Blair.'

'And Jim from next door.'

They found her in the bathroom at the back of the house, crumpled awkwardly between the radiator and the bath. Adam dropped to his knees.

'She's alive,' he said, feeling warmth and fumbling to find a pulse. 'Agnes, can you hear me? It's Adam Blair.'

She had cut her head. Blood had trickled down her face and dried, so she'd clearly been there some time.

'Agnes. Miss Buchanan!'

There was a soft moan.

'I'm calling an ambulance right now. You're not to worry about anything. You're going to be just fine,' Adam said with more conviction than he felt.

The paramedics were there in less than ten minutes.

While they examined Agnes, Adam wandered into the hall and the kitchen. In the dining room, he stopped, surprised. The room was full of paintings. He spotted a large canvas that looked remarkably like a Joan Eardley, and another that had the hallmark of an Alberto Morocco. Prints, of course, they had to be – both were well-known Scottish artists whose works sold for thousands of pounds. He walked over to the Morocco and touched the canvas with a tentative finger. It was a great copy, that was for sure. The colours were faithful to what he knew of his style, and it had been printed onto canvas.

In the living room, another large canvas dominated the room. Barbara Rae's bright, colourful hand was unmistakeable.

They had to be copies. Unless Agnes had come into a fair legacy from her parents, there was no way she would be able to afford work such as this.

'Looks like she might have had a stroke.'

Adam turned. The paramedics had moved Agnes onto a stretcher and into the hall. She still seemed to be unconscious.

'Is it bad?'

'Hard to say. Depends how long she's been lying there. The cut on her head almost certainly happened when she fell. Anyway, best get on. Are you coming to the hospital with her?'

'Hospital? No,' Adam said, disconcerted. 'I'll call later to find out how she's doing.'

While Agnes was being transferred to the ambulance, he took out his phone and quickly photographed several of her paintings. He'd ask Patrick Mulgrew later what he knew about them. Patrick would know.

'Messages for you, Mr Blair,' said the girl on reception as

soon as he stepped inside the office.

He took the notes she handed to him and glanced through them. Adrienne Keir had been on the phone several times – why hadn't his father talked to her? A number of clients had been trying to get hold of him. Had word got out already?

He spoke to a panicky and incredulous Adrienne and promised to drop in to see her as soon as he could get away.

He called each client and gave them the line he'd been advised to give by the Law Society.

Finally, he called Molly.

'I know Adrienne is worried, Molly. I've spoken to her. Yes … Yes … It's true, no-one knows where he has disappeared to. No, really, I have no idea.'

He gripped the phone tightly. 'Molly – I'm sorry, love. There's something I have to tell you about your brother—'

PART TWO

PART TWO

Chapter One

Molly didn't need to open her eyes to know that she was in the flat she shared in London – she could hear the gentle lapping of the waves of the Thames on the small mudflat outside her window. Gulls were squabbling angrily over some titbit washed up by the tide. A boat sped past, its wash smacking against the houseboats moored on the bank.

Her first thought was that living by the river had been an unexpected bonus – it had compensated greatly for losing her beautiful apartment at Fleming House.

Her second thought was ... where's Logan?

The change in the sequence of thoughts was an improvement, but the feeling of deep desolation stayed with her after the boat had passed and the gulls had fallen silent.

A gentle rap on the door heralded Julian's voice. 'You awake, darling?'

Molly hoisted herself to a sitting position and her mouth softened into a small smile. 'Sure.'

She ran her hands quickly through her hair to neaten it – not that Julian would mind, however sleep-tossed it was. Julian Granger's friendship was solid and comforting, and in the whirlpool of emotion and activity into which she had been plunged, she clung to it, sometimes with desperation.

'I brought you some tea. Can I come in?'

Barnaby had introduced her to the softly-spoken banker soon after she arrived in London – he'd just broken up with his partner and was 'right off men, darling'. Sharing suited them both. The door inched open and Julian appeared, a mug in each hand. His dark hair was damp, but he was dressed already, his pale pink shirt ironed to pristine crispness, his suit trousers neat as new. She caught a faint whiff of his aftershave, light and fresh. He always judged things nicely.

'Wanted to be sure you were all right, sweetie. Haven't seen you for days.'

Molly switched on her bedside light and accepted the mug with a grateful 'thanks'. Julian was one of the best-looking men she had ever set eyes on. He had magazine-model looks, with dark hair and eyes, and eyelashes that were impossibly thick. He was naturally slim, his fingers were long and elegant, and high cheekbones lent his face stunning definition. It was a crying shame that he was off limits, but it did make life simpler.

'What star did you zoom down from, Jules? I swear, you're an angel sent from heaven.'

Julian sank down on the corner of her bed, smiling. 'You do say lovely things. Seriously – how are you? We've been missing each other all week. I needed to know you were still alive.'

The tea was hot and strong, just as she liked it. Julian had a knack of knowing what she needed, and providing it at exactly the right time.

'I'm fine. It's been a busy week.'

He shrugged lazily and raised an eyebrow. 'What's new?'

Molly closed her eyes and sipped at the tea. Every morning, the memories flooded back and she had to work her way through them in order to face the new day. It wasn't all gloom. Fletcher Keir Mason had been registered as a company in January – a milestone to celebrate, because for the couple of months after Logan had disappeared, the possibility of it ever happening had seemed very remote indeed.

Julian said, 'Don't think about it, sweetie.'

She opened her eyes and gave him a crooked smile. 'About what?'

'You were thinking about your brother.'

'How do you know?'

'You had that look.' He shook his head sympathetically. 'There's nothing you can do to bring him back, so don't waste your energy.'

'I just wish I knew where he was.'

'Darling.' Julian extended a hand. She took it. 'It's working out. Logan will be swigging cocktails in Brazil; you're not to worry about him. Your dad's fine. Your nephews are doing well. Your career has taken off. What's to fret over?'

Adam, Molly thought, though she would never say it, not even to Julian.

'We need,' Barnaby Fletcher said, 'to keep ahead of the game, and the game is changing very fast.'

Molly looked round the table. There were five of them in the meeting – herself, Barnaby, Kenneth Mason the third shareholding director, a branding specialist they'd brought in to beef up the team (and the capital), and two young and ambitious men who were more savvy than she would ever be about the 'new order': social media and marketing in the digital age.

'It's getting harder and harder to persuade businesses to part with money for traditional marketing.' Barnaby was never happier than when he was building strategy. He glanced at Molly and broke into one of his big bear grins. 'We can beat the pack if we're smart.'

Molly smiled back. I'm a split persona nowadays, she thought. Melancholy in the mornings and a vibrant shooting star of thrilling ideas and full-on animation as soon as I get into the office.

As she spent far more hours in the office than anywhere else these days, she decided that life wasn't so bad. While she was here, she more or less forgot about Logan and the appalling trail of devastation he'd left in his wake. She was making her mark in a fast-moving, challenging industry, and she was having a ball.

Kenneth said, 'What did you have in mind?'

'Peer influence and community orientation. We need to hook in to social media, and we can develop new ways of informing and persuading.'

Molly loved this buzz. Her strength might be event management, but she was learning about other key areas fast. She was a leader, not a follower, and she was on top of her game.

She chased a stray lock of hair away from her face and thought, it's been this length for far too long. I'll get it cut.

The thought pleased her. She had transformed her life; now she would transform her image as well.

Barnaby said, 'There's a new contract up for grabs. It's a huge public health campaign and it's worth a lot of money. There'll be some very big players competing for the contract, but I believe we can win it by switching to smart, creative thinking.' He paused and looked around the table. 'It'll be a lot of work. Are you up for it?'

'Of course,' said Kenneth.

'Sure,' the young men chorused.

'Why else,' Molly said, 'are we here?'

She telephoned her father later as she walked briskly in

the thin March sunshine to get a sandwich.

'Hello, love. How are you?'

'Fine. You?'

'Cooking stew.'

'For supper?'

'A huge potful. I reckoned it would be a good idea to do enough for several meals and freeze it. There's never enough time these days, and they eat so much.'

Molly laughed. If she hadn't experienced her father's recently acquired cooking skills for herself, she would not have believed him, but having his grandchildren in the house had transformed him. Adrienne, shocked rigid in the first days after Logan's disappearance, had been unable to think past the next hours, let alone what the future might hold. One morning, denial had given way to anger, and anger to determination, and she had marched round to Billy's bungalow.

'I can't live like this,' she'd announced. 'I can't sit around moaning and feeling sorry for myself. I have to do something.'

'I agree.' Billy had always been direct, but his manner was so affable that no-one ever took exception.

'I have to go back to work. We can't afford private schools for the boys, and the house will have to go. I need you to look after the children while I'm working, and we'll pay our way. Will you help us?'

Billy had embraced his daughter-in-law and grandchildren with open arms.

'It'll give me a purpose in life,' he'd declared to a shocked Molly, 'and company.'

Molly had been livid at Adrienne's effrontery, but her father had been right and so far the effects of the arrangement had all been positive. The Adrienne that Molly knew – spoilt, demanding and extravagant – had become a new woman. Any selfishness had been redirected towards survival and the protection of her children. She snapped up a well-paid job as cabin crew on international flights and became a whirlwind of efficiency, economy and order, while Billy and his grandchildren began to bond in all kinds of unexpected ways.

He imposed a kind of mild-mannered discipline that the boys accepted without demur. Time spent on computers or phones, or watching television, was monitored and restricted. Instead, the boys made themselves useful around the house, learned new skills, and took it upon themselves to became responsible for Billy's safety and wellbeing. During the weeks when Adrienne was off rota, she had time to help in the home, and she and Billy provided much-needed mutual support.

Molly laughed at her father's words. 'If you think they eat a lot now, Dad,' she said, 'just think what they'll be like when they're teenagers.'

Billy groaned. 'I've got a year or two yet, hopefully. I remember what Logan was like when he was—'

He broke off.

They both did this all the time – they forgot that he was gone.

'It's all right, Dad,' Molly said gently.

'I just wish I knew he was safe.'

'I know. Me too.' Trying to make light of it, she said, 'Julian says he'll be sipping cocktails in Brazil. I can just see it, can't you?'

'Cocktails? If he's knocking back cocktails while we're all—' He broke off. 'Did I tell you Alastair's been picked to play in goal for the first team on Saturday?'

'Fantastic!' Speculating about Logan's fate would consume them both, if they let it. Better to avoid the subject.

'And Adrienne will be back tomorrow.'

'Where is she this time?'

'America, I think. Or is it India? I've got her shifts written down somewhere if you—'

'No, it doesn't matter. I don't suppose she even knows where she is half the time. Those long-distance flights must be exhausting. Any news on Agnes Buchanan?'

Billy got news from Rosemary Blair, who had made it her business to let him know anything she knew.

'The stroke's left her quite damaged, they say, but there seems to be plenty of evidence that she and Logan were in it together.'

'It's hard to feel sorry for the woman,' Molly said, struggling to fight the intense anger she felt every time she thought about what Agnes had done. 'I suppose until we find Logan we won't know whether he made her move the cash around or she persuaded him to fill in all those wretched forms and set up false accounts.'

Billy sighed heavily. 'Who knows? Maybe Adam has more information. You haven't spoken to—'

'No,' Molly said curtly. 'Listen, if you're OK I'd better go. I'm at the sandwich shop.'

'Fine, lovey. I've got a load of things to do. Ian's room's a tip. I've told him he'll get a beating if he doesn't tidy it, but he takes no notice.'

Molly laughed, because the idea of Billy lifting his hand to anyone was so absurd. He might grumble, but he loved having the boys there. It was a comfort – as she made lists and organised meetings and events, wrote pitch documents, rehearsed other pitches, met with clients, pacified clients and thought about clients' needs before they had even thought about them themselves: in short, lived her dream – to know that.

The only way to find time for such personal indulgences as a haircut was to convince herself it was a necessity rather than a luxury. As soon as she'd reached this tipping point, Molly took advice, and called a smart salon near Bond Street. She put the appointment in the diary in indelible pen.

'Just a trim?' Rowena, the stylist, asked.

Molly shook her head. 'I'd like it just like yours, please,' she said, eyeing Rowena's smart chin-length bob.

'Really?' The stylist lifted handfuls of Molly's long blonde tresses and let them fall, shimmering, through her hands. 'But it's so beautiful.'

'It's just hair. And I need a change.'

'Cool.'

As always when she had any time to herself, Molly's mind began to replay everything that had happened in the last few months.

The weeks after Logan's abrupt disappearance had been nerve-shredding, and she hadn't been able to reassure an increasingly desperate Barnaby that she would be able to join him.

One day, miraculously, her bank had telephoned. The money she needed had been lodged in her account. No warning, no explanation, it had just appeared. Adam, when she'd called him, had been stiff.

'I'm glad I was able to do it,' he'd said. 'Happy Christmas.'

Typical Adam. A sense of humour so dry you could trickle it through your fingers like sand.

She'd said, 'So what's happening at Blair King?'

He hadn't been in the mood for conversation. 'The law will take its course, and the law, as you know, always takes its time.'

There was sometimes a fine line between dry humour and pomposity. She hated it when he deployed that kind of self-importance. It had been December – and it was the last time she'd spoken to him.

'What do you think?'

She stared in the mirror. Rowena was standing behind her, angling a hand mirror this way and that to let her see the back. She hardly recognised herself.

Molly put a hand up to the back of her neck wonderingly.

'It feels so odd!'

'But good, I hope? You do like it, don't you? It really suits you.'

Molly shook her head and watched the bob settle back into place. She said, 'Thinking about the past gets you nowhere, does it?'

The mirror wavered. 'Sorry?'

'Don't mind me.' She twisted her head from side to side and watched the hair flick and swing. 'I feel lighter.'

'You will do. That hair was really long.'

'No, I mean inside.'

'Right.' Rowena sounded doubtful.

'The past couple of years have been rubbish, but getting this lot chopped … it feels like I'm sloughing off dead skin. Like a snake?' she added, seeing that Rowena still looked puzzled.

'Oh.'

'It's good,' Molly stressed. 'It's a new beginning, don't you see?'

'Oh. Oh, ta.'

Molly emerged into Bond Street smiling at everybody. From now on, she vowed to herself, I'm only going to look forward.

Chapter Two

Adam thought a great deal in the grim days that followed the revelation of Logan's dishonesty. He thought about what he would lose and about what his life now meant. Had everything to this point been meaningless? Had he squandered his education by using it for a career he had never wanted and now stood to lose? He wasn't sure he knew who he was any more.

He hadn't expected to feel jealousy. He'd never expected he would be lonely, but although he loved spending days alone in Scotland's wild places, he had been astonished to discover that this was different from coming home every night to an empty house, and that he did not cope well with loneliness.

What he had thought to be natural self-confidence, he learned had depended on the knowledge that Molly loved him. Her belief in him had been a necessary prerequisite to self-belief.

Most of all, he was amazed to find that, facing ignominy and failure, he turned like a cornered beast to fight for survival.

Could it be that the law was, after all, important to him? Or was it just that all he could do was react, minute by minute, hour by hour, as events unfolded?

He met with Patrick Mulgrew at Capital Art and showed him the photos he'd taken at Agnes Buchanan's bungalow. Patrick – assured, stylish, successful art dealer personified – slipped on his reading glasses and examined them carefully.

'I sold her this one,' he said, jabbing his finger at the Barbara Rae, unmistakeable with its explosion of reds and gold. 'Fabulous painting. I could have sold it a dozen times over.'

'Not cheap, then?'

'She's one of Scotland's foremost artists. Why do you ask?'

Adam sat back and looked at Patrick. He'd been a Blair King client since he'd set up his gallery, long before success had made him wealthy. Adam liked the man, and trusted him. In any case, the bad news would be public knowledge soon enough.

'You know she's our chief cashier?'

'Sure.'

'I thought it might be a good print.'

'A print?' Patrick yelped with laughter.

'What about the others?'

Patrick took the phone again and scrolled through the images.

'Some of these were definitely handled by other Edinburgh galleries in the last few years. I keep tabs on what's around. We all do. I can't speak for the others, but I'd hazard a guess they're all genuine. Miss Buchanan is astute and a very particular buyer. She knows what she likes, and what she likes is quality.'

Adam struggled to square this fact with the Agnes Buchanan he knew – or thought he'd known. The mousey woman they'd all relied on but had never valued.

'They must have cost a fortune.'

'And your point is?'

'She doesn't earn that much.'

'Adam, I shouldn't really be talking about a client like this.'

'I have good reason to probe.'

Patrick shot him an appraising look. 'I believe she came into money.'

'Hmm. Any idea when? I mean, has she been buying from you for some time?'

'She was one of my first clients. So – fifteen years or so?'

Cash-flow problems ... Agnes saying, 'It's only temporary, a loan will tide us through.'

They'd all remortgaged their homes.

'Is there something wrong?'

Adam cleared his throat. 'You could say—'

The house sold at once, and Adam made bad decisions. He took most of his books and CDs to a charity shop, then immediately regretted it. The music had been a bank of memories shared with Molly and he felt its absence keenly. Many of the books were old friends, some he'd had since childhood. It wasn't enough to tell himself he could download them all to his e-reader – his e-reader didn't have the fatty mark where he'd dripped bacon grease out of his sandwich because he couldn't bear to put the book aside while he read, or the pages that had curled with damp when he'd taken that book up some mountain to read by torchlight inside his sleeping bag.

He agreed to put a couple of crates filled with Molly's things into storage alongside his, then wondered why he was doing it when they no longer had any kind of shared life.

He forgot about the garden shed until the day he was due to hand over the keys to the new owners. The shed's contents had to be divided between the nearest charity shop and the local recycling and landfill facility, and that was that.

As soon as the house was sold, the bank took its share, and before he could think too much about it, he transferred the entire balance to Molly's account. She called him the next day.

'Thank you for the money. I thought you said there was going to be a problem with the bank.'

'They didn't take as much as I'd thought.' He didn't want to explain.

'But what about your share?'

'I've taken what I need,' he said.

He no longer cared about the wrongs or the rights of what had happened between them. He'd been neglectful, she'd had an affair, he'd lost his temper, she'd left. How could you put those things on the scales and weigh them against each other? He could only go by what he felt was right.

Weeks of sofa surfing round tolerant friends followed. He tried to develop a nose for a change of atmosphere before he exhausted his welcome.

When Molly moved to London, Lexie called him, catching him at the office on a particularly difficult day.

'Camp out in my studio,' she said without preamble.

'Studio?'

'It's at Fleming House. The garden cottage. I couldn't suggest it while Molly was living across the way in the big house, but now that she's gone … Well, anyway, why don't you come and look at it, see what you think?'

He drove out to Fleming House the next morning. What was a couple of hours off work? However many hours he put in now, it wasn't going to do the firm any good.

Lexie was waiting for him.

'Where is it?' he asked, looking around. He didn't know Fleming House; he'd never been there. This was where Molly had fled after she'd left him; this had been her retreat.

The big house was behind him, and all he could see in front was a stand of trees and the tall wall of the kitchen garden.

Lexie rubbed her crimson crop and grinned. 'Behind you. Look.'

She took him by the shoulders and turned him through thirty degrees. He spotted a path of sorts, and under the thick canopy of a chestnut tree, an old wooden door.

Adam had always liked Alexa Gordon. She was thoughtful and loyal, but there was a streak of rebelliousness about her that you couldn't help but admire. When he heard she'd got together with Patrick Mulgrew he'd been more than a little surprised, unable to envisage the sophisticated, sharp-suited entrepreneur and the eccentrically-dressed artist together. His doubts were proved wrong. Lexie had softened Patrick's sharper edges, while his unswerving belief in her had freed up her creativity. Her career had taken off, until motherhood had put it on hold again.

She led the way to the door and pulled a heavy key out of her shoulder bag. The door creaked and swung inwards.

On the threshold, Adam hesitated. 'But you said this is your studio. I can't—'

'I'm not working at the moment, because of Keira. I'm not using the studio and I haven't slept here since Patrick and I got together. Go in. It's cold right now, but once the stove is lit it gets warms really quickly.'

'What's the rent?'

He had to ask because, for the first time since he'd been a student, money was an issue. Blair King was managing to run a skeleton operation and he still had a salary of sorts, but that couldn't last. The end was in sight, and he knew it.

'Nothing. Patrick's paying the rent anyway. It'll be good to have someone here making sure the pipes don't burst.'

'But—'

'He can afford it. He says Blair King have been good to him over the years and it's the least he can do. You'd be doing us a favour.'

'In that case – what can I say? I'd love to take it.'

His intention was just to camp in the cottage, but the appeal of the place was unexpected. He found himself standing at the windows, cradling a hot mug of tea and staring vacantly into the garden. That was the clue: vacantly. The cottage had a kind of stillness that brought serenity. It didn't matter how difficult the day had been (and most days were verging on impossible), when he returned here at night, he was able to find peace.

He found himself avoiding Sunita, fobbing her off with poor excuses. Sometimes they met for dinner. On the odd occasion, he found himself staying over at her flat. She was beautiful and affectionate, but because he knew he didn't love her, he always regretted it the next day.

He didn't want her at the cottage; he protected it jealously, as if her presence might violate his sanctuary.

It was not a good situation.

Chapter Three

Adam had often dreamed of leaving Blair King, but he'd never foreseen anything like this. He looked around the boardroom. The few staff who hadn't already fled the sinking ship were standing around despondently, heads down, shoulders hunched. The other partners had found posts elsewhere, and today only he and his father remained of what had once been a proud family law firm.

There were thirteen people in the room. He'd known most of them for years. They were decent, loyal employees who didn't deserve what had happened to them.

'Everyone got a glass?' he called. He'd gone out and bought champagne – Moët, nothing cheap – out of his own pocket, because he was determined they would not go down hanging their heads.

James Blair was standing looking out of the window. How often had he stood there over the years? Pondering some difficult case, considering a staffing issue, or maybe just stealing a quiet moment of satisfaction at everything he'd achieved, despite his own father's divisive will. What must he be feeling now?

Adam put the thought aside and adopted a determinedly cheerful expression. 'Then let's raise them in a toast,' he said, his lips tightening into a smile that he hoped looked more natural than it felt. He glanced around. 'To each other – you've been a terrific team and I can't thank you enough – and to the future.'

'To each other, and to the future,' came a ragged echo. James, a half full glass of bubbly in his hand, did not move. He was still looking out of the window.

'Now, no looking back. Let's keep in touch. You all have my personal contact details. I know most of you have already found jobs. If there's anything I – or my father – can do to help those of you who haven't, please let us know.'

Deirdre Shaw was in tears. Most of the women, huddled together at the far end of the room, were either crying or nearly so. Caitlyn Murray, standing separately, hadn't touched her champagne. He watched from across the room as she braced herself against the wall. She'd be feeling guilty because she'd been the one to uncover the fraud. She shouldn't. He must tell her that. As he crossed the space between them, snippets of conversation drifted his way.

'Who'd've ever thought Agnes would—'

'I'm still in shock—'

'My hubby says she'll get ten years—'

'—if she's well enough to stand trial.'

'Serve her right, I'd say.'

'Ooh, don't be so bitchy.'

'Well, it's put us all out of work.'

'And what about Mr Keir? Bet he was the one who—'

'—and they haven't even found him yet.'

Caitlyn stood apart from them all in self-imposed isolation.

'Are you all right?'

Her head swivelled towards him, her eyes blazing. The impact of her gaze was so intense that he instinctively took a half step back.

'If you must know, I'm bloody furious.'

His eyes rounded. In all his years in this building, he'd

never heard a junior member of staff swearing in front of a partner.

'What right did they have? Their greed has destroyed this firm. It's robbed people of their jobs. It's taken away their dreams.' Her dark eyes narrowed. 'Aren't you furious? You must be.'

He stared at her. There'd been so much to do. He'd had to stay in control. He and his father had been catapulted into a world of deceit and deception. They'd had to help the investigators to uncover the trail of lies and falsehoods left by Logan and Agnes, while all the time trying to defend their own innocence and keep the business going.

In the end, the last hadn't been possible, but so far he had not felt anger. Fear, yes, but even that had been subsumed in the day-to-day effort of keeping going.

Behind him, someone laughed. He sidestepped her question.

'How's the job hunt going?'

She shrugged. 'I'd like to find something in Hailesbank if I can, but I don't want to go back to stacking supermarket shelves. There's been nothing.'

'Well, keep looking. I always believe that when one door closes, another opens,' said Adam, who did not believe any such thing. His marriage, to the only woman he had ever loved, was all but over, and his relationship with Sunita Ghosh was doomed. All he needed was the courage to tell her so.

It didn't take courage, as it turned out. It was more a matter of cowardice.

When he set the alarm and pulled the front door of the Blair King office shut behind him for the last time, he knew exactly what he wanted to do for the rest of the evening – light a fire in the stove in Lexie Gordon's studio cottage and crash out in the magical healing space. Alone.

Forty minutes after he left the office for the last time, he steered his car round the side of the big house and past the windows that had been Molly's apartment. He didn't look up. Thinking about Molly still saddened him. He left the gravel drive and pulled on to the grass under the trees. It would be the last time he'd use the car for a while. Now that he was going to have time on his hands, he would cycle everywhere – even to the station in Hailesbank, if he landed an interview in Edinburgh. It was time he got some air into his lungs.

The cottage was freezing – there was no heating, only the wood-burning stove in the studio room and a couple of portable fan heaters. Adam changed quickly into jeans and a sweater and hung his suit on the back of the bedroom door. Maybe he'd take it to the cleaner's. Now would be a good time because he had every intention of having a break before he started looking for another job.

Adam liked the cold. He liked its unforgivingness. You couldn't argue with cold; it bit into skin and turned blood to ice. The only way to ward it off was with fire, and fire was a life-giving force. There hadn't been an open fire in the Trinity house, and since he'd moved in to the studio he'd taken a particular pleasure in the ritual of laying the fire and of tending it – scrunching newspaper into tight sausages, laying on kindling, watching it catch light. The stove was old, but efficient. Within minutes, the fire was alight; in less than ten, it was sending its comforting heat out into the room.

He stood over it until it felt established, then crossed to pull the heavy curtains across the tall French windows. He guessed they were probably cast-offs from the big house, because although they were shabby and worn, they were clearly good quality. He fumbled for the switch in the neck of the table lamp that nestled on the bookshelf by the television (his sole import into the cottage), and soft light flooded the space. He pressed a button on a floor switch and the standard lamp behind the sofa glowed. To his left, the rest of the room – Lexie's studio – remained in darkness. He hadn't touched her space. He didn't need it, and one day soon, she probably would.

He didn't want to think about Lexie coming back here, because that would mean he'd have to move out, and he loved this place. He loved being alone in it. So far, he'd successfully defended it against Sunita's hints.

'It's too basic,' he told her, 'you'd hate it.' Or, 'You couldn't stand the cold. I promise you, it's Baltic.'

He didn't feel like eating. What he felt like was getting grandly drunk.

There was a bottle of whisky on the bookshelves. Macallan – The Macallan – his favourite. He found a glass and filled a small jug with water, then switched on the television. Some drama was on, dark and confusing, but watchable. He poured himself a glass of whisky, shoved another couple of logs into the stove and stretched out on the sofa.

What better end to a difficult few months? Dark drama and drunkenness. He smiled at the empty room, and at his thought.

Some time later, he awoke to the heavy thump of the iron knocker on the front door.

'Wha'? What the—?'

He sat up abruptly. The half-empty glass of whisky that had been resting on his stomach, cradled in his loose grasp, went flying across the rug and there was the sound of glass shattering.

'Shit!'

The stove was almost out and the room had grown chilly.

Again, there was a battering at the front of the cottage.

Half asleep, he stumbled along the corridor and hauled open the heavy door, which scraped over the flagstones.

'What is it?' he grunted, peering into the darkness outside.

'That's not much of a greeting,' said Sunita, tiptoeing up to kiss his cheek.

'What the—?'

'Can I come in?'

Adam reached out for the switch and light flooded across Sunita's face.

'Oh, it's you.'

'That's even less welcoming.' She was smiling. One thing you could say about Sunita was that she always met challenges with courage and grace.

'Sorry.' He opened the door wider and stood aside to let her in. 'I'm half asleep. I was asleep when you knocked. The place is freezing, sorry. Straight ahead.'

She gazed around the half dark space. 'Interesting.'

'It's Lexie Gordon's studio.'

'I know. You told me. Can we get the stove going, do you think? And do stop saying sorry.'

'Sorry. I mean, yes. It'll only take a minute. Sit down.'

The fire wasn't out; it glowed promisingly and he could feel vestiges of heat as he opened the glass door. He pushed a few pieces of dry kindling into the stove and they caught at once.

'Glass of something?'

She looked at him, amused. 'I'm driving. Unless you'd like me to stay?'

It put him on the back foot. 'I – I was just about to make a pot of coffee,' he lied.

Her eyes flickered, but she controlled herself well. Sunita was always about control.

'Coffee would be lovely.'

'To what do I owe this pleasure?' he called from the kitchen, pulling mugs from the cupboard and setting milk and sugar on a tray.

'I was worried about you.'

He twisted round at the nearness of her voice. She'd followed him and was at the door, leaning against the frame, her coat buttoned high, a scarlet and purple wool scarf twisted round her neck. She looked lovely. She always did. Why, he wondered, could he not love her?

'I mean, it was your last day—'

'Oh.' He poured boiling water over the coffee grounds and set the cafetière on the tray. 'That was good of you. I suppose it's the talk of the town.'

She pulled a face. 'There's talk, but it's not spiteful. It's more a case of, "There but for the grace of God". Everyone knows it could happen anywhere, no matter how tight the controls.'

'Yes, well, it happened to Blair King.' He picked up the tray and moved towards the door. 'The living room should be warming up. Let's go back there.'

'No sign of Logan Keir?'

'Nothing.' He set the tray down on Lexie's lovely cherry wood coffee table, the only piece of furniture in the place that wasn't battered or upcycled. 'There's a European Arrest Warrant out for him, but no-one's sure where he went. It might not have been Europe. It could have been South America, Brazil, Argentina—'

'He'll run out of cash, surely?'

'Maybe. But it's perfectly possible he'd prepared for

this. False passport, bank accounts in other names. The police have found three accounts so far and frozen them all, but there may be more they haven't unearthed yet.'

'What a mess.'

'Yup. A mess.'

She unbuttoned her coat and slipped it off, then unwound the scarf and draped it across her shoulders. In the dancing light of the fire she looked mysterious and exotic.

'You don't have to live here, Adam.'

He smiled. A sinking feeling somewhere in his gut heralded the inevitable.

'You could move in with me.'

He laid his own mug down, took hers and set it on the table. He held her hands in his and studied her face with grave courtesy.

'You're very kind. Thank you. But I have to do this on my own.'

'Do what?' Her hands twitched, but she didn't withdraw them from his grasp. 'Half starve yourself in some freezing workshop?'

'Salvage my pride. Get a new life.'

'We could work on the new life together. As for pride, it wasn't your fault. No-one attaches any blame to you.'

'Mud sticks.'

She was silent for a while. At last she pulled her hands free. Adam made no attempt to stop her.

'We need to book the tickets to India. For the wedding. My family are—'

'I can't go to India with you, Sunita.'

Her eyes glittered.

'I'll buy the tickets. My treat. No—' She held out a hand to stop him interrupting. 'It's not charity, Adam. Take it as a birthday present. It's a family wedding, my family, and I want you to come. I'd like to do this.'

He stood up and stepped away from her.

No, this did not require courage. He knew he could not do this thing. He could not travel with Sunita Ghosh to her uncle's smart house in Kolkata. He could not face being introduced to her family as 'Adam Blair, my boyfriend'. For Sunita's family, such an introduction would be tantamount to the announcement of an engagement, and he could not spend his life with this woman, beautiful though she was.

She was on her feet in one easy movement, her stare so intense that he almost quailed before it. He closed his eyes to block it out.

'You're still in love with her, aren't you?' she said, the words so soft and low that he thought for a moment that he'd imagined them.

'What?'

'Molly. You're still in love with her.'

'You're being ridiculous. This isn't about Molly.'

'Isn't it?'

She blinked. Adam was horrified to see that her eyes were full of tears.

'Sunita, I—'

'Don't. I've seen it for myself. I saw it at Loch Melfort, and I saw it again at your Uncle Geordie's funeral. I thought I could fight it. I thought I was clever enough, beautiful enough to win your admiration, and maybe, following that, your love. But I can't. She has won. Your wife has won.'

'That's not true! Molly and I are getting divorced. It's what she wants and—'

'And you, Adam? Is it what you want?'

'No, I—' he stopped, trapped. 'I mean to say, yes, the divorce is what I want.' He tried to salvage the situation.

'It's not you, Sunita, and it's not Molly. I don't mean it to sound a cliché, but this is all about me. I know it's selfish, but I've had quite a battering and I need time out to reflect and decide what I'm going to do for the rest of my life. That's all.'

'If you say so.' She bent to pick up her coat and looked at him again. She stood very straight, her head back, a small, strained smile playing on her lips. 'I'd say let's be friends, but that's not what I want from you, Adam. So I guess this is goodbye.'

The abruptness of the end took him by surprise. He bent and kissed her forehead, unexpectedly taken aback by the realisation that it would be the last time he would be near her like this, the last time he would inhale that faint smell of her perfume or touch the smooth brown skin. He lifted a hand and stroked her cheek with regret.

'You're an amazing woman. I don't deserve you. I never did. You'll find someone who does, and I'll be the first to shake his hand and wish him well.'

She snorted. 'You're an idiot, Adam.'

He heard the front door scrape across the flagstones, then close. A moment later, he heard an engine start and caught the crunch as her wheels spun on to the gravel.

In the stove, a log fell heavily and a cascade of flame shot up behind the soot-darkened glass.

Fire is a life-giving force.

Chapter Four

'Assistant required. Apply within.'

Caitlyn nearly missed the notice in the solicitor's window in the High Street. She'd walked past the narrow frontage twice already this morning. Either it hadn't been there or she just hadn't spotted it.

She stopped abruptly. It was handwritten on a piece of paper no bigger than A5. What way was that to advertise a job? She'd do things very differently if she were handling it.

She glanced up at the lettering above the door. Fraser, Fraser and Mutch. Stupid name for a solicitor if ever there was one. Still, she knew enough about how these things worked to realise that it must be a family firm that had maybe had to take on another partner at some time, maybe as a way of keeping the business going after the father retired. Maybe there was only one Fraser now. Maybe there wasn't even a Fraser at all.

She couldn't help thinking of James Blair. Once, he'd been the 'big boss', authoritative and commanding. She hadn't exactly been afraid of him, but then, she had never had much reason to meet him either. Over the past months, it seemed as though he'd grown smaller. He'd lost weight, that much was obvious, but he'd got shorter too – or did she just imagine that? As the investigations continued and appalling fact after appalling fact began to emerge, he'd grown withdrawn and defeated.

Caitlyn's gaze returned to the notice. 'Assistant required. Apply within.'

It looked right up her street – but could she face another job in a lawyer's office? Would they even think of taking her on after the whole Blair King episode? She hesitated, reached her hand out to push the door open, then backed away abruptly and walked on.

When she got home, an hour or so later, she found a note in Ailsa's girly handwriting propped against the kettle: TAKEN ISLA MAY TO THE PARK. There were small hearts in pink felt tip dotted round the words. Caitlyn picked it up and smiled. Ailsa might have a boyfriend who looked like Ross Kemp, but she was still quite young in many ways. It was great that they'd gone to the park together – there'd been a time when Ailsa would have flatly refused to do anything more than she had to with her little sister.

The twins were at after-school club. They'd tumble home in an hour or so, escorted to the end of the road by one of the mums.

Her mother was working.

Caitlyn was tempted to brew a cuppa, grab one of the old magazines Joyce had rescued from some resident's waste basket and put her feet up for a blissful hour – but now that she wasn't earning, there was no excuse not to pull her weight. She unhooked the rainbow-striped pinafore she'd bought at the pound store last year because its bright colours cheered her up, loaded the big pocket on the front with dusters and polish, then tugged the vacuum cleaner out of the cupboard in the hall and hefted it upstairs. One of these days she'd treat Joyce to a new one – this old thing was not only heavy, it was inefficient too.

Listen to yourself! A new vacuum cleaner? Hardly a treat! A day at a spa or a voucher for a nice dinner somewhere, now they would be treats.

She set the machine down at the top of the stairs, fished a tissue out from her sleeve and gave her nose a good blow. It was no use feeling sorry for herself because if, by some miracle, she landed an interview somewhere, her self-pity would show. Confidence was a trick, and one that she'd begun to think she'd mastered before everything had fallen apart again.

Cleaning Joyce's room didn't take long. There was little furniture and only a small floor area. She pulled a duster out of her pocket and started on the bedside chest.

There was a new photograph, a small picture in an old frame. She didn't recognise the frame; perhaps her mother had bought it in a charity shop somewhere. She recognised the two people smiling out of the photograph at her though – her mother, looking happier than she'd seen her in an age, and Reg West, unmistakeable with his fading ginger hair and round smiling face. Joyce had been 'seeing' the cook at the care home, as she obliquely phrased it, in recent weeks.

'His wife died,' she explained to a curious Caitlyn, 'and Reggie was shipwrecked.'

Caitlyn dusted the frame and set it back down. She smiled, a picture in her head of her mother rowing across a choppy sea to hoist Reg into the safety of her little boat. All her life Joyce had supported people in need, usually without so much as a thank you. Maybe this time she'd get her reward.

Perhaps Joyce would need the bigger bedroom soon. If Caitlyn moved out of Farm Lane, Ailsa could have this one – but she'd need another job if that was going to happen.

The boys' room took longer, mostly because she had to spend so long picking up discarded toys, clothing, sweet wrappers – even, under Harris's bed, a plate smeared with chocolate buttercream. So he had sneaked the last piece from the cupboard, despite his vehement denials the night before! She'd have to have a word with him about telling the truth.

Isla May's room was a temple to pink. A year ago, Caitlyn had picked up a roll of pale pink wallpaper with fairies on it for next to nothing in the oddments bin at the local DIY store. It had been her first try at decorating, and she'd enjoyed it. She'd painted the windowsill, doors and skirting in pink paint and done a surprisingly neat job with the wallpaper, following instructions she'd found on the internet. A pink tutu hung on the back of the door – a fairy costume Joyce had picked up in a charity shop in Hailesbank High Street for the princessly sum of fifty pence.

Caitlyn neatened the bed. As she reached across to tuck the duvet down the far side, next to the wall, her foot struck a hard object with a dull clang. She dropped to her knees and pulled out an old biscuit tin. A neat label on the top read, 'SUMMER CAMP FUND'. It was unmistakably Ailsa's writing, down to the pink hearts in felt tip decorating the background. Summer Camp Fund? Where would Isla May find money to save for the camp? They couldn't even afford new football boots for the boys, who were complaining so vociferously about cramped feet that she'd threatened to cut the toes off the ones they had.

She gave the tin a shake. It rattled noisily, but it didn't feel heavy. Poor Isla May, Caitlyn thought, I'll see if I can slip in a few coins now and again to top it up for her. It would never be enough to pay for the camp, though – probably not even the deposit.

She prised open the lid and her jaw dropped with surprise. The tin was full of notes, mostly fivers, but even – she picked it up, amazed – a ten-pound note.

Quickly, she counted the cash, a sick feeling in her stomach. Eighty-three pounds and eight pence.

How could Isla May have got all this money?

Caitlyn's head was whirling. She'd uncovered one fraud, and the outfall from that had been catastrophic. She couldn't bear the idea that her sweet little sister had been doing something wrong. Stealing, perhaps? But who from? She hadn't noticed money disappearing from her own purse – or had she? Certainly, cash seemed to melt away like snow on a summer's day. Had Isla May been taking money out of Joyce's wallet? Her mother would be too tired to notice a lot of the time.

Downstairs, the front door slammed and Ailsa's voice called, 'We're home!'

Caitlyn rammed the lid on the tin and shoved it back under the bed.

'Shall I put the kettle on?'

Ailsa was standing at the bottom of the stairs, looking up at her. Her face was shining, her eyes bright with exercise and the cold. She looked happy.

'Tea would be lovely. I've nearly finished here.'

'Cait-lynnnnn,' Isla May sang, wrenching off her bobble beanie and dancing up the stairs in her pink wellies, arms outstretched for a cuddle.

Caitlyn buried her face in Isla May's soft hair. She couldn't bring herself to say anything, not until she'd had time to think about it, and talk it over with Malkie.

Malkie was late. Caitlyn, sitting in the corner of the bar, tried not to feel worried, but there he was at last, pushing past the crowds at the door and looking stressed.

'Sorry, love, sorry! I was on time, then the boss caught me.'

'Ibsen Brown? What did he want?'

'Let me get in some drinks, then I'll tell you.'

'Malkie?' Caitlyn said suspiciously. 'What are you hiding? Tell me right now!'

'Peach schnapps and orange juice?'

'No, I – Malkie!'

She sat drumming her fingers on the seat, watching him order.

'There you go.'

He placed her drink on the table and downed a large draught of his beer.

'So what was it? What did Ibsen want?'

'Ibsen?'

'Malcolm Milne!'

His grin was irrepressible. 'OK, sweetheart, I'll tell you. There's a wee cottage on the edge of the Fleming estate that's become vacant, and Lady Fleming says one of Ibsen's gardening team can use it. The rent's really low. Ibsen's offered it to me. I thought you could move in with me.'

'Oh!' She hadn't seen it coming. She stared at him, horrified, while a thousand thoughts spun round her head and her insides did a cartwheel.

'Caitlyn?'

In so many ways it was tempting. She could move out of the chaotic household in Farm Lane, get herself clear from the endless babysitting and chores, leave the way clear for her mother's new man to move in, if that was what they wanted. And yet …

'Have I said something wrong? You and me—'

She interrupted him before he could go any further. 'No.' She shook her head. 'It's a lovely thought, Malkie. But I'm sorry, I can't.'

He was so transparent. She watched, crucified, as shock, hurt and misery chased themselves across his face.

'Don't take it badly!' she cried, laying her hand on his arm. He shook it off vehemently.

How could she get him to understand that she had spent her entire life watching her mother living her life through one man or other, each experience taking more from her than the last? She'd had five children, and she was still giving everything she had to them. Joyce was smart. She'd got a bunch of qualifications before she left school; she could have gone on to further education and made something of her life. Instead, she'd been like a busy bird with a nest full of chicks, mouths open, protesting and wailing constantly until they were fed, then starting all over again.

'I want a life,' she said, trying to explain.

Malkie recoiled.

'I didn't mean … Malkie, I'm sorry, I only meant—'

'Never mind.'

He drained his pint and stood up.

'Don't go.'

'There's nothing to talk about.'

'Don't, Malkie!'

He grabbed his jacket as she tried to catch his hand.

'Call me, at least?'

He grunted, his kiss on her cheek barely more than the brush of a feather.

Idiot! How could she have expressed her feelings so badly? She'd messed everything up.

Chapter Five

Perhaps it happened because she was thinking about Malkie. Perhaps it was because it was still early – only nine-thirty. But it was dark, and she was on her own, and she should have been alert as soon as she'd first heard the laughter and seen the youths swaggering down the dark street.

'Well hello, darling!'

Ricky McQuade was with a bunch of drunken friends – a runt among snarling pups, determined to claw for position. It was the worst possible combination.

He put a bottle to his lips and tossed his head back, draining the beer in greedy gulps, then throwing it aside. It exploded against the wall and shards of glass arced across the pavement. Somebody laughed.

'Get in there, Ricky,' someone growled, and the single laugh became a chorus.

Caitlyn stepped to one side and tried to carry on walking, as though she hadn't even noticed.

A shadow fell across her path.

'I'll see you home, darlin'.'

'I'm fine, Ricky.' Caitlyn lifted her head and looked at him squarely. On his own, she could handle him, but being with these hooligans gave him courage.

He slung an arm across her shoulder. She tried to shrug it off.

'Don' be like that. Gie's a kiss.'

The grip round her shoulders tightened and he swung

her towards him, grasping the back of her head roughly and planting his lips on hers.

She kept her mouth shut as tightly as she could. He stank of beer and cigarettes and the stubby bristles on his unshaven chin rasped against the delicate skin on her face. She tried to wrench her head aside, but he slammed her against the wall, her head hit brick and a bright pain flashed behind her eyes.

She was only two blocks from home. They were quite near the pub. Surely someone would come and see what was happening. But it was just a crowd of young people, enjoying a night out – wasn't it? There was laughter all around, and shouts of encouragement.

'Go for it, Ricky boy!'

'Give her a doing. I'm after you.'

'Get in the queue, Jimbo.'

'Need a hand?'

If she opened her mouth to scream, he'd stick his tongue in. Caitlyn needed to throw up, but she couldn't with his weight against her, crushing the breath out of her. *Stop*! she wanted to yell. *Stop it, you bastard*!

She was pinned against the wall. He was cupping her chin with his hand, trying to force her mouth open, his fingers digging into her flesh. His hand shifted and there was a flash of relief, only to be replaced by panic as she felt him yanking up her skirt and feeling for the top of her tights.

She lifted her knee sharply and hit soft tissue.

'Bitch!'

This time the flash became a white blaze of pain as his fist connected with her cheek and her head crunched sickeningly against the wall. She crumpled and sagged and he used the momentum of her fall, throwing himself on top of her on the cold, hard pavement. He had one arm across her chest, pinning her to the ground. The other was wrenching at her tights and her knickers.

'Go Rick, go Rick, go Rick!'

The chanting from the background was rhythmic. Someone started a slow handclap and it was taken up.

It seemed to spur Ricky on. Caitlyn was fighting like a maniac, wriggling and squirming every time he moved, but her strength was failing. She opened her eyes. He wasn't looking at her. He had his eyes shut tight, his head thrown back, a frown of concentration between his heavy eyebrows. There was something extraordinarily childlike about his face – how could that be possible? Above her the moon shone clear and bright in a cloudless sky. Was there no-one who would help her? Her tights were below her knees, and a patch of hard-edged pebbles on the pavement was grinding into her buttocks. Ricky was fumbling with his zipper. She had just a moment left.

She opened her mouth and screamed at the top of her lungs, 'Help! Rape! Help me!'

She expected laughter and jeering. What she didn't expect was pounding footsteps and yelps of surprise.

A deep voice called, 'What's going on here?' and another, a girl's voice, clear and steady, announced loudly, 'I'm calling the police.'

On top of her, the weight eased, and she wriggled onto her side, frantically pulling down her skirt and coat.

'What the—?'

Ricky McQuade receded like magic into the night, yanked upright by a strong hand. An arm appeared round his throat, holding him in a tight lock. His jeans, newly released, began to slither down his scrawny thighs, which gleamed like ghostly white sticks in the moonlight. His hands reached down to grab them, then flew up to his throat as the grip around it tightened.

'You're fucking killing me!' he croaked.

She scrambled to her feet and flattened herself against the wall, shrinking back into its shadow, shaking uncontrollably. The crowd had disappeared. Ricky McQuade's so-called friends had fled into the night at the first sign of trouble. To her right, a girl was punching numbers into a mobile. Caitlyn peered through a rapidly closing eye. It looked like … it couldn't be …

'Ailsa?'

The girl stopped jabbing.

'Caitlyn? Oh my God!'

Ailsa crossed the yards between them in an instant and threw her arms around her, and Caitlyn folded into her sister's embrace, clutching at her like a child hugging a comfort blanket after a nightmare.

Caitlyn slept for eleven hours. Sometime after nine, when she should have been alone in the house, she dreamed of a grotesque bear-brown monster, snapping and snarling in her face, and woke with a yell.

A door creaked, someone called, 'She's awake!' and there was a thumping of feet on the stairs. And then her mother was beside her and she was in her arms, sweating and shaking, but safe.

'You're all right, Caitie. Everything's all right.'

Joyce hadn't used her baby name for years. It was comforting.

'Let me look at you. Oh my pet lamb—'

She held Caitlyn at arm's length and studied her. 'You're getting a real shiner there. How are you feeling?'

Caitlyn tested each muscle, every joint, with care. 'My back's really sore. I'm sore all over, but particularly my shoulders and my head.'

She shuddered. 'Oh Mum – if Wallace hadn't come along—'

'It doesn't bear thinking about. He's such a nice young man, isn't he? A real gentle giant. Ailsa's a lucky girl.'

Caitlyn hung her head. 'I misjudged him so badly. Just because he's covered in tattoos and he shaves his head—' Caitlyn managed a slightly crooked smile. 'It's a good thing he acts like a bouncer though, isn't it? What time is it?'

'After nine.'

'Really? Why aren't you at work?'

'I managed to swap my shift. Reggie's here too. He's got a day off, as it happens.'

'You're so good to me.'

Joyce shook her head, smiling. 'You're my daughter. I don't suppose you've thought yet about whether to lay charges against that vile McQuade boy?'

Caitlyn shrank back at the sound of his name. 'God, I was so stupid! He's been coming on to me for ages but I never thought he'd have a go. He was drunk, of course, and the others egged him on.'

'We should call the police.'

'He didn't actually rape me, Mum.'

'He assaulted you. Look at the state of you, girl. On the other hand,' she wriggled quickly round to put herself between Caitlyn and the mirror, 'maybe that's not a good idea. Not yet, anyway.'

'Let me think about it, OK?'

She wanted, more than anything, to call Malkie, but the memory of their disagreement came in the way. Within a few hours, shock made her retreat into herself. When the young ones rushed back from school, agog to know how their big sister was, she told Joyce she wanted to rest and shut her door.

At some point Ailsa crept in, but she feigned sleep. She wasn't ready to dissect her feelings. During the long night, she wondered if she ever could.

Chapter Six

'Check that out, Molly, will you? You're the best at rooting out business babble. We need to make sure the pitch is in the same language as the material we're using to reach our target customers.'

Molly turned away from the computer screen and the final instructions she was issuing for a high-impact rebranding event that was planned for next week, and took the print-out from Ken. The team at Fletcher Keir Mason was developing all the materials it needed for the public health campaign pitch which they were due to submit by the end of the week, and everyone was working flat out.

'Jody says you look terrific, by the way.' Molly had joined Ken and his girlfriend for a drink after work last night, grabbing a much-needed hour's relaxation before heading home to Battersea. 'She reckons it's the hair.'

Molly's hand went up to her shorn locks. It had been weeks now; it was almost ready for another trim, but she still couldn't quite get used to the feeling of lightness.

'Thanks! What's the deadline for this?'

'Yesterday.'

He moved away, on to the next task already. Their submission proposal was radical – built on the idea that customers would decide the next steps through consultation. This set the traditional marketing strategy of a campaign pushed out to customers from a central point on its head, which would make selling the concept at the presentation doubly hard.

She finished her email quickly, reached for a red biro

and bent her head to the documents. It was always easier to read this kind of material off screen.

Her pencil hovered, then dropped. She'd forgotten to call her father yesterday, she realised with an anguished pang. How could she have done that? She'd been so caught up with the whole submission, as well as masterminding various other events, that she hadn't had a minute. But there should always be time for Billy; work was no excuse.

She picked up the pencil again and tried to concentrate. She'd call her father at lunchtime, when she went out for a sandwich. That had been the problem yesterday – there had been back-to-back meetings, and one of them had been over lunch, so sandwiches had been provided.

Barnaby laid a light hand on her shoulder. 'How's it going?'

'This'll take me a couple of hours, Barnaby,' she flashed, immediately defensive.

'Hey! It wasn't a criticism,' he said, startled. 'It was a sympathetic question.'

'Sorry.' Her shoulders hunched. She wiped the back of her hand across her forehead. It wasn't midday yet and already she was tired. But that was no excuse – everyone was tired.

Barnaby grabbed an empty seat and rolled it across the floor to sit next to her. 'Don't drive yourself too hard, Molly,' he said, his deep voice lowered so that only she could hear it. 'What time were you in this morning?'

She'd got home around eleven and spent an hour winding down with Julian – precious time. She didn't know how she'd function right now without Julian's loyal support. At four she'd been awake again, her mind whirring with everything that had to be done in the next few days. To-do lists rolled past her eyes.

- Write pitch documentation
- Book venue for Exco conference
- Check invoice for Oodles rebrand (check project management and graphic design hours)
- Cost ...
- Phone ...
- Email ...
- Meet ...

At half past five, she'd given up trying to get back to sleep, got up and showered, forced down a bowl of cereal, and set out along the river.

There was something calming about the water, especially at that time in the morning. There wasn't too much traffic around, and you could still hear the birds. As she strode along the bank, there was something else, too – a sense of awakening. Around her, people were stirring behind shuttered windows, sharing a precious early-morning cuddle, showering, getting ready for work. By the time she arrived at the office, around six thirty, she was ready to face the day.

Or so she'd thought. Now it was only eleven, and already she was flagging.

'Quite early,' she said in response to Barnaby's question.

'I know it's a tight deadline, Molly, but we'll never make it if you keel over.'

'Everyone's working hard.'

'I know.' He studied her carefully. 'But you've had pressures the others haven't suffered. The move to London, your brother – everything. You need to look after yourself.'

She straightened and stretched. 'I am looking after

myself. I'm fine. You don't need to worry about me. Now, can I get on?'

He stood up. 'Make it sound like you're explaining to your granny.'

'Or my dad.' She grinned, thinking of Billy and his steadfast refusal to use a computer.

She watched Barnaby's retreating back, still smiling. Barnaby was what made this whole venture worthwhile. He was her rock, her mentor and her friend. He had handed her the key to the box that contained her ambition, and she had turned it.

'Social media is the best way to reach today's consumer,' she read, 'but users of social media are tech savvy – they know how to filter unwanted messages. So in order to reach your target audience, you have to earn their permission. Our strategy to take you to this point is—'

Words swam before her eyes. Perhaps a coffee? She glanced at her watch. Only an hour till lunch; surely she could get through till then?

Ten minutes later, her phone rang. Molly glanced at the screen. It was Lexie Gordon. The interruption was both a pleasure and an irritant. She'd just got her head into the document and had found a seam of concentration – but it was always good to hear from Lexie. In the headlong, giddy world she'd plunged herself into, it was all too easy to forget there was another world outside – a world of friends, and family, and babies.

'Have you got a minute? You're not in a meeting or anything? I never know when's best to call you.'

'You're fine. I'm just working on some papers.'

Molly stood up and walked across to the window. The office Barnaby had located had a stunning view of the London skyline, and because the river flowed past the windows, there was light, and space and a feeling of being able to breathe. She tilted her head from side to side and rolled her shoulders. The cramped muscles in her neck eased and she felt the stress begin to fall away.

'How are you?' she said. 'How's Keira? Are you painting yet?'

Lexie laughed. It was good to hear her laugh. Molly could picture her in her mind, sitting in the airy nursery at The Gables, holding the baby to her chest, the sunlight streaming onto her ladybird-red hair. Motherhood became Lexie in the most surprising of ways. Molly was used to her friend in paint-smeared dungarees, lost in a world of her own creation for days on end, or – the flipside of that intensity – passionately arguing some cause. Being a mother had brought her slap up against pressing practicalities, like changing a nappy or feeding, and had softened her sharper edges.

'Painting? Not a chance. I never realised just how much a baby takes over your life.'

It had happened quickly for Lexie. She'd been at such a low ebb after Jamie died, she'd fallen out with Patrick, started out along a false trail, then found happiness. Within a year, there had been three of them. Deep inside her, Molly again felt the tugging ache she could only define as emptiness. To have a child … to be loved as Lexie was loved …

'I thought you swore it wouldn't make any difference to your life.'

'Hah! Talk about naive!' Lexie's familiar laugh rang down the line. 'You should see Patrick, Moll. He's totally besotted. He's discovered Skype and whenever he's away he's on the line every spare minute. He can't get back quickly enough. I swear he's more in love with Keira than he is with me.'

The tugging turned into a stab. 'I'm sure that's not true.'

'I'll get back to painting soon. Mum's desperate to look after Keira. She's offered to do a couple of days a week to give me some free time. But it's a bit difficult because of Adam – oh!'

She broke off.

'Adam? What about Adam?'

'Shit. I didn't mean to say anything. Forget it.'

'Lexie? You can't stop now. What about Adam?'

'I suppose I … What the hell. I let Adam have the cottage at Fleming House.'

'Your studio?' Molly's forehead creased into a frown. A police boat raced past on the river, its wake crashing onto the banks with a rolling white-topped wave. 'Adam's in your studio?'

'It's only temporary. He sold the house.'

'I know he sold the house. He gave me my share. So he hasn't bought anything else yet, and he's sponging off you? Lexie, you shouldn't let him take advantage.'

'He's not. It's not an issue. I offered.'

'Can't he stay at his parents' place?'

'I think they've sold up too,' Lexie said vaguely. 'I don't really know. Anyway, it's only temporary.'

Molly realised that she was desperately out of touch. That was her choice, of course. She didn't really want to know what Logan had done – it was bad enough knowing the effects of his misdeeds on Adrienne and the boys. Blair King would survive. They'd paid the money they owed back to the bank. Adam had told her everything was fine; he and his father hadn't done anything wrong.

'He is looking for somewhere, I take it?' she said. 'He isn't just taking advantage of your good nature?'

'No, honestly, I offered it to him. Anyway, he's going

to visit his folks in Italy soon. I'm planning to get some work done while he's away.'

'A holiday,' Molly said. 'How nice.'

It was uncharitable to feel irritated, and anyway, it was none of her business.

Lexie changed the subject. 'Listen, I didn't call about Adam. I called to ask you a big favour.'

'Shoot.'

'I wondered – Patrick and I wondered – if you'd be Keira's godmother.'

Molly squealed. Around her, heads lifted enquiringly. She turned back to the window and tried to lower her voice.

'Wow! Godmother! Of course I will, thank you, thank you, thank you!'

'Fantastic. The service is a fortnight on Tuesday. You will be able to get here, won't you? We'd have it on the Sunday but, typically, Patrick's going to be away.'

'I'll put it in the diary this minute.'

'You'll write it in indelible ink?' Lexie knew how Molly operated.

'Thick marker pen. Promise.'

After that, there was no need for coffee – excitement took her through the day.

It was the first day for weeks that she managed to get home at a decent hour. As a bonus, Julian was there too.

'Darling! I didn't like to ring, but I was hoping you'd be here. I've bought steaks. Are you on?'

'Yum, totally.' She pulled open the fridge door. There was precious little inside. 'Listen, I'll nip out and get a few luxuries in as well. Olives to pick on? Or would you prefer nuts? I'll get a good bottle of claret to go with the steak. Are there potatoes? Do we need salad? I'll go now, then we can both flop.'

'Whoa there!' Julian eyed her with amusement. He started to tick off a list on his fingers. 'Steak: check. Green salad: check. Olives: check. Red wine: check – but it's a Chilean Merlot, is that all right? Two bottles, by the way. Spuds? I bought one of Ricardo's special gratin dauphinois, all ready to pop in the oven, will that do? I can't cook chips and I couldn't bear the thought of those soggy things from the chippie down the road. It's all in that shopping bag by the sink. I haven't had time to decant stuff yet.'

'You've thought of everything, you darling. But what can I get? I want to contribute too. You're too good to me.'

'No-one could be too good to you, sweetie. Tell you what, if you really want to fetch something, why not nip down to the deli on the corner and get some ice cream for afters?'

Molly pulled her coat back on. 'If you open one of those bottles, I'll be back before you even pour my wine.'

Julian laughed. 'Righty ho. I'll slip into something more comfortable while you're out.'

She bought ice cream. At the checkout she spotted two double chocolate and hazelnut brownies, the last in a tray of home-baked goodies, and bought those too.

They'd finished the steak and all the side dishes, they'd demolished the ice cream and brownies, and they'd nearly finished the second bottle of wine as well, when Julian said sleepily, 'Forgot to tell you, darling. A hideous-looking official envelope arrived today.'

'For me?'

Molly was feeling very mellow. She was full of great food and the wine was making her head spin just ever so

slightly, in a happy kind of way. It was the first time –
probably since she'd arrived in London – that she'd felt
truly relaxed.

'Wonder if it's a jury duty summons. It's marked
"Sheriff Court" on the outside. They won't be able to
make you do it now you're down here, will they?'

'Shouldn't think so. I'll have to let them know I've
moved. How did it reach me? I suppose Lady Fleming
must have forwarded it.'

Julian rolled onto his side on the deep down-filled
cushion of the large sofa and reached out to the small
occasional table at the far end.

'Here it is. I meant to give it to you earlier. Just as well
I remembered. It wouldn't do not to answer them or you'd
end up in jail for contempt of court.' He giggled. 'Don't
worry, sweetie, I'd smuggle you in red wine and ice
cream.'

Molly curled her long legs under her and took the
proffered envelope. 'That's odd. It hasn't been
forwarded.'

'What d'you mean?'

'It's been addressed here. Look.' She thrust it under
Julian's nose.

He squinted down at the window. The address was
clearly typed and hadn't been scored out or tampered
with.

'They must've got the address from some other
documentation somewhere.'

'Suppose so.' She slipped a finger under the flap and
ripped it open.

'Oh my God.'

'What?' He sat upright abruptly. A few drops of red
wine splashed onto the cream carpet. It was a measure of
his concern at her reaction that he didn't notice.

Molly's hand was across her mouth. In days gone by she might have tried to hide her shock behind a curtain of hair, but now there was no hiding.

'What?' Julian demanded again.

'It's my divorce papers,' she whispered, dropping the letter onto her lap. 'There's an affidavit from Adam. And—' she turned it over, 'another one. A statement from Alexa Gordon.' She stared at Julian, her eyes pale. 'She's my best friend, Julian. My best friend has signed a sworn statement that my marriage is over.'

'Well,' Julian said, but not ungently, 'isn't it?'

Chapter Seven

Jean said to Adam, 'I need to speak to you.'

'I'm listening.'

He was in the cottage, looking at the small screen of his tablet and sifting through the jobs listed by one of the top recruitment agencies. It was a thankless task. He'd promised himself a break with his parents in Italy, but they'd only just finished packing up and gone out there, so it seemed a little unfair to arrive on their doorstep. They needed time to themselves and a chance to adapt to their new situation. Besides, he might be handed a paintbrush.

'I'd rather you came to the farm.'

Adam stopped looking at the screen and sat upright. 'Are you all right, Jean? You sound really—'

'What do I sound like? Don't answer that,' she said quickly. 'Just come. I'll fill you in when you get here.'

'OK, fine. Of course I'll come. When would suit you?'

'What about elevenses? I've baked a carrot cake.'

Adam laughed. 'You don't need to bribe me, but it works. I'll be there by eleven.'

'See you then.'

Adam cut the call and sat in the studio, frowning. His aunt was as sharp as anyone he knew. She was tough too, but although she never complained, he knew Geordie's death had hit her hard. Since Blair King had folded, he'd been up at the farm every other day, doing what he could to help, particularly with the heavy work, but the strain on his aunt was evident in her increased stoop, the way she found any and every excuse to serve cups of tea, and the unexpected and sudden lowering of her standards of dress and presentation. She'd never been glamorous, but she'd always been neat and correct, with her perfectly matched twin sets, her tweed skirts (straight save for a kick pleat at the back), her laced flat brogues. Recently, she'd taken to leaving her hair loose and often unkempt instead of twirling it into the tidy bun at the base of the neck, and it made her look witchy. She kept her wellies on in the kitchen, a lifetime no-no. And the twin sets were gone – or, at least, never worn with the correct matching piece. A forest green jumper was topped with a pale yellow cardi, a heathery purple top with scarlet. She didn't even seem to notice, and Adam hadn't the heart – or, indeed, the words – to say anything.

He closed the tablet down. There were no jobs worth applying for today anyway. There were precious few at all in the legal world. It wasn't as if he was eager for another job as a lawyer. There wouldn't be another partnership; anything he scraped up would be some lowly associate position, and that only if he were lucky. He was sliding down a very large snake in the board game of careers, and most of the ladders had been removed.

There was a heavy thud at the front door. He'd been so absorbed in his thoughts he hadn't even heard a car.

'Lexie! Hello!'

Lexie Gordon was standing on the doorstep, Keira in her arms, snuggled under a cosy blanket. He lifted one corner carefully. Dark lashes curled long on a plump cheek, softly curved lips formed into a peaceful 'O', then sucked with unconscious contentment at an imaginary nipple.

'She's so perfect.'

Lexie laughed. 'All babies are perfect when they're asleep. Little angels. Just wait till she wakes. She'll turn into a demanding monster, yelling for service. Milk now, Mummy! Clean bum, Mummy! Cuddles now, Mummy! Play with me, Mummy! Sing to me—'

'OK, I get the picture.' Adam laughed. 'Come in.'

They made for the studio, where the wood burner was merrily ablaze. Lexie laid Keira down on the rug. 'I'd forgotten how perfect this room is when it's like this. I almost like it better than any other time of the year. The light's fabulous, you don't feel you're missing out on the sunshine, and it's so cosy with the stove on.'

'You just caught me. I'm heading over to the farm. Coffee?'

'No, I'm fine. Thanks.'

She slipped off her coat and sat, cross-legged, by her baby, one finger tracing the contours of her cheek with gentle delicacy.

Adam gazed at her enquiringly. 'So—?'

'I can't believe I've produced her. It's such an incredible thing to do. You know – one minute, it's just you, then suddenly there's another being here, and you've made her and you're completely responsible for her. It's a beautiful thing.' She glanced up at Adam. 'Awesome.'

The urge to reproduce – no, more than that, to be a *father* – had been working its way up to the skin from somewhere near the core of his being for some time now. Longer, maybe, than he had understood. He and Molly – they'd had one conversation, then that had been it. One brief passing comment when they'd been little more than teenagers. *I don't want children, do you? God, no.* Neither of them had ever broached the subject again. She was so darned ambitious, that was the problem.

Or – had it just been Molly? Did he not bear some

responsibility too? Maybe she thought that he still thought …

'It's lovely to see you, Lexie,' he said, pulling himself together, 'but if you don't want coffee, and I'm assuming you weren't "just passing", would it be rude to ask why you've come? Only, I have to go out.'

'Oh, yes, sorry.' Lexie smiled up at him. Keira whimpered and she scooped the baby up in her arms and rocked her gently to and fro. 'You've kept this place looking really nice,' she said, looking around the room.

Oh, so that's it, Adam thought, despondency hovering like a rain-laden cloud preparing to burst over him. She wants her studio back.

'Mum's offered to look after Keira a couple of days a week—'

'And you want to start painting again. That's fine, Lexie, I'll move out as soon as you need me to. Just say the word.'

'You don't need to move out,' she said quickly. 'I can work in this room even if you're still sleeping here. It would only be, like, nine to four a couple of days a week.'

'It's really kind of you, but you'd be more comfortable having the place to yourself. When were you thinking of starting?'

She grimaced apologetically. 'Soon. Ish. Whatever suits you.'

'Leave it with me. I'll start looking around. OK?'

'Oh, Adam, I don't want to turf you out, really I don't. I feel so mean. I can wait, there's no rush.'

The first few drops of rain began to splash, the cold drips of the depression he'd been struggling to keep at bay for so long. He'd only staved it off by moving here – for a short time, he'd felt safe, but now he realised the feeling had been fragile. This was Lexie's place, not his.

Wherever he was going to end up, there was no future within these four walls for him.

'Don't apologise. It's your studio. Give me a couple of weeks. Will that work?'

'Perfect.' Lexie scrambled to her feet as Keira began to grizzle. 'Listen, I'm going to head home. If I start to feed and change her I'll be here for ages.'

'You can stay. I don't need to be here.'

'No.' She shook her head. 'It'll be easier at home. I can be back there in fifteen minutes. She'll probably doze off in the car anyway.'

The kitchen door at the farm was open, as it always was. Adam stepped into the room and felt the tug of the familiar, tinged with sadness. The lights were all on, but there was no sign of Jean.

Once, there would have been dogs to greet him. Bruno and Jack, Rufus and Caro – he remembered them all, from across the years. Working dogs. The farm was their territory, and the kitchen. Only the last one, Caro, had ever been allowed further into the house. Jean had told him that Caro had been so insistent on sleeping with Geordie during his illness that she'd whined at the kitchen door for hours until Jean had finally given in and let her go to him. But Caro died the day after her master, and Jean hadn't replaced the dog.

She should, Adam thought. A dog would help. She wouldn't have to get a puppy. A rescue dog would be less work.

He leant on the back of a chair and surveyed the room. She hadn't changed anything in years, so far as he could see. The same old kettle sat by the Aga, and the special Aga toasting gadget, blackened with age, was propped next to it, as it always had been. The clock on the wall was a relic from the 1960s and the plastic holder for the tea towel next to the sink dated back even earlier; the pot stand with the battered Le Creuset pots had been there for ever; the wooden towel rail on the back of the door, with its roller towel in a perpetual loop – when had that gone out of fashion, for heaven's sake? The towel that was on it now was white with a single peppermint green stripe. He remembered it from when he'd used to visit as a boy.

Only the lack of human presence made the room feel different. No dogs, no Geordie – no Jean, for that matter. Where was she?

He was just about to head out to the farm to look for her when the handle of the back door turned, the door gave its familiar creak, and Jean appeared, pushing her grey hair back from her face distractedly.

'I saw your car outside. Sorry I wasn't here when you arrived. A fox had got one of the ducks and I wanted to give it a decent burial.' When she smiled, as she did now, he could glimpse the old Jean. 'There wasn't enough left to eat.'

She shoved the door closed and turned her face up to Adam's for a kiss. 'You haven't put the kettle on?'

'I'm just in. Here.' Adam pulled a chair out from under the table and helped her to sit. 'I'll do it, you take a rest.'

'I'm not completely incapable, you know,' Jean grumbled, but an appreciative sigh escaped as she settled herself.

Adam filled the kettle and lifted the lid of the hotplate. Water hissed out from under the kettle as it made contact with the heat. Familiar, comforting sounds. He leant back against the Aga and crossed his arms. Jean was looking tired. Geordie's death had diminished her, although she still had grit. Look at how she was sitting – bolt upright, her back ramrod straight, her hands on her knees.

'What did you want to talk about?' he asked.

'I'll wait till you've made the coffee. The cake's in the usual place.'

He found the old cream and green cake tin and lifted plates out from the cupboard and knives from the drawer.

'There are paper napkins in the other one,' she said, watching him.

Adam smiled. She might be aging, but everything still had to be done correctly.

He found the napkins and pulled two out, folded them neatly into triangles and laid them on the plates under the knives, just as she liked them.

'The cake looks superb, Jean, you're such a great baker.'

'Just a small piece for me, dear. Half that. Now,' she said, the cake untouched on her plate, 'here's what I wanted to say, and please don't interrupt until I've finished. This place is too much for me. The house is demanding enough, but running the farm as well – I know we've got – I've got – good people helping, but honestly? It's the responsibility. And the never-endingness of it all. I've had enough, Adam.'

Adam opened his mouth but she held up a warning hand. 'I've been thinking about it ever since Geordie died. In fact, Geordie and I discussed this, but I haven't talked about it till now because I wanted to be sure.'

She's going to sell it, thought Adam. *She's going to sell Forgie End Farm and another precious part of my childhood will have gone for ever.*

'If you'd talked about this before Blair King folded, I'd have been able to take care of everything for you, Auntie. But right at the moment – I'm sorry, but I can't handle the sale. It's a shame, because it'll add quite a lot

269

to the costs of—'

'Didn't I ask you not to interrupt?' Jean's smile held a hint of exasperation.

'Sorry.'

'There will be legal work involved, but it's probably right and proper you don't do it anyway. Not when it involves you.'

'Sorry?' he said again, the inflection quite different.

Jean lifted her hands from her knees and placed them flat on the table. 'Here's what I'd like to propose. I want you to manage the farm. I'll move out of here so that you can have the house to yourself, and I'll move to the cottage near the south perimeter gate. I'd like to fence off half an acre or so around it – I couldn't give up my hens and I'd like to grow flowers. I've had enough of crops to last me a lifetime, but I really fancy surrounding myself with colour and beauty.'

Astonishment silenced him.

'Well? It seems to me to be a good solution. After all, as I understand it, you haven't got a job and you haven't got anywhere to live now that your folks have sold up and moved to their house in Umbria. Your mother told me you gave all your money to Molly,' she leaned towards him, 'which I thoroughly approve of, by the way.'

'You'd like me to manage the farm? But I've got no experience at all.'

'I'll teach you. You've got a good head and there's men to help on the land.'

'It'd be such a change.'

'You don't want it.' Jean slumped back in her chair. 'I was afraid of that. You're a lawyer. I told Geordie that but he was quite sure you had farmer somewhere deep in your core, and I thought that now life has changed for you—'

That clock had always had a loud tick. It seemed to be

exactly half the speed of his heart.

'Of course, it's not the best place for a single man. We thought – we could see Molly – it seemed to us she'd fit right in here.'

'We're getting divorced. She's signed the papers.'

'Oh dear. Well, I suppose that might make a difference to what you want to do.'

Jean looked around at the faded walls. 'It needs freshening up. I've been too busy, and anyway, when you live in a place you don't notice. But I do look at those telly programmes sometimes and someone with a bit of an eye for these things could make this place look pretty. I believe Belfast sinks and flagstone floors are quite the thing at the moment.'

'How would you see the arrangement working?'

'The farm is a business. You'd get a salary as the manager, and the tenancy of the house would be part of the salary. If it works out, we might look at making you a director in a year or two.'

Adam's brain was whirling with the unexpectedness of it.

'I've spoken to your father about it.' She smiled at Adam. 'Your father's all in favour.'

'Really? But he always wanted me to be a lawyer. He was so angry when Geordie walked out of the family firm.'

'The old feud? He's got over it. They made it up. Your father may be wiser than you think, Adam. Maybe he never wanted to recognise it, but he knows your heart wasn't in lawyering.'

James hadn't forced Adam to study law. The assumption that was what he wanted had been Adam's.

'Well, there it is. It's an offer. If you don't want to take it up, I'll advertise for a manager. I don't want to talk you

271

into something else your heart's not in – farming's a hard life, I can't pretend it's not. You've got to have a love for the life. You can't pick it up and put it down. You're out there all weathers, and it can be chancy. However hard you work, there are always risks – blight, infestations, the weather. And the paperwork gets worse and worse—'

'You're not doing a good job of selling it.'

Adam stood up and walked across to the window. It looked out over the backyard. However tired she might be feeling, Jean still kept it tidy. A tractor parked in the far corner was the only sign that the place was still a working farm. It was surprisingly pretty. Across the yard, the wall of one of the double-storey stone outbuildings was pierced by two large arches, leading into the space where carts would once have been housed. The coachman would have lived in the flat above. There were other outbuildings too, all empty. Geordie had long since erected modern barns further down the paddock, out of sight of the house and much more functional than these cramped old spaces.

They were ripe for conversion.

'If we could find some money to invest, those buildings would make fantastic holiday lets, you know,' he said thoughtfully. 'Or you could let some of them to businesses. Building the new barns was very farsighted of Geordie. There's a lot of potential at Forgie End other than just farming the land.'

He turned. Jean was smiling.

'I'm thinking,' she said, 'that maybe that's a yes.'

Chapter Eight

'We got through! We've made it to the next stage!' Barnaby was more excited than Molly had ever seen him.

Molly looked up from her screen, trying to switch her focus from the running order for the new whisky launch at the Gherkin she was in the middle of organising to tune in to whatever was prompting Barnaby's excited outburst.

'Great! What are you talking about, by the way?'

'Only the public health campaign.' Barnaby looked smug.

Around her, people started to clap and chatter.

'Oh my God!'

'Fantastic!'

'Thank God for that, after all the work we all put in.'

Molly stood up and flung her arms around Barnaby. 'That's brilliant,' she said, rather more quietly, 'and you really deserve it. Now all we have to do is go in there and wow them.'

'We'll need to start rehearsing.'

'Who did we decide was going in?'

'Just you, me and Ken. Me as principal, you on the event-management side of it, and Ken on the digital and social media elements.'

'Yes, that sounds right. When's the pitch?'

'Next Tuesday, at their offices. There'll be—' he scanned his notes, '—six of them. A bit intimidating, but we'll keep our team really tight. If there are too many people we'll lose control.'

'Next Tuesday?' Molly picked up her diary. 'Oh God, no. I can't do it, Barnaby.'

Barnaby looked startled. 'Can't do it? What do you mean?'

'That's the day of the christening. Lexie and Patrick's baby, Keira. I'm godmother. Remember, I told you? I've got the air ticket already.'

'Can't be helped.'

'What do you mean?'

Heads were swivelling in their direction. A public row was unthinkable. Molly put her diary down and nodded in the direction of Barnaby's glass-walled office. In the open plan space, he was the only one to have any kind of privacy.

'I can't do it,' she hissed as soon as the door had swung shut.

He crossed his arms. 'There isn't a choice, Molly. This isn't some game, this is business. Our business, let me remind you.'

'I've made a commitment. It's the first time I've asked for even a single day off, Barnaby.'

'You're committed to Fletcher Keir Mason. Don't think I'm unsympathetic, but it's impossible.'

'Can't you take someone else in with you?'

'No.' He uncrossed his arms and looked at her more compassionately. 'I really am sorry, Molly, but it won't do. It has to be the three directors for this one.'

'Can't we change the date?'

'You know that's not on. We have to go in, every inch eagerness; we can't mess them around before we've even got the contract.'

Molly could feel tears pricking and made a ferocious attempt to blink them away. She'd have to let Lexie and Patrick down – how awful was that? They probably wouldn't even want her to be Keira's godmother if she couldn't make the effort to get to the christening, and she didn't blame them in the least.

'This is what you wanted, Molly,' Barnaby said, his voice gentle. 'This is the life you've chosen. You're doing a terrific job. Things are just beginning to work. Your friends will understand.'

'I expect they will.' Molly made a big effort and pulled herself together. She ran her fingers through her hair and smiled. 'We'd just better get the damn contract, that's all.'

'Good girl. Want me to call Lexie and explain?'

'Certainly not.'

'Right then.'

'Right.'

She tested the water with her father first, choosing the words of her confession with care as she strode out for a sandwich. The day had turned blustery and damp and she hadn't come prepared. She could feel drizzly drops of rain on her face as she walked. Too bad.

'I can't do it. You do see that, Dad, don't you?' she said into her mobile, dodging out of the way of first one car and then a bike as she tried, ill advisedly, to cross the road against the flow of traffic. 'I feel caught in a trap, but I don't see what else I can do. The business has to come first because there are many other people involved. People whose mortgages are depending on us winning new business.'

'It can't be helped, love. Lexie will understand.'

'Do you think so? Maybe she will, but I'm hating the thought of having to tell her. You know I can't stand letting people down.'

'I'm sure she'll find a way round it. She knows how important the new business is to you.'

'It shouldn't make me break promises to my friends.'

'These things happen. In the scale of things—'

He went quiet and Molly knew instantly what he was thinking of.

'I'm guessing there's still no news of Logan,' she said, without any hope.

'Not yet, love, no.'

Molly had arrived at the sandwich shop. Rain had started to trickle down her neck. She shrank into her jacket. It didn't help.

'You would tell me,' she said, 'if there was? Even if it was bad?'

'Course I would.'

Three people pushed past her, then a fourth. She didn't feel like standing here and she couldn't go inside and keep talking on the phone, not about things like this. She turned and carried on walking. A few yards further on, she stepped under an archway. There were still many passersby, but no eavesdroppers.

'I don't like not being up there with you,' she said.

'I'm fine. Adrienne went away again yesterday, so the boys are playing up a bit, but they're fine too.'

Molly sighed. She'd never thought that following her dream would be so difficult.

'Stick with it, darling,' Billy said, some intuition leading him to her innermost thoughts. 'It'll work out.'

'Thanks, Dad.'

'I won't keep you, love. You must have a million things to do. Call me tomorrow?'

'I will. Love you, Dad.'

'And you.'

She called Lexie at once, before she had time to think too much more about it. There was no choice, she'd accepted that, but she hated doing this.

Lexie was surprisingly philosophical. 'Ah well. I should have guessed there'd be something.'

'Lexie! I hope you don't think so badly of me.'

'It's just that you're always so busy. I know what your life's like. It's always been like that, and I'm guessing it's even worse now you're in London.'

'I don't let my friends down. At least, I try not to. You know I'd move heaven and earth to get there if I could.'

'I know. Don't upset yourself, Molly, it's not the end of the world.'

'It is to me!'

Lexie would have made the christening a priority. Lexie had always put her family first, even sacrificing her career to be with her parents after Jamie died. Molly, fiercely loyal though she was, found such choices more difficult.

'Keira's crying, I'll have to go.'

'Lexie – I guess you won't want me as a godparent now?' Molly held back tears.

'Of course I want you, honey, but I'll have to check if the godparents have to be present. I think they do.'

'Ohhh—'

'I'll get back to you. Don't beat yourself up, there'll be more.'

'More what?'

'Children. At least, I hope there will be.' The whimpering in the background became a wail. 'Got to go. Speak soon. Love you, bye!'

Molly stared at the phone. Why was it that everyone she knew was surrounded by family and she was on her own?

Don't be childish, she reproached herself, you've made your choices, just get on with it. By the time she'd queued for a sandwich and started marching back to the office, the rain had stopped and a watery sun was fighting its way through the clouds.

She didn't expect to hear from her father again so soon, but he called her at four. He never called her during working hours. Mostly he waited for her to call him. She snatched her mobile up from her desk and answered it at once.

'Hello, Dad? Is something up?'

'Logan's been found.'

'Logan!'

She bounced off her seat and ran out of the office.

'Logan's back? Tell me what happened. Where is he? Is he all right? What's happening? Do you need me?'

'Shhh, let me talk.'

'Sorry, Dad. Sorry. Tell me.'

She was breathless with nerves.

'I've just had a call from Adam—'

Of course Adam would know before she did. He'd be the first the police would tell. All the same, Molly couldn't help feeling cross. After all, Logan was her brother.

'—because his parents have just phoned him.'

'You're not making sense, Dad.'

'Give me a chance, will you? The Blairs have a place in Italy. They've moved out there permanently, and they came across Logan yesterday in their local bar.'

Umbria. The house on the hill. Molly pictured it instantly – she'd been there with Adam half a dozen times. It wasn't big, or pretentious, but it was very pretty, a rose-brick building in a quiet street in the village. It had breathtaking views across a valley full of olive trees. The bar was less than ten minutes away by foot. It was a small place, one room only, with tables that spilled out across

278

the pavement and, in high summer, onto the street itself. Bar Tosca. She could even see the neon sign above the door, a modern addition the locals liked to scoff at, although the owner, Gianni Lazzaro, was stupidly proud of it.

Logan and Adrienne had been there once. They'd dropped in for lunch when Adam and Molly had been visiting. She remembered a searingly hot summer's day. The boys had been tiny, Alastair grizzly and out of sorts in the oppressive heat, and they'd all wandered down to the bar and sat in the shade and fed the boys messily with pasta and ice cream.

If Logan had been found in the bar, it was because he wanted to be found.

'Is he all right?'

'He was drunk, apparently, and very scruffy.'

Logan, scruffy? Molly pictured him in his Savile Row suits and immaculate shirts and found 'scruffy' difficult to imagine.

'I think he'd run out of money. Rosemary and James got him back to the house and cleaned him up. They let him sleep till this morning, then fed him coffee and *bomboloni con la crema* and persuaded him to turn himself in to the police.'

'So he's in custody?'

'Apparently so. I think there'll be some formalities to go through, then they'll escort him back here.'

Molly sagged back against the marble clad wall. She was trembling. 'Thank God,' she said. 'Thank God they've found him, Dad.'

'Yes. It's not going to be easy, pet, but he's alive and he's safe.'

Billy's voice cracked and Molly found she was sobbing.

'Oh, Dad!'

'Molly, love—'

The lift halted and two members of staff walked out, staring at her curiously, then averting their eyes, embarrassed, but she didn't care about the tears. Logan was safe! The boys had a father. Adrienne had a husband. She had a brother. Billy had his son back. Whatever Logan had done wrong, they'd get through it.

'I'll come up.'

'I thought you—'

'I can't make the christening, there's something really important on that day, but I'll come up this weekend. To hell with the cost. I want to see Logan – and you and the boys and everyone.'

The need to be surrounded by her family had become overpowering.

Chapter Nine

Caitlyn decided not to inform the police about the incident with Ricky McQuade.

'I couldn't face the endless questions, Mum. I'd have to make statements, maybe stand up in court … I'd have to relive it again and again, be questioned by some eager young barrister keen to make his mark. They mightn't believe me.'

'There are witnesses – Wallace and Ailsa—'

'No! I won't have Ailsa dragged into it. She's shaken enough as it is.'

'Well, I do understand, lovey. If you're sure. But Ricky might—'

'He won't do that again. Not to me, anyway. You should have seen his face, Mum, when Wallace had him in a headlock. He was terrified.'

'Serves him right.'

'Yes, it does. Wonder if he confessed to his mother.'

'He didn't. But I told her.'

'You didn't!'

'I saw her down the street and gave her a right piece of my mind.'

'Bet she didn't believe you.'

'She didn't, not at first, but then she remembered Ricky coming in that night in a right old state with some cock and bull story about a fight and began to think about it.'

'Weren't you afraid she'd have a go at you?'

'Angie McQuade?' Joyce scoffed, laughing. 'I've known Angie since we were in school. She was all mouth and no brains then and she's no better now. She's not all bad, though. My reckoning is she'd have gone home and given him a skelping, or got that lout of a man of hers to do it, never mind that the lad's the same age as you. They always did beat their kids, the McQuades.'

'Didn't have much of an effect, not if they meant to teach them how to behave.'

'You're right at that.'

Malkie didn't phone for a week.

'Hi, Caitlyn, how's things going?'

His careful cheeriness hurt. He loved her, but he had no idea what had happened. If they hadn't quarrelled, he would have been taking her home, as he always did, and she would never have been exposed to Ricky and his friends.

She couldn't find the words to tell him. The whole episode was too vile, too painful, too degrading. If he'd dropped by instead of phoning, he would have seen the bruises and asked questions, and perhaps she would have fallen into his arms and everything would have been just like it was before.

'I'm fine,' she said coolly. 'You?'

'I'm OK. Been busy.'

'Right.' She paused, aching for consolation – but her hurt had begun to curdle into resentment, and distress was making her cool. 'Have you moved into the cottage yet?'

'Not yet. They're going to give it a lick of paint. Caitlyn?'

'Yes?'

'We need to talk, don't we?'

Despite herself, she was touched. Malkie was more of

a listener than a talker, and the suggestion must have cost him. She remembered her bruises.

'OK. Maybe next week?'

Now it was his turn to sound hurt. 'I get the point, Caitlyn. You want your independence. Fine. Give me a phone when you're ready.'

He cut the call abruptly.

Caitlyn closed her eyes. Why did life have to be so complicated?

'There's someone to see you,' Ailsa said. She'd closed the door to the hall, which Caitlyn thought was odd because normally they didn't bother unless it was very cold and they needed to keep out the draught.

Caitlyn was watching *Pointless*. The boys were playing upstairs and Isla May was round at Mariella's. She zapped the remote and the sound went off.

'Malkie?' she exclaimed, hope in her voice.

Ailsa shook her head violently. She was pulling strange faces and gesticulating at the hallway. 'It's Ricky McQuade,' she hissed. 'What do you want to do?'

Caitlyn leapt to her feet. 'Ricky's here?'

'Yup.'

'On his own?'

'Yup. Shall I send him away?'

Demons, Caitlyn thought, are better faced. She could not spend her life jumping at shadows. 'No. Show him in.' She clutched at Ailsa's hand. 'But stay with me?'

Ricky looked smaller by daylight. The face she'd last seen distorted and ugly was showing distinct signs of nervousness. His thin shoulders were hunched and he seemed to be fascinated by a spot on the carpet.

'Hello, Ricky,' Caitlyn said quietly.

He shifted his gaze reluctantly and looked at her, then

away again quickly. He cleared his throat. He clasped his hands together and started wringing them, then thrust them deep into the pockets of his jeans. He'd cleaned himself up for this visit. His hair, usually toneless and dull, looked recently washed, and his T-shirt was wrinkle free. He was wearing black leather shoes, not trainers. They even looked polished.

'Came to say I'm sorry,' he mumbled.

'I didn't hear you. What did you say?'

'I said I was fuckin' sorry!' He spat the words out like sour sweeties, but when he looked at her, he flushed. 'I didnae mean it, Caitlyn. It was all just words, you know, all that stuff I said. Just joshin'. I never thought you'd fancy the likes of me. You're sharp. You've always been clever. Me, I'm a waster, like my pa.'

Caitlyn almost felt sorry for him.

'I was drunk, ken? Too much o' the old—' He made a swigging gesture, lifting an imaginary bottle to his lips. 'An' the lads were cheering me on, ken? I didnae mean it—'

'No.' Caitlyn's voice trembled with suppressed fury. 'But you would have done it all the same, wouldn't you, if it hadn't been for Wallace and Ailsa.'

'No, I—' he flushed again. 'Maybe. Like I said, I was fu'. Blootered. Rat-arsed.'

'It's not an excuse for rape, Ricky.'

'Naw. Sheesh, Caitlyn, gie's a break. I said I was sorry, an' I am, honest.'

She wanted him to go. 'OK. Thanks for coming to tell me.'

He turned, obviously relieved.

'Ricky?'

'What? You're no' going tae tell the polis, are ye?'

'You could make something of your life. You're not so

stupid as you make out. Get a grip, get a job, do something useful.'

He shuffled his feet. The carpet held his attention completely.

'Aye,' he said at length. 'Mebbe yer right.'

Chapter Ten

Nothing on television or in the cinema, Molly decided, could prepare you for the stark reality of prison. She went in through the doors as uncertain sunlight faltered and died, and the rain began. She felt one single drip as she locked the car. It splashed on her arm and she studied it, unsettled. Another arrived on her hand even as she looked. By the time she had crossed the carpark and reached the formidable building, the splashes had turned to a torrent and the mood of determined cheerfulness with which she had left Billy's house had washed with it into the gutters and drains.

She steeled herself for the meeting she had longed for so keenly. Now that Logan was here, she found that the relief she had felt at his reappearance had changed into something altogether more complicated.

'You must hate me,' Logan said before she had a chance to catch her breath. 'I hate myself.'

Molly clutched the edge of the table as if its hardness could steady her, appraising her brother with a newly critical gaze, because he was no longer her hero. It was difficult not to be shocked by the way he looked. It wasn't the absence of expensive tailoring – he seemed clean and comfortable. The change in him came from inside. There was a restlessness and uncertainty that was new in him. He was still handsome, though the high cheekbones that had always defined his face seemed more prominent than ever. She no longer noticed the long eyelashes she had always admired, because the eyes they framed appeared so troubled. He had lost weight. The unremarkable sweatshirt and jogging pants – so far removed from his usual style – hung loosely on his frame. His fingers, which had always been elegant, looked as fragile as twigs as he tapped them restlessly on the table between them.

She said, a little uncertainly, 'I'm not here to judge you. That's the job of the court.'

'Believe me, there is no sterner judge than me.'

She'd lain awake half the night, planning everything she wanted to say. About how he'd let Billy down and destroyed his family. About the clients whose money he had stolen and spent for his own enjoyment. About the way in which he had brought down Blair King and caused the loss of livelihood of dozens more families. About the way he'd nearly destroyed her chance of a career, because if there hadn't been enough left over from the sale of the house, she would not have been able to buy her way into Fletcher Keir Mason. The list had formed in her head in the hours before dawn and was there still.

It was a sizeable list of victims by any standards. She couldn't begin to imagine what had prompted his behaviour, but all the sentences she had formed in her mind deserted her as she looked at him. She'd thought she would be furious, but she only felt saddened. He looked broken.

She reached across the table. He yielded his hand without resistance, but it felt limp and lifeless.

'I don't understand, Logan. Why? Why did you do it? You earned a good salary.'

If he'd shrugged, the anger might have flooded in, but he didn't.

'There was never enough.'

'Tell me who started the deception – you or Agnes?'

'Agnes had been fiddling the books for years, but she was so clever at it that no-one had spotted it. I did though. And once I knew—'

'You did what?' Comprehension came in a flash. 'Logan! Don't tell me! Instead of revealing her fraud, you persuaded her to become a party to yours. Je-sus.'

'The day I realised, I was in a tight spot. I needed to find cash quickly for the boys' school fees. I had an idea – but I couldn't do it without her help.'

My brother, thought Molly. My brother has done this. She could find no words.

'I forged a false new client, set up a bank loan on his behalf, and suddenly there I was with a hundred thousand in a false account. It was that easy. Agnes helped move the money around. She got a big cut. And the more clients I invented, the easier it became.'

'You must have known it couldn't go on.'

'There was always that fear, but there was a wild excitement as well. I was on a weird high. And as time went on and everything kept going well, a kind of madness seemed to get into me. I began to feel invulnerable.'

He made a sudden gesture with his arm, startling her. She sat back abruptly.

'Didn't you ever think about what it would do to the firm?' Now the anger was coming. Molly could feel it bubbling to the surface and feared that it might become uncontrollable. She sat on her hands and forced herself to control her tone. 'You put the livelihood of dozens of people at risk.'

'I didn't think about that then. I have since.'

Logan sank his head onto his hands and looked beaten. She softened. 'Why did you run away, Logan? Why put us through all that frantic worry?'

She thought he wasn't going to answer. Silences, she was learning, marked another change in the brother she'd known. Eventually he said robotically, 'When Adam called … I was going to go into the office and face him … I opened the drawer for my car keys—'

'And?' she prompted as another silence began to drag out.

'I remembered I'd hidden a couple of false passports under a pile of stationery.'

'Oh God.'

'I know. It was stupid. But at the time, it was surprisingly easy. I drove all night. I was on a ferry to France before anyone realised I'd gone, and I kept going for months by operating a couple of the false accounts.'

For the first time, he lifted his head and met her gaze squarely. 'I knew it was going to end badly, of course. But that wasn't what made me give myself up to the Blairs.'

'Don't tell me it was your conscience,' Molly snapped with a sudden return of wrath, 'because I'm not sure I could believe that.'

She regretted the words as soon as they were out of her mouth. Logan shrank away from her and she sighed.

'Oh, forget it. Just tell me. You still had money, so why did you decide you'd had enough?'

'I was lonely.'

'Lonely?' She started to laugh. 'Well, that's the last thing I had imagined.'

'What did you imagine, Moll?'

She shrugged. 'God knows. Dad and I spent for ever wondering about you – if you were safe and well, if you'd been murdered by some gang you owed money to, if you might be in South America enjoying endless cocktails in Rio.'

'I didn't think about what you must be feeling. I was

too busy being sorry for myself. This whole thing has been about selfishness. Believe me, I've spent hours picking apart everything I've done, and there's no credit in any of it.'

She laid her hands on the table and spread her fingers. She still wore Adam's wedding ring on her left hand. It had never even occurred to her to take it off.

'So. You were saying you were lonely.'

'I spent months living more or less on my wits. There was little pleasure in it, I promise you. It's no life.'

Molly opened her mouth.

'Don't lecture me. You can believe it or not, but I missed Adrienne. I missed Dad. You too. But most of all, I missed the boys. Nursing a bottle of local vino plonko night after night in some tawdry local hostelry was no fun. You think about a lot of things, like what life's really for. It sounds trite, but believe me, that period I was on the run was probably the first time in my life I'd ever thought about stuff like that. And it didn't take me long to realise that without my family, none of the rest mattered at all. I was scared. Scared about what Adrienne would say, about what my boys would think of me and about Dad's opinion. But unless I came back, I'd never know.'

His smile was gone almost before it was there.

'It was sheer luck that I found myself near James Blair's place and remembered you raving about it.'

Molly knew the story by heart; she'd been over it a dozen times with Billy. How James and Rosemary had walked down to Bar Tosca one evening, as they often did, and been greeted by an agitated Gianni.

'There is a man,' he'd told them, 'says he knows you. I do not think this is possible. He is very – how do you say it? – *ubriaco*.'

'Drunk?'

'*Si.*'

It was a polite word for the state Logan had been in. He'd been almost too drunk to stand, his hair had been long and unkempt and he'd been sorely in need of a shower. Somehow, they had managed to get him home and into bed. To their credit, Molly thought, they had refrained from calling the police until the morning. Instead, they got him cleaned and fed, and were given some kind of rambling explanation of everything that had happened.

She said, her heart expanding painfully in her chest, 'Thank God you did.'

Again there was a flash of a smile, before it was gone and the restlessness was back.

'What can I do to help?'

'Just be there for my boys. It's going to be some time before I can be.'

When she left the prison, the rain had stopped and the air smelt fresh and damp. The sun was sinking lower on the horizon, but there was warmth on her skin. She closed her eyes and tilted her face to the skies, inhaling deeply. It had never occurred to her before what freedom meant.

Molly had picked up a hire car at the airport and driven straight to the prison. When she arrived at her father's house, it was Adrienne who answered the door.

'Oh! Hi!' she said, kissing her sister-in-law on both cheeks. 'I didn't realise you were going to be here.'

Adrienne was looking good. She was as neat as she'd always been, her hair well cut, her nails perfect. Molly would expect nothing less, because good grooming was second nature to Adrienne. But there was no sign of expensive designer clothes. She was wearing skinny jeans and a fuchsia pink sweater Molly recognised as from a high-street store.

'I finished a day earlier than expected. I'm really glad, because I haven't seen you for ages. Come on in. Billy's out at the park with the boys; he'll be back soon.'

Being invited into your own childhood home was the first of many strange moments. The second was the sudden realisation that with Adrienne at home, there would be no room for her.

'Been to see Logan?'

'Yes.'

'What did you think?'

'About?'

'How did he seem to you?'

Molly eyed Adrienne cautiously. They had never been close and she was uncertain how to handle the question, so she parried it with another.

'What's your impression?'

Adrienne's face crumpled. It was the first time Molly had ever seen her display any kind of weakness. She caught Adrienne's arm.

'Sit down. Here.' She guided her to the sofa and put an arm across her shoulder. 'You'll get through this. We all will.'

Adrienne took out a tissue and dabbed at her eyes. 'I know. Thank you.' She smiled shakily. 'I try not to let the boys see me like this. I try to be positive all the time, but it's hard.'

'I bet.'

'Your dad's fantastic. I couldn't have survived without him.'

Molly's earlier moment of resentment at Adrienne's presence in her home evaporated. 'He loves having you here. It's given him purpose.'

'I know.' Again there was a wry smile. 'Thank

heavens something positive has come out of this sorry mess. And if I'm honest, I'm loving working again too. Now that I look back on all those years I swanned around doing nothing, I can see they were pretty hollow. Being forced to fend for my boys has brought meaning to my life too.'

How odd, Molly thought, that they should all turn full circle. Lives that had been empty were filled with new meaning, but her life, which had once seemed so satisfactory ... What did what she was doing signify?

While Adrienne made coffee, she called Lexie, realising that she should have arranged to see her as soon as she'd known she was coming. She'd been too busy.

There was no answer at The Gables. She tried her mobile. It was switched off. Perhaps she was painting. Keira might be with her grandmother. Maybe Lexie and Patrick were travelling.

It occurred to Molly that she knew almost nothing about Lexie's life these days. Once she would have known her friend's every thought and feeling. The day the baby had been born ...

She remembered every detail of that day, the hours of waiting and helping, of being needed, of excitement and nervous anticipation. That day, she had truly been whole.

'Molly love, you're here!'

'Hello, Dad, hello, boys.'

They arrived back from their walk glowing.

'Look what I found!' Alastair said, holding out his hand to reveal a dark feather. It shone, iridescent green and gold, in the sun streaming in the kitchen window.

'It's beautiful.'

'Grandpa says it's from a starling. I'm going to look it up.'

Ian was not to be left out. 'I found a pebble. Look.'

She took it and closed her hand around it, enjoying its smooth warmth. 'It's very pretty, Ian. What a lovely shape.'

'Grandpa's got a book about stones and things. He's going to help me iden ... idenny—'

'Identify,' Alastair scoffed.

'That's what I said.'

Billy smiled. 'Now, boys, let's find the right books. Great to see you, Molly love.'

'And you.' She hugged him close. It was good to be here. 'Listen, while you're doing that, I'll call the Travelodge down the road. You're overflowing here.'

'You will not. I'll sleep on the sofa. It's just one night.'

'Don't be silly, Dad.'

Adrienne said, 'There's no problem. The boys can share my bed for one night. You and I can use their bunks.'

Alastair groaned. Ian pulled a face, but gave Molly a cuddle.

'I like it when you're here, Auntie Molly,' he said, looking oddly vulnerable.

She put her arms round him. 'And I like being here,' she said, burying her face in his hair. 'And most of all, I like seeing you.'

That made Alastair want a hug too. They might be boys, all bravado and swagger, but underneath they must be bleeding. Their relationship with their father could take years to rebuild.

Adrienne cooked supper, moving round the kitchen with ease and familiarity. Earlier, Molly had believed that Logan's dishonesty had crowned no winners. Now she saw that that wasn't true.

'I'm exhausted,' Adrienne yawned, ascending the

ladder neatly and collapsing on the upper bunk. 'Still, it's good to keep busy, isn't it?'

By the time Molly had worked out a reply, she realised that all that could be heard from above her was the steady sound of the deep breathing of someone who was fast asleep.

Chapter Eleven

Molly flew back to London the next afternoon. Far from resolving the queries in her mind, the visit had opened up new issues.

She called Julian as she joined the queue to get through security.

'Hi, it's me. Are you going to be in this evening?'

'I was thinking of going out to a pub. I met a guy last night at a party – he's pretty cool.'

'Oh.'

'Did you have something in mind, sweetie?'

'Never mind.'

'I haven't decided yet. I don't have to go.'

'Julian, I don't want to get in the way of your happiness. Go,' she said, not meaning it. She wanted Julian to be there. She needed a friend.

She slipped the phone into her bag and rummaged around for her cosmetics. She was still a long way from the scanners – the queue snaked along and back, along and back several times, but it was moving quickly. She straightened up, and found herself staring right into the eyes of Sunita Ghosh.

She looked away quickly. The last thing she needed right now was to have to talk to Adam's girlfriend.

The queue moved. Sending up a little prayer of thanks, she moved with it.

Thirty yards further, she found herself doubling back, and half way along this length, she realised that it was inevitable that she'd pass Sunita again. She saw the dark, glossy hair approaching – six people away, five people, four – and had to make up her mind how to react. Ignoring her completely would be bizarre. Now there was just one head between them.

She gave a small, quick smile. The queue moved raggedly on, and she was safely past.

Molly felt the stress building. There was still one loop to go before the queues diverged, and there was no way they could pretend the coincidence hadn't happened. She glanced ahead. An elderly couple, towing large cases, were deep in conversation. Behind her, two Japanese youths were chatting incomprehensibly. There was no chance of engaging anyone in conversation so that she could pass Sunita without having to acknowledge her existence.

When they were next to each other, Sunita said, 'Are you going back to London?'

Molly nodded. 'You?'

'I'm off to London too. I've got a meeting first thing tomorrow morning.'

'You don't like the red-eye?'

'I don't mind, but I have to see my cousins. There's some family business.' She smiled, her teeth white and perfect. 'There's always family business.'

'Tell me about it,' Molly said, in heartfelt accord on this, at least.

How long would they have to stand here like this? Thank God Adam wasn't with her. That would have multiplied the embarrassment a hundredfold. She hadn't spoken to Adam since Logan had been brought back to face justice. He'd be pleased about that, naturally, while Molly's feelings at seeing her brother again were heavily tempered by the thought of the months that lay ahead while the case was being prepared for court, and the horror of all the publicity that was sure to follow.

'Hope the flight's not delayed,' Sunita said. 'What flight are you on?'

'British Airways. You?'

Molly's heart sank. 'British Airways too.'

'See you, then.'

'See you.'

The queue moved and their paths diverged. Thank heaven.

Molly was sitting in one of the many cafés scattered around the airport when Lexie called.

'Hi! Sorry we missed you. I didn't know you were coming up; I thought you were far too busy.'

'It's just Tuesday that's the problem, Lex. I did explain we have a critical pitch on Tuesday.'

'Oh, that's right. Listen, I've sorted that. Apparently you can have a proxy godparent; you don't actually have to be there, so I'm arranging for Adam to be your proxy. That's what I was doing yesterday.'

'*Adam*'s going to be my proxy?' Molly was shocked.

'It's only a formality, Molly. You're the real godparent.'

'But why Adam?'

'I bumped into him when he was getting the last of his things out of the cottage. It seemed like a good idea. That's all. Don't read anything else into it.'

'Oh.' Exclusion was one thing, Adam being her substitute was quite another. 'How is he?' she managed to say.

'He's terrific. He's moving into Forgie End Farm.'

'Forgie End? His uncle's farm?'

'Yup. Didn't you know?'

'No, I didn't. What's he doing there?'

'His aunt's asked him to manage the place. She's

moved to one of the cottages, apparently. She's had enough of farming; she just wants to keep hens and grow flowers. Can't say I blame her. She is in her seventies, after all.'

'What does Adam know about managing a farm?'

Lexie laughed. 'Nothing. But I imagine he's a quick learner. Jean Blair will still be around and there are a few guys who've been working there for a while – they'll keep him right. Anyway, you know how much he used to love that place as a boy, and he'd definitely had enough of law after Blair King went belly up.'

Molly shuddered. 'Don't.'

'Sorry. Listen, it's hard for everybody. Adam's still not over it, but he's obviously thrilled that he's got something else to do with his life. But that house is vast. He's camping out in one room and the kitchen at the moment. I've told him he needs a woman to do the place up. I'm sure it's got bags of potential, but there's no way he'll have time. Or the inclination, for that matter. Molly? Are you still there?'

Molly cleared her throat. 'I'm here.'

'Sorry, was I being tactless?'

'What about Sunita?'

'Who? Oh, the Asian woman. The one we met at Loch Melfort? I believe that's over.'

Molly put her cup down because her hand had started to shake. 'Is it? Why?'

'Heavens, Molly, I don't know Adam well enough to probe into stuff like that. Anyway, I told him to join some online dating agencies. He'll never find anyone unless he does. He's going to be stuck away in that place with precious little chance of socialising.'

'Good idea.'

'And what about you?'

'What about me?'

'Have you met anyone else? London must be full of yummy men with the same aims and ambitions as you.'

'I imagine it is, but I've been too busy to find one. There's Julian.'

'Who's Julian?'

'My flatmate.'

'The gay?' Lexie laughed. 'Great as a friend, I'm sure, but—'

'He's as much as I can cope with right now, believe me.'

'Oh – I forgot to tell you.'

'Tell me *what*?'

'Patrick proposed. We're getting married.'

Molly yelped. 'What? Oh my God! When did this happen?'

'A couple of weeks ago. Mum had Keira overnight – the first time she's done that. By the way, it went really well. She told me she'll have her again any time—'

'Lexie!'

'Oh, sorry. I guess you're not wanting all the details about my beloved daughter. I forget not everyone's as besotted as we are. Yes, well, we left Keira with Mum and Patrick took me for a special meal at Martin Wishart's in Leith, my all-time favourite restaurant, and he proposed.'

'And you haven't told me till now?'

Molly felt desperately hurt. Once upon a time Lexie would have dashed off to the Ladies to text her there and then.

'I didn't realise I hadn't. Sorry, Molly, honestly, but life's just so hectic these days, what with Keira and the christening and everything. Aren't you pleased?'

'Course I'm pleased. I'm thrilled. Truly. You'll be so happy.'

'I know. I can't believe it. All my dreams have come true. Except Jamie won't be there, of course.'

The grief Molly had felt when Jamie Gordon died had never left her, only now it had dulled to an ache that only surfaced on occasion. That whole period of her life now seemed unreal – not as though it had never happened, but shadowy and distant.

Lexie cut in on her thoughts. 'Listen, Molly, I know you won't mind, but I can't ask you to be a bridesmaid. It's just that – well, you can have a proxy godmother, but you can't have a proxy bridesmaid, can you? I mean, of course I hope you'll be there, but I can't take the risk. You do see, don't you?'

Molly tried to be brave. 'Of course I do. Don't worry about it. Who are you asking?'

'Cora Spyridis, Patrick's half sister. You remember her, don't you.'

'Of course I do. She ran The Maker's Mark, where you had your big exhibition.'

'She's coming back from Greece for the wedding.'

'When is it?'

'Next month. The third Saturday. I know it's really soon, but we're just keeping it small. We don't want anything fancy. There's too much to do with Keira around, and anyway, neither of us wants that whole showy thing. We're having the supper room at Fleming House, not the ballroom – that's far too big. The guy who took over from you is organising everything. You will come?'

'I'll put it in my diary in—'

'Indelible ink.' Lexie laughed. 'I know you will.'

Molly glanced up at the departures board above her head.

'Heavens, I'll have to run or I'll miss my flight. I'm so

pleased for you, Lexie, honestly.'

'Thanks. Love you.'

'You too. Bye!'

She slid into her seat, her mind whirling. Adam was to be her proxy. Adam and Sunita had split up. He was going to manage Forgie End Farm – a new life was opening up for Adam and she was as far removed from it as she could possibly be.

Lexie was getting married. And she was not going to be her bridesmaid. That hurt.

'Hi again.'

Molly looked up. Sunita was standing above her, smiling. 'I think I'm in the window seat,' she said, gesturing beyond Molly.

'Sure.'

Molly, who had been allocated the centre seat, prayed that the flight would not be full so that she could slide across to the aisle – but events today were conspiring against her, big time. It was only seconds before a very large man arrived and installed himself in the aisle seat, sweating profusely and moaning about the lack of space.

'Good afternoon, everybody,' came the voice over the intercom. 'As we have a very full flight today, please ensure that all your luggage is installed safely in the overhead lockers or stowed neatly under the seat in front of you.'

There was to be no respite.

'So,' Sunita said after take-off, the flawless smile perfectly in place, 'how are things with you, Molly?'

It was going to be a long flight.

Later, talking to Julian – who had taken mercy on her and stayed in – Molly confessed.

'I know it's uncharitable of me, but I can't help being glad they've split up.'

'Darling, if you need to bitch, I'm absolutely the right man to bitch to.'

She grinned. Julian was the most perfect companion in the world.

'It's not that I wish either of them ill, and actually, the flight wasn't nearly as bad as I'd expected – she's very bright and quite easy to talk to. I just can't get the fact out of my head that she was there with him, at Loch Melfort, that time I went there with Lexie.'

'And what was so wrong with that? Have another olive.'

'She was absolutely like a fish out of water, with her high-heeled gold sandals and her shimmering dresses. Loch Melfort's a place for outdoor pursuits – you know, hill walking, climbing, sailing, all that stuff.'

Julian shivered. 'My worst nightmare. I'm with Sunita. Anyway,' he refilled their glasses, 'I'm not buying your story. It was really none of your business, was it, whether she looked out of place there or not? That was Adam's problem. In fairness, he probably didn't even see it as a problem. You said she's stunning.'

'Flawless bloody skin, thick, shiny hair, eyes like a roe deer's and pearly white teeth,' Molly said gloomily.

Julian took her hand. 'You're not so desperately ugly yourself, dearest Mollykins. Now, forgive me if I'm wrong – I'm only a man so I know nothing – but dare I suggest you were a teensy-weensy bit jealous?'

Molly snatched her hand away. 'Not in the slightest. My marriage, as you once so clearly pointed out, is over.'

'Ah. But are you still in love with him?'

'No! Maybe a little. Well, what if I am? It won't do me the slightest good. Now,' she emptied her glass in three quick gulps and held it out for a refill, 'you mentioned you'd met a man. I want to hear all about it – every gory detail.'

Chapter Twelve

The tin labelled 'SUMMER CAMP FUND' was still very much on Caitlyn's mind. It was an impossibly large sum for Isla May to have; she couldn't imagine how the money had got there. She waited for the right moment and sat Isla May and Ailsa down.

'There's something I have to talk to you both about,' she said.

'That sounds serious,' Ailsa said, laughing.

Ailsa had changed her hairstyle recently. It only fell to her shoulders now, instead of half way down her back, but it was stylish and sleek. It made her look more grown up. She almost was grown up. The night of Ricky's attack had been a turning point – or perhaps that had come earlier and Caitlyn hadn't noticed. Either way, dating Wallace had definitely improved her sister.

'You're not expecting a baby, are you?' Isla May said, her little face earnest.

'*What*?'

'Mariella says you get a baby when a man sticks his thing into you. That's what horrible Ricky did, isn't it?'

'No, darling, that is absolutely not what Ricky did,' Caitlyn said, alarmed that Isla May's childhood innocence appeared to be so soon at an end. She resolved to have a proper facts of life chat with her very soon, or to make sure her mother did it. 'Thanks to Wallace and Ailsa, all he did was hurt me a bit. Anyway, that's all over now and Ricky has said he's sorry, so we don't need to talk about that any more. No,' she reached under the table and produced the tin, 'this is what we need to talk about.'

Isla May's eyes widened. 'You found my tin.'

Ailsa said, 'That was supposed to be a secret.'

'How did you get this money, Ailsa? Isla May?'

'It's no great deal,' Ailsa said carelessly. 'It's not like your fraud thing at the office or anything. Keep your hair on.'

Isla May wriggled her bottom on her chair and sat up very straight. 'We worked for it. We did baking and I sold it at school.'

'You did what?'

'We set up a business,' Isla May said importantly. 'The Wallace Summer Camp Fund Cookery Company Limited. I'm the chief director.'

Caitlyn stared at her sister. 'You're six years old.'

'I'm nearly seven,' Isla May said indignantly.

'I'm the accountant,' Ailsa said, 'and Harris and Lewis are both salespeople.'

'You got the twins involved in this?' Caitlyn asked incredulously.

'They demanded ten per cent,' Isla May said indignantly, 'but we negotiated them down to seven, didn't we, Ailsa?'

'Let me get this straight. You baked things and sold them? Where?'

'I told you: at school. Only we had to be a little bit careful, cos Ailsa says some teachers can get fussy about – what is it again, Ailsa?'

'Food handling certification,' Ailsa said gloomily. 'It's a real bore, you know, one of those stupid health and safety things, so we thought it was better to just sell it on the quiet.'

'And the boys sold stuff at school too?'

'Yes. They did really well, actually, though we had to make them account for it all or they'd have scoffed the lot. We did spreadsheets, didn't we, Isla May? Most tray bakes were cut into twenty portions, and they either had to give us the money or give back the pieces they hadn't sold.'

Caitlyn's amazement grew. 'Where did you get the capital, for heaven's sake?'

'I put up the money the first couple of times. It wasn't very much. We put all the profits back into stock.'

Caitlyn's hands were over her mouth. She was trying to smother her laughter. She'd been imagining heaven knows what – extortion, pilfering, stealing from Joyce's purse, or her own – and here was a profitable small enterprise set up and thriving right under her nose.

'What's so funny?' Ailsa asked belligerently.

She couldn't contain herself any longer. 'It's not ... funny ... it's brilliant! It's just that I was thinking—' she clutched her sides. Tears were streaming down her face. Laughter was unexpected, and with it came release. All of a sudden, nothing that had happened over the past months seemed quite so bad – not the fraud or her role in uncovering it; not the loss of her job; not the assault; nothing. All that mattered was her wonderful family.

The cashbox must have been worrying Caitlyn more than she'd realised. She felt so much better that she made up her mind to go into Fraser, Fraser and Mutch and find out what the job was, how much it paid, and whether she had the right qualifications to have a chance of getting it. And she resolved to see Malkie – to hell with the bruises, now showing more green than purple.

'It's general secretarial work,' said the girl on

reception, her tongue stud flashing.

What were they thinking about, letting her come to work like that? Caitlyn thought of the scruffy felt-tip notice in the window, took in the threadbare carpet with its dark stains and the shabby chairs for clients to wait in. OK, so maybe Blair King, with its sleek contemporary furnishings and gleaming cherry wood floor, had been a bit much the other way, but if she worked here, she'd have to get this sorted. She'd bet a million pounds that Fraser, Fraser and Mutch were men. Either young guys who had been students not so long ago or old men who no longer noticed such things.

'That sounds all right.'

'We've had loads of applications, so if you're interested you'd better get something in quick. They're starting to call people in for interviews.'

'Tomorrow?' Caitlyn asked, taking an application form. Now that she'd decided to try for the job, she really wanted it.

'Sure,' said the girl, stifling a yawn.

Goodness, she needed a bomb under her!

In the high street, she ran right into Adam Blair.

'Sorry! I wasn't looking where I was going.'

He peered at her eye. 'Is that a bruise? What happened?'

'Nothing. An argument with a door.'

'You're not being … I mean, no-one's … at home?'

'What? Oh, beating me up, you mean. No, you're all right, there's no man in our house. Well only Ailsa's boyfriend Wallace, and he's a pussycat. I didn't know you lived in Hailesbank, Mr Blair.'

'I didn't till recently. I've started as manager at Forgie End Farm.'

'Really? My gran used to work there.'

'What did she do?'

'Mostly housework and cooking. It was ages ago. There was some big feud, wasn't there? The Blair brothers. Hey—' she looked at Adam, startled, '—was that something to do with your family, then?'

'It was. But it's all a long time ago. Have you found a job yet?'

'No. But there's a post going at the lawyer's down the road there,' she tossed her head in the direction she'd just come from. 'I'm putting in an application.'

'If you need a reference, get in touch, OK?'

'You'd be willing to do that for me?' she asked, surprised.

'You're not still feeling guilty about what happened at Blair King, are you? What you did was upright and honest, and pretty damn smart. I'd be more than happy to recommend you.'

Caitlyn blushed as he walked away. He'd been all right, Adam Blair.

The sun was shining, the daffodils and crocuses in the tubs along the high street had shot into bloom, and it was suddenly spring – a time of regeneration and new beginnings. Nothing could stop her feeling upbeat.

She called Malkie.

'You're absolutely right, Malcolm Milne.'

'Really? What about?'

'You said we need to talk, and so we do. I need to get it through that thick head of yours that just because I said I wasn't ready to move in with you doesn't mean I don't care about you.'

'Right.'

He was clearly going to take a bit of convincing.

'There's something else I have to tell you about too, but you have to promise not to do anything.'

'How can I promise not to do anything if I haven't the faintest idea what you're talking about?'

'You'll see. Promise?'

'I guess.'

'Right then. Are we on? For seven, at the Duke?'

'See you then.'

She spent the rest of the afternoon in WorldLink, the new internet café in Kittle's Lane. Filling in the printed application form looked as though it would be straightforward, but she asked them to make two photocopies of the blank in case she made any mistakes. Finally, she spent an hour drafting her covering letter, and asked for it to be printed.

It was half past five. She hurried back down the high street intending to slip the envelope through Fraser, Fraser and Mutch's door, but, just as she approached, a pleasant-looking man with silvery hair emerged and pulled the door to behind him.

'Are you closed?'

He turned and smiled. 'I was about to lock up, yes. Can I help you?'

She liked the man at once. He had smiley, intelligent eyes – not the kind of cold intelligence that she found intimidating, but a kind of gentle wisdom.

'I just wanted to hand this in. I hope it's not too late. It's an application for the job. Are you a Mr Fraser or a Mr Mutch?'

He laughed. 'Neither. I'm Harold Armstrong and I'm the only lawyer here. Good afternoon.'

His handshake was firm and warm.

'No Frasers or Mutches?'

'Not these days. Will you trust your application to me? I promise I'll be in touch very soon to let you know whether we need to see you.'

'Thanks.'

She had to stop herself dancing down the street because she could feel his gaze on her back as she walked away. She had a good feeling about this.

'What the hell happened?'

'I knew you'd be upset. It's all right, Malkie, there's been no harm done. If you get in the drinks, I'll tell you.'

How long had it been since she'd seen him? Ten days? Was that all? Her life had turned cartwheels since then, and he didn't even know.

'Ricky bloody McQuade? I'll kill him!' Malkie raged when she finished telling him what had happened.

'It's all sorted, I promise you.' She'd withheld the worst of the story and made the whole event sound almost comical. That took an effort, but it was worth it. She couldn't have Malkie igniting some kind of feud that he could never win. 'He came and apologised. Everything's fine.'

'He's a little shite. I always thought so. I should—'

'You should leave well alone. Honestly.'

Malkie finished his pint. 'It's all my fault.'

Caitlyn was prepared for that. 'No. You must never think that.'

'If I hadn't gone off in a sulk and left you to walk home on your own—'

'It could have happened any time, Malkie. I could have been out with my friends, or coming home late from somewhere, anything. You're not to blame yourself. OK?'

'I guess.' He cleared his throat. 'Have you thought about what I said last time? About moving in with me?'

His face was so full of earnest hope that she felt mean all over again. She had to find a way through this. She must lead him lightly towards a place of understanding and of agreement. She thought of the day he had run from her in the park, and she had chased him, laughing.

'Bet my pace is quicker than your pace,' he had said, but if he had understood what she had said that day, he had forgotten it now.

She took his hand.

'I've thought about it, Malkie.'

'And the answer's still no.' He tried to pull his hand away, but she held it fast. She would not allow him to sulk or be despondent. If they were to have a relationship, they would both need to move along the same path, inch by inch.

'I thought, after Saskia, you might have been put off living with someone.'

'Saskia wasn't you. I hate going home to an empty house.'

'But right now, that's all I want. Can you understand that?'

His mouth was pinched and unhappy. 'You obviously don't feel the same way about me as I feel about you.'

Caitlyn stroked the back of his hand softly, liking its breadth and length. It would be easy to be swayed by Malkie, but it would be a mistake. She needed time. She needed to make her own way, and to live for a time in a place where she did not have to think about the needs of anyone else – not her mother nor her siblings, and certainly not a lover who would have a particular set of demands.

'It's not about that, Malkie. Don't be grumpy, love. I need to live for myself for the first time in my life. I need to choose what I watch on the telly or whether I watch nothing at all and just stare at the ceiling instead. I need not to think about cooking for someone every night or cleaning up someone else's mess. No—'

She laid a finger on his lips as he opened his mouth to object.

'—I know you'll say you won't make a mess, that you'll cook too, that you don't mind what I watch on telly. I know you care about me, Malkie, and I'm happy that you do. You make me feel safe, and I love that feeling.'

She knew by the set of his shoulders that she had not won his understanding, not yet.

'I can't do it, Malkie. Not now, at any rate.'

'Not now?'

She glimpsed hope in his eyes and was content to leave it there.

'We haven't known each other long. I don't want to be another Saskia, making you dance to her tune then dropping you when she tired of the game. I want us to talk together, hand in hand, with love, and kindness, and optimism, and patience. Do you understand what I'm trying to say?'

'I can still carry your bag?'

Her laughter punctured the tension and she saw a tremulous smile flit across his face.

'You can carry my bag, Malcolm Milne.'

'You're that stubborn—' he grumbled, still fighting.

'So you need to know that, and think about whether you can live with it. And with my other many faults.'

'Hah,' he grunted.

But he kissed her cheek and then her eyelids, and then her lips, before the cat calls erupted across the room.

Chapter Thirteen

Molly met David Swift through Julian.

'How do you know him?'

'He's my new friend Evan's second cousin once removed, or something. Evan says he's a techie geeky entrepreneur type. He's a bit of a legend in his family.'

'A techie geeky entrepreneur type? What the hell's that mean?'

'I have no idea. I'm a mere banker. Come and meet him anyway. Evan says he's looking for lurve.'

'He's not gay?'

Julian looked affronted. 'Darling. Would I suggest it if he were?'

'And what makes you think I'm looking for lurve, as you put it?'

'Aren't you?'

'Not really, but I'll come. A night out might do me good.'

'Terrific. Can you make Vinopolis by half seven?'

'I should think so.'

'Great. He'll be wearing a red carnation.'

'Won't you be there?'

Julian smiled. 'Just teasing, darling. Evan and I will be there. To start with, at any rate.'

It was one of those evenings when nothing went badly wrong, but nothing worked out the way it might have done either. Molly warmed to Evan instantly, even though he couldn't have been more different from Julian. He was a chef, and although he could hardly be described as fat, his face had a pleasing softness. She found him approachable and refreshingly open, and she could see at once that they were falling for each other.

David Swift was another matter entirely. He wasn't at all like the 'techie geeky' types she knew from work. They tended to be skinny and intense with an impenetrable vocabulary. Not that they weren't nice guys. Some of them were even quite fanciable. If David was geeky, he hid it well. He was tall, obviously very fit, with a quick smile and smart clothes, and the kind of charm, she suspected, that would have women scurrying in his direction from all corners. She also – though she could not define why – suspected the charm might be all on the surface. She was prepared to be proved wrong.

'I hear Fletcher Keir Mason is doing extraordinarily well,' he said as they shook hands.

'Thank you.' She tried not to look startled. It was the kind of comment she might expect at a business meeting, not on a night out.

'You've only been in business for a few months, isn't that right? Yet already, my little moles tell me, you're shaking up the world of marketing.'

Instantly, she was thrown on the defensive. 'Well, we try to be innovative, but our main priority is always to provide the best possible service for our clients.'

'Sure, sure.' He leaned towards her and lowered his voice. 'And if you can add a premium for that kind of service and get away with it, why not? Good business, I'd say.'

Molly blinked and looked away. She was rapidly forming an aversion to David Swift.

'Ah, thank you,' a waiter had arrived with a bottle of

champagne on ice, 'good stuff.'

The champagne was Julian's treat, but David took charge of it.

'Did Julian tell you I have my own business?'

'He said you were an entrepreneur. What do you do?'

Molly regretted the question almost immediately, because he launched into a complicated explanation about the advanced digital technologies he was exploiting and selling on 'to companies just like yours, actually'.

Oh God. First impressions were playing out exactly as expected. It was going to be a long evening. She glanced at Julian, hoping against hope that he would see her discomfort and come up with a rescue plan, but he was deep in conversation with Evan. Did men handle these things better? she wondered. Would Julian, in her situation, be more straightforward, stand up, say, 'This is not going to work. Goodbye.'

She cursed the courtesy that Billy had bred in her. She would be polite. She tried to make allowances. He must be nervous. When he relaxed, he would offer a softer self for her attention.

But the evening did not improve. Julian and Evan excused themselves and slipped away in the throng before Molly had the wit to make her own excuses. David said, 'There's a small restaurant close by, on the up. Impossible to get a table, you know, but—' He tapped the side of his nose.

She accompanied him with reluctance.

It wasn't all bad. He had moments of promise – when talking of his sister, for example, who had Down's syndrome.

'She's a star. We're all so proud of her. She smiles at everything.' His own smile at this point was the first genuine one she had glimpsed and it gave her hope – but it vanished abruptly, as though he regretted allowing her to glimpse something of what made him human.

Was she becoming like this? Obsessed with her work, her small talk stilted, her friendships pitifully limited? She picked over her *raviolo* – single, swimming in a sea of pea green *velouté*, and quite perfect. The restaurant was a place for easy companionship. Around her, couples leaned towards each other in familiar intimacy, friends shared jokes over a fine claret or an *île flottant* and a glass of umber Sauternes. It could have been a place for lurve.

'Have you been married?' she asked, thinking of Adam.

He looked startled. 'Haven't we all?' He took her hand across the table before she could withdraw it. 'We all carry baggage, at our age.'

It was an insight, at least. And honest. She prepared to soften.

'All the more important, don't you think, to understand what we each want before we embark into our little boat on the storm-tossed waters of life?'

Oh God, such a cliché. Molly swallowed, thinking longingly of Julian's gentle perception and Evan's straightforwardness. Where were they now? Enjoying a very unpretentious drink in a fun-filled gay bar somewhere, no doubt. She reclaimed her hand.

'You're right, of course. We all have baggage.'

She tried. She sidestepped questions about her work, quizzed him on travel, on hobbies, on sport, on reading (exotic resorts, no time, squash and trade journals), but by the time the waiter arrived bearing the dessert menu, she had had enough.

'Not for me, thank you. Listen, David, it's been fun,' she lied, glancing ostentatiously at her watch, 'but I have a seriously early start tomorrow. Would you mind very much if we—?'

'Not at all. I'll see you home.'

'If you could just find me a taxi, that would be great.'

He didn't launch into more clichés. There was no 'I'll call you' or 'we must do this again soon'. They hadn't clicked, and at least he had enough perception to know it.

'Thank you for supper. I hope you find the right sailing companion.'

'You're a very delightful lady.' He lifted her hand to his lips and she squirmed at the gesture, before realising she preferred that gesture of farewell to some of the other possibilities he might have chosen.

'It was awful,' she giggled with Julian over a late nightcap at the flat.

'He seemed perfectly pleasant. Nice looking guy,' Julian said.

'Oh yes, at least I had something worth looking at all evening.'

'So what was wrong with him? He's mega rich, Evan tells me. The techno geeky whatever it is he does is rolling in huge bucks.'

'That was part of the problem. He was so focused on making money that everything else was unimportant to him.'

'Like?'

'Like being human.'

'Ouch.'

'There was one glimpse of genuine feeling, when he talked about his sister, who has Down's. I actually rather liked him for a few minutes. Then he brought down the curtain and it was all ambition, success and money making.' She stopped, appalled at a sudden thought. 'My

321

God, Julian, do you think that was how he saw me?'

'You're not like that.'

'Really not?' She sighed, missing Lexie and the old times of laughter, and friendship and silly fun. 'I liked Evan,' she said, not wanting to think about herself for a moment longer.

'Isn't he just perfect?'

'Yes. For you. Are you a couple yet, do you think? Will I have to move out?'

'Oh darling, not yet.' His smile was mischievous. 'But it's all very promising—'

They won the health campaign contract. So it was, ironically, the best day in Fletcher Keir Mason's short history when Molly told Barnaby that she wanted out.

'It's so brilliant!' Ken Mason was jubilant and hugged Molly ferociously.

'What a team,' Barnaby said, over and over again. 'What a team.'

She waited until after the champagne had been popped open and the cupcakes demolished, until the smiles and the chatter had subsided and everyone had returned to their desks to get on with the day's business, then said quietly, 'Barnaby? Can I have a word?'

She almost bottled it. He was a good man and a great colleague. She'd thought that this career path was what she'd always wanted. The glittering successes, the challenging but rewarding contracts, the buzz of being at the heart of all these new ideas and testing her skills to their utmost and beyond. In some ways, it still was – but she couldn't help thinking about David and how his ambition had shaped him into something rather distasteful. Or, at least, into the kind of person she very much did not want to be.

'Isn't is wonderful?' Barnaby said, letting the glass door into his office swing closed.

They were in a bubble of silence. Molly inhaled deeply. This was it.

'It is wonderful. You've achieved miracles, and in a very short time.'

He looked at her, puzzled by her tone. 'Is something wrong?'

'I want out, Barnaby.'

'Sorry?'

'It's not for me. I thought it was, but I've realised I was wrong.'

'I don't understand.'

'I'm resigning from the company.'

'You can't.'

'I can. I am.'

'Sorry, Molly.' Barnaby's puzzlement was changing into anger. 'It's a pity that you are feeling that way, and I'll work with you to turn your feelings around, but you are financially and contractually committed to this company. You can't simply resign.'

She'd known this side of Barnaby must exist – it's not possible to build a business with such single-minded determination unless you have a core of steel – but she hadn't run up against it before. The problem was, she could be determined too, and having made up her mind, she was fixed on her resolution. Barnaby's opposition only made her more tenacious.

'Trying to hold me here against my will would be extremely ill advised,' she said icily. 'I might adhere to the letter of my contract, but my enthusiasm would be nil. And that would show.'

'You're threatening me?'

'I'm telling you like it is.'

'You're a key part of our success, Molly.'

'I'm flattered you think so. But I'm not irreplaceable.'

'You are. People like you. You bring in business. You are top rate at what you do.'

'There's a dozen more like me out there. Women who have the hunger for success as well as the expertise. If it's a woman you feel you need.'

'You can't leave. What's brought this on, anyway? We've just won our biggest contract, for heaven's sake. We're on course for some serious profits. We're making our mark.' He grabbed her arm. 'It's what you wanted. What we both dreamed of.'

She waited until he released her.

'I thought I did. I've realised I was wrong.' She changed her tone. 'I miss my family, Barnaby. My father needs me. My brother's facing jail. I want to help his kids keep sane. I want to be part of their lives.'

She could see him soften. Family was important to Barnaby.

'Bloody hell, Molly.' He sank down onto his chair, a look of devastation on his face.

It almost made her change her mind, before she remembered Lexie and the wedding, and the fact that she was losing the friendships that really mattered to her.

'I can't release the money. It's completely tied up.'

'You could find someone to buy me out.'

'That's not so easy.'

'It's a successful business. You said so yourself.'

'Banks aren't lending. It would have to be someone who could pay cash. People are up to their necks in vast mortgages – the kind of people I'd be hoping to catch, anyway.'

She stood her ground. 'I'm going.'

'I can't release the money.'

They stared at each other, locked in an impasse.

At last, Barnaby relented. 'I'll tell you what. I can see that you need some time to sort yourself out. Why don't you take a sabbatical? I can't pay you because it'll cost us a packet to hire someone in to do your job, but you'll still get dividends, if there are any. And your name will still be on our letterhead as a director. That's really important, Molly, you do see that, don't you? I can't have a principal walking out at this point, it would send out so many wrong signals.'

Molly wavered. 'It's not ideal.'

'Certainly not from my point of view, but it's the best I can come up with.'

'Can I work? I'll need money.'

'That's a problem.' He drummed his fingers on his desk. 'Maybe small freelance jobs. Event stuff, like you were doing at that place before you joined us. Not big projects. Nothing high profile.' He gazed at her searchingly. 'I'll need your word on that.'

She nodded. 'Thank you, Barnaby.'

'Bugger thanks. I still want you back.'

Chapter Fourteen

Molly arrived back in Edinburgh in a car that was stuffed to the roof with bags and boxes and the detritus of everyday life she hadn't had the heart to junk – the paperweight her mother had given her years ago; an orchid Julian had presented to her when she'd first moved into the flat in Battersea; the heavy brass Buddha that Adam had bought for her on their honeymoon. There was no room in Billy's house and she had nowhere else to stay. Lexie's home was out of the question and she had little more than a month's wages in her bank account.

'You don't expect the nestlings back when you get to my age,' Billy had said good-humouredly. 'Look at me – quietly hobbling down the final staircase of life, minding my own business, when everything changes.'

'You don't get my sympathy, Dad,' Molly laughed. 'You know you love having everyone around. Besides, you don't even have a staircase.'

'And just what are we meant to do with all this stuff?'

She could see the pleasure under the gruffness, and smiled.

They set to and cleared a corner of the garage. As Billy no longer drove, it was a garage in name only because Adrienne had already colonised the space with most of the contents of her former large house.

'It won't be for long,' Molly said. 'Barnaby will find someone to buy me out then I can get a place of my own.'

Billy hugged her. 'I missed you.'

'I missed you too, Dad.'

She gave herself three days, then started a round of calls. She'd have to find work, and soon.

Her first call was to Sharon, Lady Fleming.

'I was wondering,' she said without any real hope, 'if you might need a hand now and again. I'm back and I'm working for myself.'

'Molly! How unexpected.'

'It's a long shot. I imagine you're well taken care of. I just thought it might be worth a try.'

She was preparing her platitudes when Lady Fleming said, 'As it happens, we're more than usually busy in the next few weeks. Hugh – your replacement – has been on his knees begging me for more help.' She laughed. 'To be candid, Molly, I don't think he has your stamina, or gift for organisation. Why don't you come in and we can talk about it. Three o'clock?'

A few years ago, Sharon Eddy had been chief reporter on the now-defunct *Hailesbank Herald*. Then she'd fallen in love with Sir Cosmo Fleming, married him after a whirlwind romance, and transformed herself – to the astonishment of the entire town – from bossy journalist to twin-set-and-pearls landed gentry with remarkable ease. More to the point, she had taken the rambling, crumbling, money-leaking Fleming House firmly in hand and started its transformation from near ruin to money-making machine with ruthless efficiency. The appointment of Molly as the estate's first events manager had been a key brick in her business plan.

'There is work,' she said over a cup of coffee in her functional office, 'but it's all short term.' She glanced at Molly and said, 'I'm sorry to say that Hugh hasn't been as astute as you were at the marketing side of things.'

'What kind of work?' Molly asked, her heart sinking at the thought of having to come in to teach her successor how to do the job. She could foresee all sorts of resentments and grievances, and besides, she didn't want the responsibility.

Sharon Fleming was not stupid. 'The best thing would simply be to hand over a few events to you in their entirety, don't you think?'

'Sounds good. I could do that.'

'Good.' She started looking through her large desk diary. 'Ah. The first thing could be the Mulgrew-Gordon wedding.'

'Oh no!'

'Sorry?' Sharon looked at her over the top of her spectacles.

'I'm sorry. I'll do anything else, but I can't do that one. Lexie Gordon is a great friend of mine and I'm a guest. I would hate to—'

'Of course. I forgot. It was you who persuaded her to rent the garden cottage, wasn't it? And rushed her to hospital to have her baby. You're quite right, it wouldn't be appropriate. All right.' She scanned the diary again. 'There're a couple of corporate dinner evenings in the Barn, two more weddings, a few family parties – I'll tell you what, why don't you and Hugh agree the diary between you? Take no notice if he grumbles, I'm sure he'll be very relieved.'

'Fine by me.'

Lady Fleming took off her glasses and laid them on the desk. 'Where are you staying?'

'Short term, with my father, but his house is really cramped and I'll have to—'

'Your apartment is still empty.'

'I beg your pardon?'

'Your old apartment. Hugh deemed it unsuitable. He has a wife and children and prefers to live in Hailesbank.'

'I see.'

'I could let you have it for a nominal rent. To be frank, I'd prefer someone in it. I always think it's best to keep these rooms warm and aired.'

'That's really kind of you, but I don't know how much I could—'

'Let's do it on a month-by-month basis, shall we?'

There comes a time when life is at such a low ebb that things have to turn around and start to go well. Or maybe it's about grabbing problems by the scruff of the neck and dealing with them.

That was how it seemed to Molly. She had faced up to her situation and made a decision that to many would appear bizarre – but to her felt so absolutely right that it seemed inevitable.

She woke up on the morning of Lexie's wedding in her old apartment, smiling at these thoughts. This place had been her bolt-hole before. Was she merely running away again? It didn't feel like that this time, but she did welcome the familiarity of the flat. It felt safe.

The wedding was not until two. It was to take place in the room that had once been the billiard room and which she and Lady Sharon had converted into 'The Wedding Room' – a calm, beautiful space with a fine aspect down towards the river and excellent natural light. They had purposely kept the decor simple. This was a space that was to be suitable for ceremonies of any denomination. After the photographs, they'd have dinner in the supper room. There was plenty of space around the great hall and staircase for guests to disperse and chat while the room was prepared for dancing later.

The format was so familiar that Molly could have run the wedding in her sleep, but there was a delicious pleasure in knowing she didn't have to.

She took a leisurely shower, enjoying, as she did each time she went through this ritual, the feel of her short hair.

She pulled on her dressing gown and breakfasted on coffee and toast, feeling delightfully decadent. It was a gloriously sunny day; Lexie's photos would be fabulous.

At ten, her doorbell rang and Hugh appeared, looking apologetic. 'Don't panic,' he said, 'but there are a couple of small problems—'

The caterer had called in. They were three staff short and none of the agencies had been able to supply replacements. The woman who played the piano for the service was sick. And the wine that had been delivered was not what had been ordered.

'I'm so sorry, Molly, but can you handle these issues? I'll be back well before the ceremony, but my youngest, Betty, has taken a tumble out of the tree in our garden and I think she may have broken something. She's downstairs in the car. I can't leave her for much longer; I'm going to have to drive her to A&E to get her X-rayed because my wife has taken our son to his judo in Dunbar and she doesn't have her phone with her—'

'Leave it with me,' Molly said, holding out her hand for the information and trying not to sigh audibly. 'Don't worry about it, these things happen. I hope your little girl's all right.'

'Sally will be back by midday,' Hugh said, heading for the door. 'I'll come straight back in, I promise. Oh,' he delved into his pocket, 'I brought up your post. I nearly forgot.'

'Thanks.'

It took an hour, and her old contact book as well as

Hugh's meagre one, to sort everything out, but it could have been worse. She glanced at the clock. Eleven thirty. She still had a comfortable two and a half hours to get ready for the wedding. There would even be time to read a couple of chapters of her latest book.

She made another coffee and settled on her favourite armchair. Seeing the letters Hugh had left, she picked them up. They had all been redirected by Julian. They must be a week or more old. She sifted through them. Some junk, an alumnus magazine, a letter from the Sheriff Court …

She seized the brown envelope and ripped it open.

It was her decree absolute.

She and Adam were finally divorced.

She would cope. Everything she had gone through had made her stronger. Molly held her head high and threw her shoulders back and led with her chin into the wedding ceremony. She saw Lexie drift down the aisle in a confection of ivory lace that might have been 1920s or 1930s, but most certainly was vintage. Wrist-length sleeves, a fish tail that puddled on the floor at the back – she would have noted every exquisite detail of the dress, except that she could not keep her eyes off Adam Blair.

Her ex-husband.

She wrested her attention back to the ceremony.

Lexie did nothing conventionally. She carried no bouquet; instead she carried her baby. Keira Mulgrew Gordon, aged eight months, in fuchsia pink satin to match her mother's hair, sat bolt upright and mute with the strangeness of it all – until Lexie tried to hand her over to Cora, at which point she started to scream.

Lexie laughed.

Patrick took his child, but Keira was having none of it.

She wanted her mother and was going to have her mother.

Lexie's laughter stopped abruptly. 'I can carry on holding her,' she said, her voice clear, 'while we do this thing.'

Molly stepped forward. 'No,' she said, 'let me. I'll take her out.'

She meant it as a sacrifice, a kind of personal penitence for having missed the christening. She wanted above everything to see her friend married, but godmotherly duties dictated otherwise.

'Oh will you? Thank you, Molly.'

The child was handed over. Molly turned to walk down the aisle between the chairs so that she could find somewhere quiet outside to entertain Keira, but the moment she had the baby in her arms, there was silence.

She stopped. She looked at Keira. Keira looked solemnly back. A solitary tear sat on her plump cheek, but she squeezed no more out.

All right then, Molly thought, we'll see, shall we? And she slipped back into her place.

Keira took hold of the gold pendant she was wearing – it was one that Adam had given her on their first wedding anniversary – and started to examine it closely.

Molly looked up. From across the aisle, Adam was staring not at Patrick and Lexie, but straight at her. She could not read the expression in his eyes.

Lexie said, 'That was miraculous, Molly,' as she turned down the aisle by the side of her new husband and reclaimed her child. 'What's your secret?'

'I'm a fairy godmother,' Molly whispered, as much to the child as to Lexie.

Keira gurgled and smiled, and as Lexie cradled her in her arms, she waved a chubby hand.

Molly fell in love.

Of all the emotions she had expected to feel on meeting Adam, shyness was not even on the list she had considered.

'You're back,' he said, unexpectedly offering her his arm as they turned, simultaneously, out of their seats and into the aisle, one from each side.

'Yes. Divorced, penniless and with no visible means of support.' She smiled at him. His face was imprinted on her soul and the shyness melted away. 'But glad to be back.'

'What happened to the hair?'

'Oh!' Molly's hand shot up to her head. 'I keep forgetting. Don't you like it?'

'I barely recognised you.' He studied her carefully, his eyes hooded so that she couldn't read them. 'It suits you. What prompted it?'

'I needed a change.'

'Change is good. Change is brave. Has it changed how you feel about yourself?'

Taken aback by his perceptiveness, she laughed nervously. 'The photographs will take an hour,' she said, evading the question, 'but there'll be champagne.'

'We could pass on the bubbles and go for a walk.'

'I suppose we could.'

He hadn't mentioned the divorce. Did he even know it had come through?

They strolled round the side of the house, towards her apartment. 'They'll come round this way shortly,' Molly said, 'to take pictures in the formal garden.'

'There's a path towards the river. It winds through the trees over there.'

'Yes,' said Molly, who knew it well.

Her shoes were not suited to walking. They were satin

and had high, thin heels. Half way across the lawn she took them off and carried them.

'You all right? We can stop.'

'No, let's walk. There's a sheltered bank down by the river; we can grab a seat for a bit.'

The sun was high in the sky. It was May, and unseasonably warm. As they reached the wood, they heard a babble of voices from the terrace behind them and turned to see what was happening. The wedding party had turned the corner of the house and was approaching the steps at the top of the formal garden.

'Quick,' said Adam.

Molly turned towards the path into the wood and ran, though why she was running she had no idea.

A few steps later, she stood on a rough pebble and cried out. 'Ouch!'

'Sore?' Adam smiled in the dappled light, the shadows playing across his face so that she could not quite read his eyes. Before she realised what he was doing, he stooped and lifted her in his arms.

'What are you – Adam?' Molly cried, laughing.

'Where's this bank then?'

'Not far. I can walk if you—'

He didn't slow down, so she shut up. She had no real inclination to protest. She hadn't been in Adam's arms for – what? – four years? It felt disturbingly pleasant.

'Down there,' she instructed as they emerged from the wood.

He stood at the top of the bank and looked at it. 'Can you walk? It's quite steep. I'd hate to drop you.'

Her dress was lapis blue satin, and short. She picked her way down the grass and dropped onto the lush grass, threaded with wildflowers.

Adam slithered down beside her, then sat up and took

off his jacket. 'I didn't think I'd have to wear a suit again so soon.'

'I heard you'd turned to farming.'

'Farm managing, yes.'

'Has Jean given up?'

'More or less. Geordie's death hit her hard. I don't think she had the heart for it any more.'

Molly picked a handful of daisies and started weaving them together. She said, 'I got the divorce papers this morning.'

'Just this morning?'

'They'd been forwarded from London.'

'Ah. It was what you wanted, wasn't it?'

She sat up. 'What *I* wanted?'

'You told me off for not getting the divorce through because it affected the bond on the house.'

'Well, it was too late by then anyway, wasn't it? So there was no need to—'

'Don't tell me you didn't want to go ahead. You never said—'

Molly crunched the daisies in her hand and tossed them away. 'I thought you wanted it.'

'I had the impression it was inevitable.'

'Oh God.'

She slumped back against the bank and closed her eyes, drained. A cloud crossed the sun and she felt the change of temperature immediately.

'How did you do that trick with Keira?' he asked after a long silence.

'Trick?'

'Made her go quiet.'

'Pure luck.'

'You looked—'

'I looked what?'

336

'So natural with her.'

Molly half opened her eyes and turned her head towards him. 'Really?'

'I always thought it was a shame we never started a family. Do you think things might have been different for us if we had?'

'You thought *what*?'

'Well, you said you didn't want children, and I—'

'When? When did I say that?'

'That first holiday we had. When we were students. We were sitting by the pool in that ghastly resort and you said the last thing you wanted was to have children.'

'We were eighteen, Adam! Anyway, you said the same thing. God, it's getting chilly.'

'Here.' He draped his jacket round her shoulders. 'Or do you want to go back? Perhaps we should.'

She shook her head. Adam reached his hand up and touched her hair. 'When did you cut it?'

'A month or two back.'

'And? You never answered my question.'

'Did it change how I feel about myself?' She forced herself to think about it. 'It's true I was trying to persuade myself that a new image was what I needed.'

'Was it?'

'No, though it took me some time to work that out.'

He didn't ask what she *did* need. Eventually she said, 'You like it?'

'I love it.' He picked a blade of grass and passed it through his fingers, stroking the length of it with a gentle rhythm. 'I love you. I always have.'

Molly sat up, her eyes wide, but Adam wasn't looking at her. He went on, his voice a dull monotone. 'Did you love him? Tell me it's none of my business if you like, but—'

She didn't need to ask who he was talking about.

They were divorced. Separate. Rent asunder. Their relationship had gone through too much ever to resurrect. So why did it feel like an important moment?

'I thought I did,' she said carefully, then immediately felt compelled to amend her statement. She could not betray her memories of Jamie. She had called him for help and he had died coming to her. He deserved honesty – and so, now more than ever, did Adam.

'No, it was more than that. Jamie was a friend at first. He was funny, and great to talk to, easy to be with. I can't deny he was attractive.'

She saw the slightest tic in a muscle in Adam's face, but he was expressionless. *Honesty*. She ploughed on.

'He offered me all the things that you were not giving me at that time. Attention. Adoration, even. Find me a woman who would not find that irresistible.'

'So it was my fault that you had an affair with Jamie Gordon?'

'Yes! Partly!' She picked half a dozen daisies in quick succession, plucking them furiously out of the ground and tossing them into a forlorn heap at her feet. 'Oh, dammit, how can I blame you when I was the one who did wrong?'

'If it was my fault, I couldn't be sorrier.'

Anger flared. 'Christ, Adam, why are we having this conversation? Why are we having it now? Couldn't we have talked when you were so busy you never had time for me? When work was the only thing that seemed to matter to you?'

'You were always busy too. You worked all the hours. You were driven.'

'There's nothing wrong with being ambitious,' she said defensively, even though her opinion on ambition had changed. 'My job always involved antisocial hours, you knew that when you married me. But I never forgot your birthday.'

'Oh, so that was it? We got divorced because of a late birthday present?'

They were staring at each other furiously. She could see sparks of exasperation in his eyes and thought fleetingly that she liked it better than the lifelessness that had characterised them of late. But her anger collided with his fury and words exploded out of her before she could stop them.

'It was more than that, Adam, and you know it. We'd almost stopped speaking to each other. We certainly never did anything together any more – any spare time you had you went off out to the hills.'

'That's because I hated being cooped up in the office. I hated law. I detested it.'

'Really?' The revelation stopped her dead. 'I never knew that.'

'Didn't you?'

'You were so involved in everything. That's why I was so angry when I found out I was still liable for that debt. You'd been so bloody busy lawyering that you hadn't even bothered to make sure my interests were protected. I could have lost my career without that money.'

'I know. That's why I gave you my—'

He stopped abruptly.

'What?' Molly demanded. 'What did you give me?'

He sighed. 'I gave you my share of the remaining capital.'

Molly's jaw dropped open. 'I didn't know that.'

'You weren't meant to.'

'So – you've got – how much left?'

He shrugged. 'Nothing.'

'Nothing?'

'That's why this job at the farm is so good. It's come at just the right time. I had nowhere to live, no job, and not the slightest wish to carry on working in law anyway.'

'Oh, Adam.' Molly pursed her lips. Somewhere inside, the absurdity of it all struck her and amusement erupted into laughter.

'What? What are you laughing at, Molly?'

'Don't you see?' Tears were streaming down her face. 'I've no hankie, dammit.'

He moved closer to her and hooked a handkerchief out of one of his jacket pockets.

'Here. What is it?'

'All that money. Everything we worked for, you and me. It's all gone. Every penny.'

She had to hold her sides, her ribs were aching.

'What about your investment?'

'Barnaby's keeping it. I might get it back. One day. But I might not. Oh. Oh. Ohhh!'

It was impossible not to join in, her laughter was so infectious.

At last she spluttered to a halt. Her face grew serious.

'You did that for me?'

'It was the least I could do.'

'Oh, Adam. What fools we've been.'

She reached out her arms and he pulled her close. After a minute, he tilted her face towards his with one finger and wiped away smudges of mascara with his thumbs. When he kissed her, it was like the very first time.

'We've made such terrible mistakes,' she whispered when she could catch her breath. 'Do you think we can ever put them right?'

'I don't know,' Adam said, looking into her eyes and smiling. 'We could try.'

Six months later

'She's home,' Adam said. 'I went round to see her today.'

'I take it you mean Agnes Buchanan,' Logan said evenly.

'She's not good. Her speech is fairly unintelligible and her face is all lopsided. Her right arm is almost useless. She has a carer in twice a day.' Adam gave a short laugh. 'She may not be able to say much, but boy, that woman knows how to harbour a grudge.'

Logan took a long drink from the glass of water Adam had poured for him before he said, 'I know.'

Adam looked at him sharply.

'Was that what it was all about? A chip on her shoulder?'

Adam had become used to long silences in their conversations. Logan had become ruminative. He accepted nothing on a superficial level; it was as though he had to digest statements, ponder them, weigh his answers. Adam didn't mind this. In fact, he quite liked it. They weren't fraught gaps – they had moved beyond those into a different dimension. There was time, in those silences, to reflect on things himself. So now he waited patiently for Logan's response.

'No-one,' Logan said eventually, 'understood Agnes Buchanan. No-one saw the resentment.'

'Except you.'

'Once I'd spotted the false entries in the accounts, it fell into place. She'd been there forty years. She knew more about that place than anyone, your father included.

Yet she felt – keenly – that no-one valued her.'

'It's probably true.'

'It wouldn't have taken much. A few words of praise now and then. A bonus. A bigger-than-inflation pay rise.'

Adam looked around the small room. This was the first flat he had restored at Forgie End Farm, and when Logan was given bail while the case was put together, he had offered him sanctuary.

'Why?' Logan had asked him.

'Why?' had also been the first question his father had put to him.

Molly had simply kissed him, which had repaid the deed a hundredfold.

He'd taken to visiting Logan Keir in prison. It had started in anger. It had started with him storming into the visiting room not knowing whether he would be able to stop himself from punching the man and beating him to a pulp for the damage he had inflicted.

Logan had sat, impassive, through the long outbursts of accusation and recrimination. Mistaking his stony face for defiance, Adam had at last come to boiling point.

'Say something, you bastard!'

'What do you want me to say?'

'Say, "I did wrong". Say, "I was a selfish bloody idiot and I ruined the lives of a lot of people".'

'I did wrong. I was a selfish bloody idiot and I ruined the lives of a lot of people.'

'Are you taking the mickey?'

Still Logan had sat, wordless. It was the nearest Adam came to hitting him – until he saw that Logan's eyes, staring at him, unwavering, were bright with tears.

Instantly, he felt his own fill, and before he knew it, they were both weeping deep, half smothered, silent sobs that they had to fight to disguise from everyone around.

He had left, ten minutes later, without either of them speaking another word – but a tentative bond had been forged between them and they began to move forward.

'She started, you know, a long time before I upped the stakes.'

'I know.'

'Those cash shortfalls. She'd been squirrelling away small amounts for years. I just found a way of getting more. Did she manage to communicate at all?'

'Oh yes. I gather the police have deemed her fit to stand trial.'

Another silence, then, 'Poor Agnes.'

'Do you know,' Adam said at length, 'even though those pictures were all purchased with my money – well, the firm's … the partners' – I found it strangely poignant to sit in those bare rooms. She felt it. The way she looked at those empty walls was heartbreaking in its own way.'

'She won't cope well with prison. But they'll probably not send her down. There will be some kind of leniency.'

'What will you do if they find you guilty?'

'They won't have to. I'm going to plead guilty.'

'Really? A good defence might be able to pick holes in the police case.'

Logan gave a short laugh. 'You shouldn't really be advising me like that.'

'Probably not. Personally, I think you've done your time already. What you did has destroyed you too.'

'Yes.'

Logan finished his water and sat staring at his glass. 'I'll serve my sentence for the rest of my life. In my head. I've paid a price with Adrienne and the boys that has sucked the blood from my veins and turned me into a zombie. I have no idea if I will ever recover the ground.'

'Your boys,' Adam said with surprising gentleness,

'will always be your boys. They'll always love you. Your job is to start, when you can, to rebuild their respect.'

'I know. I just don't know how.'

'As for Adrienne—'

Adam stopped. How did he know what Adrienne was going to do? How did any man know what was truly happening in other people's marriages? Logan and Adrienne were living apart, but he knew they still talked from time to time.

'There may be a chance,' he said lamely.

Logan reached across the table and grasped his hand.

'I never knew the meaning of friendship,' he said, 'until now.'

Malkie Milne stood looking at a point somewhere past Caitlyn's right ear and said in a voice that was quite unlike his normal cheery tone, 'I think we should stop seeing each other.'

Caitlyn stared at him, speechless.

Malkie didn't seem to be able to look at her. She watched, appalled, as a wave of blood suffused his skin, starting at his neck and creeping all the way to his scalp.

'I really care about you, Caitlyn, you know that, but you don't want what I want.'

'If you're talking about living together—'

He seemed to gather courage, and although the blush was still hot on his cheeks, his gaze was now steadfast.

'Aye. That's what I'm talking about. I want my life to be full that way. I want to have someone in my arms at night when I go to sleep and in the morning when I wake. I want to hold hands in front of the telly when I'm tired, and have someone by my side when I visit my ma. I want,' he said with uncharacteristic resolution, 'commitment.'

'I see.' Insight flashed. 'And you've found someone who'd like to play this role in your life.'

'No! Well,' the blush had returned, 'I've done nothing yet, we've just talked. I wouldn't cheat on you, Caitlyn, you know that.'

That was the hardest part. She did know it. Malcolm Milne was fundamentally a good man. She could look a long time before finding a better one.

He caught her hand and held it, even when she tried to pull away.

'Look at me, Caitlyn Murray. Look at me and tell me this isn't what you want, because if it is—'

But she couldn't say what he wanted to hear.

'How's that pile of work coming along, Caitlyn?'

Caitlyn blinked away the tears that had been threatening, pulled a hankie from her sleeve and gave her nose a good blow.

'Just one more document to do after this one, Mr Armstrong.'

'Not getting a cold, are you? Can't have our best worker coming down with flu.'

'No, it's nothing. I'm fine. Thanks.'

She'd been at Fraser, Fraser and Mutch for six months. She was good at the work because she was efficient and organised – years of having to create order out of chaos at Farm Lane had endowed her with many useful skills. Mr Armstrong seemed to appreciate what she had to offer. He'd let her take charge of some refurbishments and the office already felt like a brighter, fresher, more welcoming place. She'd made friends with Donna, the part-time bookkeeper, and Janet Reid, the senior legal secretary, who'd shown her lots of new things. She'd even managed, by a combination of cajoling and bossiness, to get Gemma, the girl on reception, to smarten up and learn to smile.

Caitlyn finished the document she was working on and read it through carefully. She prided herself on not letting Mr Armstrong find any mistakes.

Perfect. She laid it aside.

Not perfect.

She blinked.

I'm not going to cry.

Trouble was, it was all so recent. It still hurt. A lot.

Concentrate on the good things.

Good thing number one – Reg West had moved in with her mother.

This led to good thing number two – she'd begun renting a tiny box of a flat in one of the new estates across the river. Losing Malkie was the price she had paid for realising this dream. Maybe the jury was out on whether she'd made a monumental mistake or taken the right decision, but the real truth was, she was loving living there. She didn't care how small it was. She didn't mind that when you sat on the loo you could just about wash your hands in the basin at the same time, or that the kitchen area was so small that she could reach everything from one spot. She'd managed to squeeze a double bed into the bedroom, and if there was little room for clothes it didn't really matter because she hardly had any. What was important was that it was her space. Hers. She could have the telly on – or not. She could listen to music, or enjoy complete silence (apart from the sound of occasional arguments from the couple above, or the music from the guy through the wall).

Privacy was a treasure beyond price.

She picked up the last document.

Good thing number three – Ailsa had settled down to

study and was planning on going to college to do a childcare certificate.

'I've looked after kids all my life,' she joked to Caitlyn when she dropped round one evening to share some supper. 'I reckon I won't have to study too hard.'

They'd guzzled egg salad with chips from the chippie down the street.

'I want to open a nursery of my own one day. That's the way to make money, not to work for someone else.'

Was this Wallace's influence? Saying goodbye to Ailsa later, Caitlyn had been overcome with admiration for her little sister. They'd do fine, her and Isla May. Look what they'd done with that baking business. Neither of them would get stuck at home raising kids for some layabout.

She didn't have that kind of ambition. She'd never be a lawyer, and with all that she'd seen, she wouldn't want to be. But she was fast becoming queen bee in this little office, and that was the way she liked it. A steady job, well paid, where she could make sure everything was neat and in order, just as it should be. No dodgy accounting. No forged client registrations.

So the split with Malkie hurt. Well, there'd be other men, nice ones, when she was ready.

'Last Will and Testament', she typed, 'Of Jean Muirhead Blair, Forgie Farm Cottage.'

She paused, her fingers hovering over the keys. This was the trouble with working in a small office in a small town: there was always the risk of knowing other people's business. Then you had the job of keeping it to yourself. Should she go and tell Mr Armstrong she knew Jean Blair? But she didn't know her; she only knew of her and that wasn't the same thing at all.

She carried on typing, her fingers nimble and resolute.

Most of it meant nothing to her; she merely copied the obscure phrases from the templates Mr Armstrong had directed her to.

I appoint as my Executors and Trustees …

It was all the usual stuff.

Debts and Funeral expenses …

Allocation of expenses and tax …

Caitlyn yawned and glanced at her watch. She had to get this finished before she went home. She had to have time to wash her hair and change before she met her friend Jenna. They were going clubbing in Edinburgh. She was having a life at last, the kind of life she could never enjoy when she'd had to look after the kids for Joyce. It was mindless and unproductive and she'd almost certainly waste half of Saturday lying in bed wishing she hadn't drunk so much, but it was fun!

Bequests of cash sums …

Bequest in favour of …

Caitlyn sat up and stared at Mr Robertson's notes. *Bequest in favour of Adam McKenzie Blair.* Damn and double damn. It was too late. She'd seen it, and now she knew.

Jean Blair was leaving the entire farm, all its buildings and moveables, to Adam Blair.

Lucky man.

She wondered if he knew. She'd have to keep her mouth shut, that was for sure, but then, she was used to keeping secrets.

She finished typing the document. All that money and land, that was another world, but it didn't necessarily make you happy. Working to pay your way, even if it was just a small way, that was what was rewarding.

She printed out the document and put it with the others in a tray.

'That's everything finished, Mr Armstrong.'

'Thank you, Caitlyn, just leave it on the desk there, will you? Off out somewhere nice tonight?'

'Just a girls' night out.' She smiled, thinking that the evening sun would already be coming through the window right into her front room, lighting everything with its golden low-slanting rays.

Molly finished drying the dishes and draped the tea towel over the ancient plastic rack next to the Aga. She'd love to do something about the kitchen, but it wasn't their house. They were just tenants. One of these days she might have a chat with Jean about it, but in the meantime, there were too many other things to deal with, and anyway, she and Adam had no money to spare.

She glanced out of the window. The builders had already started work on the conversion of the old coach house. All the outbuildings would be ready for letting next spring. It was amazing how quickly she and Adam had managed to put together the detailed business plans, get the architects' drawings finalised, the bank loan approved and planning permission through.

She smiled. In truth, most of the work had been hers, though Adam's legal expertise had been invaluable. She couldn't have done without his eagle eye for detail either.

They made a good team. Why had they never realised that? They'd both been so focused on what they'd thought was the right path through life that they'd never stopped to think about how they might work together.

She shrugged on a fleece and headed for the back door. Time to feed the hens. She liked having hens at the big house, even though Jean had most of them at her cottage. Anyway, a few hens would be a great attraction for children when families started coming to the cottages for their holidays.

Across the field, by the far gate, she spotted Adam. Gone was the business suit and the neat haircut. His shock of brown hair had grown long round his ears and the stiff set of his shoulders had softened. His gait was easy, his stride assured. A collie trotted by his side, glancing up every few steps as if to check he was doing everything his master wanted him to.

She waved to him. He waved back, smiling.

Not my husband. She smiled, as she always did, at the thought. Being lovers rather than husband and wife had rekindled the passion they thought they had squandered. Would they ever remarry? That depended, Molly thought, on a great many things.

It was getting cool. She leaned against the doorpost to wait for her man.

Deep inside her, she felt something move.

She laid a hand on her belly, her eyes open wide with amazement. She stood perfectly still, straining for every sound, as though she might hear the new heart that beat inside her.

Yes! There it was again. A tiny flutter, like a butterfly flapping its wings. She was not mistaken.

'Adam!' she shouted, gesticulating like crazy. 'Adam! I felt it!'

He started to run. The dog ran beside him, delightedly.

'What it is?' he called when he reached the edge of the yard. 'What's happened?'

'It moved!' She placed her hands on her stomach. 'Our baby, Adam. I felt our baby!'

THE END

Maximum Exposure

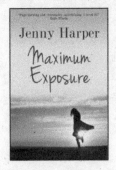

She's a professional photographer – but is she ready to expose her heart?

Adorable but scatterbrained newspaper photographer Daisy Irvine becomes the key to the survival of *The Hailesbank Herald* when her boss drops dead right in front of her. And while big egos and petty jealousies hinder the struggle to save the paper, Daisy starts another campaign – to win back her ex, Jack Hedderwick.

Ben Gillies, returning after a long absence, sees childhood friend Daisy in a whole new light. He'd like to win her love, but discovers that she's a whole lot better at taking photographs than making decisions, particularly when she's blinded by the past.

When tragedy strikes Daisy's family, loyalty drives her home. But it's time to grow up and Daisy must choose between independence and love.

People We Love

Her life is on hold – until an unlikely visitor climbs in through the kitchen window

A year after her brother's fatal accident, Lexie's life seems to have reached a dead end. She is back home in small-town Hailesbank with her shell-shocked parents, treading softly around their fragile emotions.

As the family business drifts into decline, Lexie's passions for painting and for her one-time mentor Patrick have been buried as deep as her unexpressed grief, until the day her lunch is interrupted by a strange visitor in a bobble hat, dressing gown and bedroom slippers, who climbs through the window.

Elderly Edith's batty appearance conceals a secret and starts Lexie on a journey that gives her an inspirational artistic idea and rekindles her appetite for life. With friends in support and ex-lover Cameron seemingly ready to settle down, do love and laughter beckon after all?

Sand in My Shoes

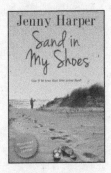

A trip to France awakens the past in this heart-warming and tear-jerking short summer read from the author of *People We Love*.

Head teacher Nicola Arnott prides herself on her independence. Long widowed, she has successfully juggled motherhood and a career, coping by burying her emotions somewhere deep inside herself. A cancer scare shakes her out of her careful approach to life and she finds herself thinking wistfully of her first love, a young French medical student.

As her anxiety about her impending hospital tests grows, she decides to revisit the sleepy French town she remembers from her teenage years – and is astonished to meet up with Luc again. The old chemistry is still there – but so is something far more precious: a deep and enduring friendship.

Can it turn into true love?